WILLIAM S. RUSSELL

Shallow Water

Newhouse Creative Group

First published by Newhouse Creative Group 2020

This novel is entirely a work of fiction. The names, characters and incidents portrayed in it are the work of the author's imagination. Any resemblance to actual persons, living or dead, events or localities is entirely coincidental.

First edition

ISBN: 978-1-945493-32-4

Cover art by Daniel Traynor

This book was professionally typeset on Reedsy.
Find out more at reedsy.com

Dedication

This book is dictated to my wife Margaret, who continues to inspire me in my writing. It has been with her help and support that I was able to plow ahead with a story related to my many years working with and for the U.S. Navy and Northrop Grumman.

Acknowledgement

Special thanks to my good friend, a great and generous editor-in-chief, Mark Newhouse. His tireless effort and careful attention to the smallest detail has helped me in the writing of the Shallow Water Predator. Thanks to Keith Newhouse of Newhouse Creative Group for his support in preparation and publication of the Shallow Water Predator.

Thanks to Mike Dorman, (MMCM(SS) USN a 26-year veteran of the submarine force. His knowledge of the operational aspects of the nuclear plant and overall performance of the day-to-day shipboard activities has helped me smooth out the rough edges.

Thanks to Duane Moss, for his technical insight of the day to day operation of Buffalo's Torpedo Room and general operation of weapon loading and handling equipment. Duane Moss, a retired Submarine Senior Chief Torpedoman served 24 years in the US Navy, four of those on the USS Buffalo. Duane currently works for the Naval Undersea Warfare Center in Newport, RI.

A Note from the Author

Dear Reader,

I have attempted to make this novel as authentic as possible. To assist you, at the rear of this book, you will find:

- A complete list of characters
- A glossary of acronyms
- A glossary of naval terminology used in this story

Smooth sailing, friends.

If you enjoy your voyage on the Buffalo, your kind reviews are sincerely appreciated.

Thank you,

Bill

Principal Characters

Note: See the back of this book for a full list of characters and their assignments.

USS Buffalo SSN-715
Commander Joseph Leo Scott, Commanding Officer
Master Chief Sonar Technician Submarines, (STSCM) Jack Norris
Lieutenant Commander Thomas Varney, Executive Officer
Lieutenant Patricia Morton
Dr. Janice Lace, Professor Oceanographic Department University of Hawaii

President's Security Council/Advisers
Mr. John Washburn, President of the United States
Mr. Raymond Richards, Secretary of the Navy
Mr. Jack Ure, Director of the Central Intelligence Agency

U.S. Navy SEALs
Commander Mike Walsh, SEAL Team Leader, and Mission Leader

Bandar 'Abbas Naval Station Iran
Admiral Al Jujair, Islamic Revolutionary Guards Corps Naval Commander

Strait of Hormuz

https://simple.wikipedia.org/wiki/Strait_of_Hormuz#/media/File:Strait_of_hormuz_full.jpg

"*A good Navy is not a provocation to war.* - **President Theodore Roosevelt**, 2 December 1902, second annual message to Congress.

"*One who knows the enemy and knows himself will not be endangered in a hundred engagements. One who does not know the enemy, but knows himself will sometimes be victorious, sometimes meet defeat. One who knows neither the enemy nor himself will invariably be defeated in every engagement.*"

Sun Tzu
The Art of War

Chapter 1

National Geospatial-Intelligence Agency; Dahlgren, VA –

Colonel Bill Johnson punched in the numbers on the security board and waited for the green light allowing him access to the National Geospatial-Intelligence Agency, NGA. He expected it to be a routine night.

Once a lecture hall, the large floor area now consisted of four semi-circles with five separate workstations in each row. They were in a staircase pattern with each circle overlooking the one below. Three LED screens were attached to the wall in front of the stations. The center featured a flat view of the Earth with the orbital pattern of every satellite circling the globe. The left displayed a topographical view of the Persian Gulf, while right showed the Afghanistan/Pakistan border. Being a holiday weekend, only duty personnel were manning four of the twenty stations. Located in the second row was Lieutenant Colonel Sandy Day.

Late, as usual, Johnson strolled over to Day's workstation. Both senior Air Force officers, their office was above the back row, behind plate-glass windows where they could oversee the entire room. Both men were single and had chosen to take the duty to allow the married officers to enjoy the Christmas holiday.

Atop each workstation was a red-lighted rectangular box two feet in length. The white letters displayed in the red field identified the name of the satellite in geosynchronous orbit. The KH-129 Spy Satellite was 336 kilometers above the earth using a 10-inch aperture telescope. The room was quiet except for the hushed hum coming from fans of the tower computers behind each station. Johnson stepped behind Sandy and peered over his shoulder. For the last several days, they had been monitoring the activity in the Straits of Hormuz, a 100-square mile area around the Bandar-e-Abbas Naval Base.

"Sorry I'm late, Sandy," Johnson said, studying the image on the right-hand monitor.

Day glanced up but returned to what was holding his attention.

"Whatcha got?" Johnson asked, stepping to the side of the console to take a better look.

Still focused on the display, Day said, "Bill, it's more like what I haven't got. I'm missing one Iranian Qaaem class submarine." He pointed to the empty dock from the previous day's satellite image. He tapped an icon opening the file and displaying a list of satellite photo folders. He then selected the fifth folder, which contained over 200 miniaturized pictures or thumbnails. Dates, time, latitudes, and longitudes appeared printed below each frame. He opened the first image.

"OK, there she is, still sitting beside her birth." Johnson pointed with his pencil.

Sandy Day selected the auto-feed and studied the pictures as they advanced from midnight the previous day. Black and white grainy satellite photographs were displayed every 15 seconds.

"There," Johnson said, placing his pencil next to an image

2

of a submarine. "A tug is pulling her from the jetty."

Fast forwarding the tape twenty-five minutes, they saw the submarine was underway and passing between two sea walls.

"Hold that picture," Johnson ordered. "Take a look in the upper right corner."

"What are you referring to?" Day leaned closer to the monitor.

"Here!" Johnson moved the pencil under the hazy image of a small surface ship sitting next to her berth. "Did we receive any infrared satellite pictures of the area?"

"Yes, I just downloaded them into a file this morning," Day responded, eyes glued to the images.

"OK, switch to the Infrared file and send the picture to the printer," Johnson said, as he headed for the Classified room. "Something's not right," he muttered, collecting the printout and returning. He placed the satellite picture in front of Day. "Sandy, see the heat signature above the ship?"

"Yeah, but why the interest?"

"It's an old missile Corvette. The Intel guys reported she was due to be decommissioned and sent to the scrap yard. Why would the Iranian navy start up her engines if she was about to be scrapped?"

"Maybe they intend to sail her to the yard," Day surmised.

"They've never done that in the two years since I've been monitoring their ship movements," Johnson said.

"There's always a first time," Day said.

Johnson moved over to an adjacent workstation and turned on the display. Within seconds he had the same images as Day. Placing the pointer on the footprint of a ship, he said, "Damn! It's been staring me in the face for the past two days!"

"What are you talking about?" Day asked, staring at his

monitor.

"Go back and restart the pictures from the beginning. Take a look at each corner of the harbor. What do you see?" Johnson asked.

Day stroked his chin as he focused on the vessels.

Johnson said, "I've never seen so many vehicles and people working at night at this Naval Base. Flatbed trucks are carrying cylindrical containers. If I had to guess, they could contain torpedoes or missiles. We need to identify the reason for the increased nighttime activity."

"You're right." Day took another look. "This is highly unusual."

"Unusual isn't the word! The question is for what are they preparing? Sandy, you can leave. I'll take over."

"Not on your life. Something's going on."

Johnson grunted. He had taken an immediate liking to Day, finding him focused on the often-tedious job of filtering through file after file of satellite images. Day never quit and was willing to spend hours scrutinizing the grainy black and white pictures, digging for every scrap of information.

Over the next three hours, Johnson and Day studied the Corvette and submarine as they headed into the Persian Gulf toward the Eastern Iranian coast. The sub appeared to be station-keeping 2,000 yards astern of the Missile Corvette.

Where are you going, Johnson thought and leaned back in the chair trying to ease the burning sensation in his eyes from staring at the monitor. After several seconds, he leaned forward and increased the magnification. *Is this what I think it is?* Adjusting the contrast on the monitor, he moved the pointer over to another footprint, the silhouette of an American Arleigh Burke-class guided-missile destroyer. "Hey, look at this," he shouted.

Focused on the two Iranian vessels, the two men had failed to see the faint, infrared lights of the destroyer flickering on and off like stars in the night sky. It was moving off the tip of the Musandam Peninsula. They also didn't detect fifteen high-speed Bladerunner boats off the coast. They couldn't know these marauders were waiting to close in on the destroyer to test their latest technology.

Chapter 2

USS Oscar Austin DDG-79 Guided Missile Destroyer; Straits of Hormuz-

The knife-edge warship sliced through the calm waters of the Persian Gulf, pushed by four General Electric LM2500-30 gas turbines. Having been released from the USS George H. W. Bush Carrier Battle Group, USS Oscar Austin, a guided-missile destroyer, was heading home after nine-months of enforcing UN sanctions against Iran. The crew was just settling down after having inspected their last commercial ship heading into the Straits of Hormuz.

The Tactical Action Officer (TAO), Lieutenant Jack Blair, had just assumed the mid-watch in the Combat Information Center (CIC). As he reviewed the Captain's night orders, he verified the men and women assigned to this duty section were relieving the off-going station operators. Except for an occasional snapping seatbelt, the only sounds in the room were the cooling fans on the operator's consoles and the chilled air blowing out of the vents in the overhead.

Lieutenant Blair was responsible for maintaining a complete tactical picture of the subsurface, surface, and air environments surrounding Austin. Although he was relieved to be able to depart for home, Blair knew to expect the unexpected when operating in the Straits. He knew it would be another 12 hours before Austin entered the Gulf of Oman.

Satisfied the operators were relieved, Blair was reviewing the night orders when the radar operator reported, "Bridge, CIC; two unknown surface contacts. Bearing 270 degrees, range 24,000 yards off the port quarter. Designated Romeo 23 and 24."

Keying the mic switch attached to his belt, Blair announced, "All stations, TAO, SPS-67, radar operator just reported two unidentified surface contacts."

Noting the time, Blair thought, why the hell can't I just sail through the Straits of Hormuz without having to jeopardize the safety of the crew? With Iranian missile sites along the coastline, I now need to worry about sending personnel to investigate if they are carrying contraband. Damn, we were almost out of here.

Having just changed course upon exiting the commercial shipping lane north of the Straits, the Austin increased speed to 20 knots. Wedged between two landmasses, Oman's Musandam Peninsula on the starboard side, and the Iranian coastline off the portside, Blair had hoped for a quiet night but now stared warily at the picture in front of him.

"Captain, this is the TAO. I've just received a report of two unknown surface ships 24,000 yards off the port quarter, paralleling the coastline. Request permission to close to within 10,000 yards to investigate?"

"Any other contacts?" Captain Leonard Willard asked from his stateroom.

"No, Sir. And the towed sonar array is streamed 1,200 yards," Blair added, standing behind the radar operator as he watched him place a track ring on the contact.

Willard responded, "Permission granted."

"Bridge, sonar detected two lines from diesel engines off our port quarter. Do you hold a visual on the two contacts?" Blair asked, rechecking the monitor.

"We hold visual on one surfaced submarine, and a Hamzeh Class guided missile Corvette," the duty officer, responded.

"Bridge, surface contacts classified hostiles," Lt. Blair announced.

As Blair was receiving the new information, Willard arrived in CIC.

"Captain the two—"

"I heard the report, Lieutenant. Thank you," Willard said, walking over to Blair. "Let's move within 8,000 yards. I'm curious as to their intentions." Hitting his intercom switch, Willard announced, "Bridge, slow to 8 knots."

"Sonar, do you still hold lines on the submarine?" Willard asked.

"Negative, Sir, our ship noise and their Corvette are masking passive returns."

What the hell's going on here? Willard wondered. "Range to Frigate?" He studied the status boards showing the surface and air picture.

"Radar, give me an update on the range to the surface ship," Blair ordered.

"Eight thousand yards and closing."

"Captain, recommend we parallel the missile Corvette," Blair said, aware their ship had entered torpedo range.

"Let's move in a little closer," Willard said. "Have an Operations Specialist deploy the towed decoy. If the submarine launches a torpedo, I want the NIXIE radiating as much noise as possible to screw with their torpedo's acoustic guidance."

8

He continued to eye the status boards as they received updates from the sonar and radar operators.

Blair knew his CO never displayed emotion. The Captain would remain steadfast, focused, and alert as he weighed all his options. So why Blair wondered, was he, himself, feeling such anxiety, as he envisioned the worst-case scenario of having to flee from what he assumed might be a Russian-made torpedo.

"TAO, Sonar is detecting faint lines on the towed array."

"TAO, Bridge holds visual on a submarine's periscope."

"What the hell game are they playing?" Willard exploded. "Why would they shadow a submarine, submerge, then return to periscope depth? Have we stumbled into a shooting exercise? I don't like it. Blair, we need to open the area. Let's get the hell out of range."

Chapter 3

QAAEM Diesel Submarine Q-104; Straits of Hormuz –

Captain Morteza Kashani of the Iranian Navy stood on the pedestal and studied the dark silhouette of the Iranian Corvette through the attack periscope. *Is this what it will feel like to hunt an American surface ship,* Kashani mused, counting the seconds. A hint of a smile formed on his face. He thought of the surprise for the Americans. As he continued to peer through the periscope, he said a silent prayer for the three men aboard the missile Corvette. *Soon they would be with Allah, the one true God, inshallah.*

Unknown to the crewmen aboard the Corvette, Kashani was about to unleash an advanced underwater weapon Iran had just acquired from the Russians. He was thrilled to be chosen to demonstrate the destructive power of the torpedo. *What could be more appealing than to destroy the Corvette with an American surface ship observing?* "Range to target?" he asked his XO, serving as Fire Control Coordinator.

"Six thousand yards and opening, Captain."

Rotating the handlebars to the bearing, Kashani shifted the magnification to high power. Perfect timing, he thought. He'd seen too many times arrogant American warships closing on a suspect craft, boarding and searching them for contraband.

He knew the American ship would approach, cocky, not suspecting the danger. *Their skipper must hold a visual on the missile boat by now. The foolish American will want a closer look. Good. Come just a little closer; I have a surprise for you, one which will remain burned in your mind for months to come.*

"I have a perfect firing solution on both surface targets," the XO announced, interrupting Kashani's thoughts. "Give the order, and I will launch."

Kashani smiled paternally at his XO. He understood very well his subordinate's eagerness to attack the American enemy. "Not yet, Nouri, be patient. Your opportunity will come soon enough. For now, we must be satisfied with the Corvette. I want to see what the American skipper does once they detect our torpedo in the water. We will record his tactics. This information will be most valuable in the future."

"Control, the American destroyer just went active," announced the sonar operator.

"Captain, the destroyer is changing course," the XO announced.

Kashani gripped the scope's handlebars tighter. What is the American doing?

"The destroyer is matching our course and speed," the XO said. "Wait! He is starting to open. If we don't launch our torpedo now, the destroyer will not witness the full effects of the blast."

Kashani had hoped the American ship would move closer to the missile boat before he launched the torpedo. Rotating the periscope back to the warship, he asked, "Range to Corvette?" He was disappointed the Americans would miss the full glory of the show.

"Sixty-four hundred meters, Captain." The XO sounded

disappointed, as well.

"Match target bearings and shoot," Kashani ordered, regretting the fun was over—at least for now.

USS Oscar Austin; Straits of Hormuz –

"Lieutenant Blair, sound General Quarters," Willard ordered.

Seconds later, a high, gong-like sound filled each compartment as GQ sounded.

Lieutenant Blair saw the Captain tapping his fingers as he waited for each department to report their status, "manned and ready." Time was critical when GQ sounded.

"Set Material Condition Zebra," Lieutenant Blair heard the Captain order over the 1MC General Announcing system.

I hope to God this is just another false alarm, Blair prayed.

"Torpedo in the water! Torpedo in the water!" the Senior Chief Sonarman shouted.

"All ahead flank; right full rudder," Willard ordered.

The destroyer keeled over pushed by the four turbines to a top speed of 30 plus knots. The twin propellers cut into the water, creating massive knuckles, releasing millions of bubbles.

Willard, beads of sweat on his forehead, listened for sonar to provide the status of the torpedo. "Talk to me, sonar," he shouted into the open mic.

"Down Doppler, Captain. The fish is moving away from our ship. It appears to be targeting the surface ship, not us." Blair replied relieved.

"Range to surface ship?" Willard barked.

"Seven thousand yards," responded radar.

"Bridge, come to course 270 degrees and continue to open. Sonar, ensure decoy is activated." Willard's eyes were glued to the status board. *We've got to exit out of the torpedo danger zone.* Lieutenant Blair, have Fire Control mark the location of the submarine and prepare to launch a torpedo on my command. Let's hope our weapon will force him to break contact and run before he fires at us."

"TAO," the Bridge Officer shouted, "The frigate. It just exploded. It's a huge fireball."

"They fired on their ship? What the heck is going on?" Willard saw flames shoot into the night sky where a ship and a live crew had been seconds ago.

Iranian Bladerunner Squadron; Straits of Hormuz –

The Bladerunner's Squadron Commander saw the fireball ahead as his squadron closed on the American destroyer. 'Allah Akbar,' he rejoiced. The destroyer had turned and was speeding toward his location. "Standby," he announced to the other boats. "Maintain formation and speed. Keep a sharp lookout for guns along the railings of their ship. Boatswain, range to target?"

"Ten thousand meters, at a closing speed of 30 knots."

The Commander smiled. *How close can we get before they see our boats?*

Holding on the side rail, the boatswain pushed the throttles forward.

"Control your speed and don't bunch up," the Commander urged the ten boats, hungering for the order to attack.

National Geospatial-Intelligence Agency, Dahlgren, VA –

"What the hell just happened?" Colonel Bill Johnson exclaimed as an enormous explosion consumed the missile boat he'd been observing.

The two analysts working below Johnson and Day's row stopped keying in data as the orange fireball lit the lower half of their stations.

The satellite was providing real-time imagery of the destruction of the Corvette.

Johnson's mind raced as multiple explosions of flame appeared where the frigate was formerly marked. "I don't understand why they torpedoed their boat," he murmured.

Day shook his head. "It had to be more than one torpedo. Look at that destruction. I don't believe the Iranians have such a powerful weapon." He peered harder at the monitor. "Bill, I've seen videos of Iranian live-fire exercises. I've never seen anything like this before."

Johnson searched the screen for any sign of the submarine that fired the torpedo. "There! She just surfaced."

Day stared at the sub. "Do you think that sub fired the weapon from underwater?"

Johnson felt a chill race down his back. "Sandy, I think the Iranians just sent us a pretty scary message."

USS Oscar Austin –

Willard moved over to the screen. "Bridge, do you hold visual on the surface contacts off our port bow?"

"Negative, Captain."

"Lieutenant Blair, pass the order to man the 50 caliber machine guns," Willard said, and added, "We're not going to be caught with our pants down. Range to contacts?"

"Four-thousand yards," The Operation Specialist, (OS), replied, "and closing."

Willard noted alarm in the officer's voice.

Bladerunner Squadron –

"Range to target?" the Squadron Commander asked the boatswain.

"Three-thousand yards and closing, Commander. I see their sailors operating deck guns."

"Boat captains, reverse course."

USS Oscar Austin –

"Captain, the contacts are moving away from our position," the OS reported.

"What was the final count on hostiles?" Willard asked.

"I counted ten contacts."

"They're just outside our firing range," Blair announced.

"Remain at GQ until we are midway through the Straits, Lieutenant Blair."

"Yes, Sir." Blair knew it wasn't time to relax with Iranian boats near. He wondered what the Brass would say about this latest provocation by the Iranian navy and if it might impact Austin's return home. The torpedo could have done a lot more than sinking a Corvette. It could signal a new confrontation between Iran and the United States.

Chapter 4

The Office of the President, Washington, DC –

"Do you agree with the recommendations made by the Security Council?" President Washburn asked Raymond Richards, Secretary of the Navy, (SecNav), Dr. Jack Ure, CIA Director, and the President's Chief of Staff, Ian Williams.

Reclining in his red leather chair, the President's six-foot, 250-pound frame, appeared relaxed. The appearance was deceiving. Washburn was known never to make snap decisions, always taking the measure of every recommendation and comparing it with as much information as he could get from his advisory team. Today, CIA Director Ure suspected might be an exception. "Yes, Sir," he replied. "The situation is urgent. We must place SEAL Team 6 on the ground to pull 'Alias' out of Iran as fast as possible."

"Alias? Who the hell is Alias?" Washburn poured another cup of coffee.

"Alias is the code name of our Iranian counter-intelligence operative," Ure responded. "Alias may help us determine if Iran is placing nuclear warheads on their new torpedoes."

At the slightest mention of the Middle East, Washburn jumped to attention. It was an election year, and the polls showed Washburn had a 10 percent lead over his Democratic challenger. His understanding of foreign policy, especially dealing with Iran, had won him the election four years ago, so he knew he had to be sensitive to all foreign policy changes. Polls showed the public still demanded the President try to keep the lines of communication open with Iran, long considered a significant threat to the United States and its allies. What most American's didn't know was how hard the administration, including Dr. Ure, was working to eliminate the on-going threat by Israel, reacting to Iran's calls for the Jewish state's annihilation, to destroy her nuclear facilities. The administration was doing everything possible to lessen the tensions. All was now in danger if anyone made a wrong move. Arming nuclear torpedoes would easily qualify as a wrong move.

Washburn was deep in thought. "You want me to use the SEAL Team?"

"Yes, Mr. President, SEAL Team 6 must be placed on the ground as soon as possible," Dr. Ure replied.

The President trusted Jack Ure. They were classmates at Harvard and graduate students at Columba University. Ure was the best man at Washburn's wedding. "You know how I feel about acting precipitously," Washburn said.

Dr. Ure nodded. "Sir, recent events indicate the revolutionary guard may have a nuclear or some form of a new torpedo they can use against our ships." Pausing to refer to his notes, he added, "One of our warships witnessed the sinking last week of an Iranian Corvette. Satellite images convince our analysts the Iranians may have weapons we know nothing about." He glanced uneasily at the President.

"Well, Jack, what do we know?" The President placed the coffee cup on the table.

Ure turned to the Secretary of the Navy.

"Based on observations by our destroyer Captain and analysis by our experts, and the distance from the firing submarine and the target Corvette…Sir, the torpedo may well have been traveling as fast as 170 knots." Secretary Richards said.

Washburn frowned. "One-hundred and seventy knots?"

Ure nodded. "Our analysts estimate the warhead yield to be at least 700 kilotons."

Washburn looked worried. "Are they sure the warhead was that powerful? Isn't it possible the Corvette might have been packed with explosives for a better show?"

"Yes, it is possible, but not probable, based on the analytics," Dr. Ure said. "We don't know much yet. But the size of the explosion and the speed of the torpedo are indisputable."

Washburn aimed his eyes at the Naval Secretary. "Can we stop a weapon traveling at 170 knots?"

"No, Sir," Secretary Richards answered, shifting in his chair. "Our ships are defenseless against this type of weapon."

Dr. Ure interrupted, "Once we extract Alias, we will know much more about these weapons."

Washburn sighed. "Jack, this could be very serious. If Israel becomes convinced Iran can deploy nuclear weapons, they won't hesitate to attack and destroy their facilities. We all know what kind of a firestorm the U.S. could be drawn into if that happens."

Dr. Ure nodded. "And that, Sir, is why we are not making any of this known. The Persian Gulf and the Straits of Hormuz are powder kegs." He sighed. "There is something else. We believe sinking their ship that close to one of our own is a warning."

"You think Iran is threatening us?" President Washburn

asked.

Ure replied, "All of our reports, when added to the images captured by our satellite, leave no other explanation for the torpedoing of one of their vessels when they knew we were close."

"But you're not sure of any of this yet?" Washburn peered into Ure's eyes.

"We can't be certain of anything at this time. Once we extract Alias, we'll know more."

"This is risky. You're confident the intelligence from Alias is reliable?" Washburn asked. "We can't have a repeat of the Iraqi WMD debacle where American soldiers died based on false information. No way! The American public will crucify us if this administration pounds the war drums for no good reason."

"We've never had to question Intel Alias provides. He's been a vital source for over ten years. He's risking his life every day. Only three people know his identity, which ensured his safety—until now. We have to get him out before they grab him."

"Okay! I get it. You want the SEALs to extract Alias, so we can protect him and verify our intelligence. I agree. How can I help?" Washburn stood up and stretched his legs.

"Your intervention is required to expedite this mission," Secretary Richards said.

Washburn shot him a look. "OK! I'm guessing you have a plan, so let's hear it. You have a plan. Right?"

"Yes, Mr. President, we do. To start, we'll need a submarine to land Team 6 on Iranian soil," Richards answered.

President stiffened. "I was led to believe it's almost impossible to deploy a submarine in the Persian Gulf and the Straits of Hormuz. Far too shallow. Is that wrong?"

Ure shot an anxious look at Richards.

Richards said, "It is challenging. Yes, Sir, but not impossible," He pulled a folder from his case. "We placed SEAL Team 6 near the Bandar-e-Abbas Naval Base three years ago. We can do it again with the right submarine, skipper, and the new prototype advanced SEAL Delivery Vehicle."

"And you think you'll be able to extract Alias if I grant your request?" Washburn asked.

Richards nodded. "That's one of our objectives."

"One?"

Ure placed a map on Washburn's desk and indicated a black square. "We've located their nuclear weapons facility. The red mark is the location."

Washburn leaned over the map and then stared at his two advisors. "You want the SEAL Team to destroy this building?"

Secretary signaled Dr. Ure to respond. "Satellite pictures taken at the Bandar-e-Abbas Naval Base indicate unidentifiable containers, most likely these new weapons, being delivered to this facility. We strongly believe the weapon fired yesterday was assembled at this plant."

"Do you believe or know? I'm not going to risk American lives on conjecture." Washburn stared at the satellite pictures.

Richards replied, "I contacted Admiral Westfield, Commander, U.S. Naval Forces Central Command, to discuss the matter. He agrees we need to place SEAL Team 6 on the ground and destroy the building. And soon."

Washburn looked incredulous. "I don't believe this! You want me to authorize the destruction of their weapons manufacturing site without conclusive evidence? Do you know the risk if the American people find out about this?"

Richards looked grim. "Yes, Mr. President. But we don't see any other choice. If the Iranians get high-speed nuclear-tipped torpedoes with unknown capabilities and place them on their submarines, every ship in the Persian Gulf could be a target. It will be a bloodbath."

"Why wasn't I informed of this earlier? When was this information received?"

"I just received the results from our analysts two hours ago," Dr. Ure said.

Washburn glared at the map. "Gentlemen, I don't like this. It feels too rushed. We don't have enough information."

"Mr. President. Alias will provide the information we need. Time is of the essence. Mr. Richards identified the submarine essential to this mission. We need your immediate approval." Ure said.

Washburn headed for his desk, an angry look on his face. "I don't like this at all. But you're sure. Okay. Secretary Richards can handle it."

Richards looked anxious. "Sir, there's one more matter. We need you to authorize this assignment to one of the finest submarine captains in the Navy—"

"Personnel? That's what I pay you for, Ray," the President said only half-joking.

Richards squirmed. "Sir, I've selected the submarine for this mission, but I need you to agree on the officer we recommend."

"I don't understand. As Secretary of the Navy, you have the authority to pick whoever you want."

"Yes, Sir." Richards felt more anxious.

"So, what's the problem?" President Washburn asked, aware both Richards and Ure appeared extremely nervous.

"Sir, I've designated USS Buffalo for this mission. The submarine is the same one that placed SEALs along the coastline in the Persian Gulf three years ago—"

"Great. I approve. Is there something else?" The President was growing impatient.

Dr. Ure stepped in, "Mr. President, the problem is we need a submarine commander who has experience in operating in shallow water and has conducted covert missions with a submersible. He also has to have the specialized experience of having worked with Team 6 and is familiar with this dangerous theater."

"I understand all that, but doesn't every submarine in the fleet have an experienced CO?" The President asked.

"Yes, Sir; I mean no, Sir," Richards answered. "The problem is no one officer in the fleet possesses the hands-on experience needed for the extraction of Alias, placing the SEALs on the beach, and operating in such shallow waters. Sir, we need a commanding officer who has this combination of experiences and the operational knowledge to pull all this off. This combination is critical to the success of this dangerous mission."

The President glared at Ure. "Gentlemen, it sounds like you have someone in mind? We're wasting valuable time—"

"Commander Joseph Leo Scott," Richards said, handing the President a folder marked Top Secret.

"Scott? I've heard that name before." Washburn opened the folder.

"Yes, Mr. President," Richards responded. "Scott was removed for dereliction of duty. His submarine plowed into a seamount—"

"What?" Washburn lifted his eyes from the folder.

"Yes, Sir. His ship struck an underwater mountain—"

"Scott was judged derelict? Are you kidding? What makes you believe I'll reinstate someone like that?" Washburn slammed the file closed.

Richards said, "Mr. President, he was not negligent, Sir—"

"That's not possible. The Navy ruled him at fault—"

Ure spoke up. "Sir, since the hearing, we learned the Government Survey Office provided inaccurate charts of the sub-lane Scott had orders to transit."

"Are you kidding?" Washburn asked, slowly reopening the folder. "I don't believe this—"

Richards shook his head. "Sir, in my opinion, Scott is our best hope for placing a team on the ground and destroying the weapons facility without getting caught. He has a history of making on-site decisions essential for this mission. That's why we're asking you to intervene."

Washburn stared at Ure. "I still don't like it. Where is Commander Scott now?" the President asked, skimming the pages of the folder.

Richards glanced at Ure and replied, "At present, he is working as a desk jockey at the Pentagon. We think he'd welcome a shot at reinstatement."

The President sighed. "If he's your choice, but I want to speak to him in person. This thing is too damn risky. Schedule a meeting as soon as possible."

"Yes, Sir," Ure said, giving Richards a fast smile.

There was a knock on the Oval Office door and the Press Secretary entered. "Mr. President, Tonight's press release for your approval."

"Thanks, Jeff. Excuse me, gentlemen." The President read the first page then looked up at his Press Secretary. "The statements are too weak. I want the American people to understand that except for humanitarian aid, the U.S. supports the UN Security Council's decision to place additional sanctions on Iran. Please rewrite this?" He handed it back to the Press Secretary, who left the office.

"Gentlemen, are we done?"

"Yes, Mr. President."

"Ray, would you remain a few moments? I want to go over Scott's file with you before I meet him. Dr. Ure, I expect to be kept up to date at all times."

"Yes, Mr. President." Dr. Ure walked out of the office, knowing he was risking more than his career on a disgraced officer. He was risking war.

Chapter 5

Washington, DC Oval Office Waiting Room –

Commander Joe Scott stared at the painting of George Washington mounted on his white horse overlooking Valley Forge. *I wonder what was going through old George's mind when he saw his sick bedraggled troops, starving and freezing at Valley Forge? The pressure had to be enormous. I guess I'm lucky. I only lost my command. Washington almost lost the country.*

Scott's hands clutched his khaki hat. He tried to straighten his wrinkled pants and shirt, concerned he might not make the right impression for whatever the reason he was summoned to the Oval Office. He didn't have time to change into a fresh uniform. As an ex-SEAL, the Commander was trained to maintain calm but still felt tightness in his neck at this uncertainty. *Show no fear. Stay calm no matter what they throw at you.*

Scott heard the door open. Another surprise. The Secretary of the Navy walked in. He jumped to attention and saluted.

The Secretary didn't waste time with a greeting. "We don't have much time, Commander."

"Why am I here, Sir?"

"You'll find out soon enough."

You've got to be kidding.

As Richards was about to speak again, the door to the Oval Office opened.

"The President will see you now," Dr. Ure announced.

Richards stepped in front of Scott. "Just answer the President's questions. Give concise responses unless he asks you to explain."

Explain what?

Secretary Richards had reviewed Commander Scott's military records and read the review board's recommendations. At first, he agreed with the findings, but after new information, he felt Dr. Ure was correct in wanting Scott reinstated for this mission. He had come to believe the Commander was a victim of the government's unwillingness to admit responsibility for the near destruction of a nuclear submarine. It was not the first time a cover-up killed the career of an excellent officer, but the SecNav knew recommending Scott was a huge risk. He felt there was little choice. "This is crucial. Good luck, Commander Scott."

"Yes, Sir." Scott entered the Oval Office behind Richards, his nerves on high alert.

The President stood at the front of his desk as Scott entered. He noted the gold Trident badge pinned on the officer's khaki shirt. He wondered if a disgraced officer could muster the respect of a crew.

Scott remained at attention, wondering how long before they lowered the boom on him.

"Commander Scott, please sit." Washburn motioned to a leather chair. The President took his seat behind his desk. "I won't waste time. Commander, you were involved in a covert mission in the Persian Gulf?"

Scott glanced at Dr. Ure and Secretary Richards. *Why is he bringing that up again? Were they reopening the case for a possible court-martial? I will answer honestly and hope for the best.* "Yes, Sir, Mr. President. I was the boat's Executive Officer, but forced to assume command after our commanding officer became ill."

The President leaned forward. "According to Secretary Richards, and Dr. Ure, although not your original mission, you ordered SEAL Team 6 back to pick up stranded operatives."

"Sir! I—"

The President held up his hand. "Let me finish, Commander. Were the SEALs on board when you took command?"

Scott had believed this matter had been closed at the hearings. "No, Sir! We placed them on the beach the previous night. The Captain became incapacitated, just before their extraction." He saw no reaction, so continued. "I saw no alternative. After taking command, we received a message two SEALs were injured and couldn't swim five miles back to the boat—"

"You had a submersible aboard?" the President interrupted.

"Sir, the submersible was down hard with an electrical problem. I judged it would take too long to repair. Time was short. I—"

"Scott, how did they return to Buffalo?"

Scott glanced at the Secretary of the Navy as if asking for help. "Sir, I drove the submarine into the shallows by the coast and sent two divers to swim in. They helped the wounded SEALs return to the boat."

The President looked grim. "What happened after you picked up the SEALs?" He stared hard at the officer.

Scott felt the President's eyes were boring holes in his brain but refused to show any fear. "Sir, I after we picked up the

28

SEALs, we learned two CIA operatives were stranded on the shore. Lieutenant Keenan, the SEALs commanding officer, asked me if we could go back to retrieve them." He stared at Washburn. "They were in imminent danger of being found by the enemy—"

"And?"

"I did what I thought any commander would do. I turned the boat around and went back. Two of the SEALs went in and pulled the operatives out."

The President's voice was stern. "You're aware you put your ship in jeopardy? This office would have been in an awkward position if you were detected. But you did it anyway?"

Scott kept his eyes locked on the President. *This interview was not going well.* "Yes, Sir, I knew, but it was a risk I determined I had to take. If we had not rescued the SEALs, and the Operatives, Iran would have found out there was a submarine along their coast. I wanted to avoid a major crisis." He wet his lips. "I felt I had no alternative, Sir. Leaving the men was not an option."

The President stood.

Scott sprang to attention. He was surprised when the President extended his hand.

"Thanks for coming Commander," the President said, grasping Scott's hand firmly. "You're dismissed."

Scott left the office. Once in the waiting area, he sank into a chair. *What the hell just happened?*

Back in the Oval Office, the President turned to the Secretary of the Navy. "I like Commander Scott. I feel you made the right decision. He's willing to take risks to accomplish his mission and is loyal to his crew. Not many skippers would do what he did, risking his career." He handed Richards the file. "OK, set

29

up the necessary meetings and cut through the red-tape. Get Scott to sea. Failure is not an option. I want constant updates. No excuses."

Richards felt relieved but understood there were significant obstacles ahead. "Now comes the hard part," he muttered, leaving the President's office.

"You just make sure it gets done," Ure said. "We're sitting on a time bomb, and Iran is holding the match."

Chapter 6

Joint Region Marianas, Naval Base, Guam –

Rear Admiral Tom Armstrong, Commander Submarine Group Seven, was at his desk. He was going through inspection documents for the Forward Deployed Naval Units stationed at the U.S. Naval Base Guam when summoned for an urgent teleconference with the Secretary of the Navy. He couldn't remember when, if ever, Secretary Richards had requested such a meeting. *Something's cooking,* he thought.

The Admiral entered the teleconference room and sat down in front of three high definition monitors. The words 'No Signal' were stepping across their surface. He glanced down at his watch, 18:04. *Dammit! My schedule's too tight! Two hours until I fly back to Yokosuka, Japan.* The following day he was scheduled to be onboard the Amphibious Command Ship, USS Blue Ridge, to monitor Marine landings. *I hope the Secretary is brief!*

At Armstrong's left, the duty Information Systems Technician was tapping on the keyboard. "Good morning, Sir," he said, springing to attention.

The Admiral nodded, looking at his watch. "I wish they'd hurry," he muttered.

"Yes, Sir," the IT replied, wishing the meeting was over so

he could relax again. The Admiral's spit-shine attitude always put him on edge.

Armstrong glanced at the communication equipment, impatiently. I don't have time for this, he thought, as Secretary of the Navy's face appeared on the middle screen.

"Afternoon Tom," Richard's voice blasted from the speakers. Sitting at the table with him were Dr. Ure and the President's Chief of Staff, Ian Williams. "Has Admiral Westfield joined us?"

"Not yet, Sir, I'm having trouble connecting with the SIPR-Net secure channel," the IT replied, working on the Secret Internet Protocol Router.

"Please hurry up? We've got to kick this meeting started," Richards said.

The right monitor flashed, revealing Admiral Samuel Westfield at his desk, then the signal was lost. Static poured out of the speakers.

"Fix that, will you," Armstrong gruffly ordered his IT.

Seconds later, Commander U.S. Naval Special Warfare Development Group, at Dam Neck, Virginia, filled the 60-inch panel.

"Good afternoon, Admiral," Secretary Richards said.

"Good afternoon, Mr. Secretary," Westfield replied, placing his pen down. "I was about to fly to Bahrain to meet with SEAL Team 6 when I received your urgent message."

"Then we caught you just in time," the Secretary said. "Gentlemen, we've grave concerns about Iran's new Qaaem Class submarines. As you know, Iran is expanding its fleet. This new diesel submarine is lethal. It will carry the Shkval torpedo, the Sushant anti-ship missile, and the AS-Tasban air-to-air missile. I don't need to tell you the threat these well-armed submarines pose to our fleet. They're ultra-quiet, can remain submerged for extended periods, and can operate in shallow conditions." He eyed the camera. "They may very well be beyond the reach of our submarines—"

"The Russian's sold Iran Shkval torpedoes?" Armstrong interrupted. "Are you sure?"

"Yes, Admiral." Dr. Ure replied. "Intel tells us Iran is waiting for a shipment of ten Shkval and two six-kiloton warheads from Russia."

Armstrong shook his head. "Are you sure your source is reliable, Dr. Ure?"

"Yes. I have one hundred percent confidence in the source."

"What are you recommending, Dr. Ure?" Admiral Westfield asked.

"Admiral, this is not a recommendation. It is an action approved by the President—"

"He agreed already?" Westfield was surprised.

"The President feels we must move fast."

Armstrong was not happy about being left out of the loop. "This is most unusual—"

Ure interrupted, "Admiral, the President wants us to place boots on the ground to extract our informant out of Iran as soon as possible."

"That could provoke a war," Armstrong said, wondering, as he often did, how non-military types could make such decisions.

"We've considered the risks. Our operative getting caught would be far more disastrous," Ure said.

Armstrong was silent.

Ure continued, "There's more."

There always is, Armstrong thought.

Ure's eyes were intense. "Following this extraction, we must destroy the Weapons Depot. Timing is critical. The nuclear warheads and the Shkval torpedoes must be in the facility."

There was a long moment of silence.

"What do we know about these weapons that makes them such a threat?" Armstrong asked, bristling that he wasn't informed earlier of these developments.

Ure hated these delays. "Admiral, we now know the new Shkval torpedo can travel four to five times faster than our most advanced torpedoes. These weapons are far more lethal than anything we possess—"

"How is that possible?" Westfield asked, still not convinced.

"The Shkval," Ure explained, trying to remain patient, "is a supercavitation torpedo. It flies in a gas bubble created by the outward deflection of water from its pointed nose cone and gases from its engine. At 170 knots, it's a killer."

Armstrong looked stunned.

"How do we defend against this thing?" Westfield asked. "Do you realize, such a torpedo fired from 10,000 yards would only take three minutes to impact? Make it just ninety seconds if launched from 5,000 yards. Our ships would be sitting ducks, with precious little time to react. Our acoustic countermeasures are useless against the damned thing."

Armstrong sputtered, "We should have known this earlier."

"I just received this information." Dr. Ure sounded annoyed. "In one week, the cargo ship, Volga Balt, is scheduled to leave the Russian commercial port of Vladivostok with a shipment of these torpedoes and two nuclear warheads, destination Iran—"

"Where did you get this information?" Westfield asked.

"Admiral," Dr. Ure interrupted. "Rather than discuss

specifics, let me just say we had a deep-cover operative in Russia for the past six years. We have confirmation that the Russians fabricated these deadly weapons and sold them to the Iranians."

Secretary Richards broke in. "Yesterday, during our intelligence briefing, we were warned that Iran's threat to disrupt shipping in the Persian Gulf might soon be within their grasp. Iran has increased the total size of its diesel fleet to 25."

Ure sighed. "There's another wrinkle. If the Israelis decide to launch a preemptive attack against Iranian nuclear facilities, the President believes Iran will close the Straits of Hormuz. I'm sure you're aware of the economic and political consequences of such action—"

Armstrong shook his head, vehemently. "If what you say is true, and Iran decides to attack our ships, there is no defense, as Admiral Westfield pointed out, against their damn new torpedoes. It will be like shooting fish in a barrel."

"The President is aware of this and that is why we must move quickly," Dr. Ure responded, annoyed at the time this was taking.

"What are the President's orders?" Armstrong asked, wishing he was in charge instead of a civilian who didn't know anything about the needs of the Navy.

Dr. Ure replied, "My orders are to select a commanding officer to drive the USS Buffalo into the Persian Gulf and place SEALs on the ground—"

"You're selecting an officer? I don't follow," Admiral Armstrong jumped in. "Our subs have experienced commanders, trained to undertake missions of this nature—"

"If that were true," Richards said, "this meeting would not be taking place. There's only one commander with the hands-on experience of operating a submarine in the shallows and supporting this kind of incursion in the Iranian theater of operations. He also has experience with the advanced SEAL Delivery Vehicle vital for this mission."

Armstrong snapped, "So, who is this officer with all these capabilities?"

Richards smiled, "Commander Joseph Scott."

Armstrong was quick to react. "Scott? Scott was relieved of his command." He laughed but saw Richards was dead serious. "Ray, you know I was a member of the Board of Inquiry that found Scott derelict. He almost destroyed his ship. Are you questioning our decision?"

"Admiral. The President wants Commander Scott reinstated and placed in command of the USS Buffalo. His operational orders will follow once he is aboard," Richards stated with authority.

"With respect, Mr. Secretary, once an officer's record is tarnished like Scott's, they're forced to retire, or placed on non-command duties," Armstrong said. "This interference is unprecedented—"

Admiral Westfield added, "After 200 years, we can't go against navy tradition."

Secretary Richards anticipated their resistance. "Gentlemen, the President is all for respecting tradition. But not at the risk of our ships and an incalculable loss of life. It is also where I draw the line. Knowing your proud records, I am certain you do, too."

Armstrong felt cornered. "And you agree to this, Mr. Secretary? The man was found guilty. This action undermines our services' judicial system—"

"Damn the judicial system, Admiral," the Secretary snapped.

"Under these precarious circumstances, I completely agree with the President. We must act now."

"I don't know," Armstrong said, "the man is a disgraced officer—"

Dr. Ure tried to remain patient. "New evidence reveals that Scott lost his command due to the Defense Survey Office's (DSO), incompetence—"

"What do you mean," Armstrong asked, still bristling that the President was countermanding a judicial verdict.

"The truth, which is FYI, is we discovered errors by the DSO resulted in the near grounding of three other submarines over the past year alone." He held up a file. "If you want to hang someone, start with the DSO."

"I'm not aware of such findings," Armstrong grumbled, suspecting this was a fabrication.

"I haven't either," Westfield said.

"I assure you," Richards replied, "This is a fact, a tragic fact."

"If this is true, then it must be dealt with," Armstrong said, still suspicious.

"The President has ordered an investigation and will take appropriate action," Dr. Ure replied. "But we can't wait given what we suspect about Iran's capabilities."

"Admiral, our orders from the President, are to reinstate Commander Scott and put him to sea as soon as possible," Richards said. "Any more questions?"

No one spoke.

Armstrong broke the silence. "I'm still against reversing disciplinary board decisions. But if the President's need for Scott is this great, I am compelled to obey. However, I will brief Commander Scott myself."

Richards nodded. "OK, Admiral Armstrong, we'll set up a video briefing for you with Commander Scott." He aimed his eyes at the Admiral. "This is just a formality, you understand. The President made his decision."

We'll see about that, Armstrong thought, fuming at this break in the chain of command.

Richards turned to Admiral Westfield, "Admiral Westfield, prepare SEAL Team 6 to embark aboard Buffalo in two weeks. This mission is going down, and soon, gentlemen. The President wants no surprises, delays, or disclosure of what we discussed today. Understood?"

"Yes, Sir," the others replied.

Richards sensed this was not the only opposition he would encounter in reinstating Scott, but that was the least of his problems. Iran had long been a thorn in his side, and now posed an imminent threat to world peace.

Chapter 7

Washington, DC; Commander Joe Scott's Apartment –

The siren blared in his ears. He recoiled at the shock of the collision, knocking him to the stateroom floor, pressed against the bulkhead. Turning onto his back, it took Joe Scott several seconds to grasp what happened.

The banshee wail of the alarm cycled up and down. Dazed from being slammed against the bulkhead, Scott picked himself up just as the deck pitched down. His head throbbed. Blood dripping from a laceration above his left eye blurred his vision. His ears echoed with the sound of sailors running in the passageways, shouting as they headed to damage control stations.

Making his way from his cabin, gripping the walls of the tight passages, he started for Control. He heard the Officer of the Deck (OOD) and the Diving Officer (DO) shout, "Emergency! Blow main ballast tanks!" He caught the split-second response of the duty Chief, "Emergency blow, Aye!"

Scott stumbled forward as the OOD announced on the public address system, "Emergency Surface! Emergency Surface!" He braced himself. He knew the Chief would slam the forward ballast-tanks emergency-blow-valve up, followed several seconds later by the after-group valve. He waited for the sound of 4,500 pounds per square inch of air to slam through the four-inch piping to flush out the seawater. He felt the submarine quiver as the bow pitched up. At first, the rate of rising was maddeningly slow, but as the air poured in and displaced the water in the ballast tanks, the sub rose with increasing speed. He heard the alarm still in his ears. "I won't lose my boat," he screamed.

The scream jerked him awake. It took several seconds for his vision to clear and his heart to stop pounding. He breathed a sigh of relief. It was another nightmare.

Scott picked up the duvet he threw on the floor and saw the twisted sheet on the bed. He closed his eyes. It was the same dream that had tormented him before. Even with his eyes open, he suffered its effects.

Bright yellow beans of sunlight slanted across the disheveled bed.

"I'm going to be late." Scott sat up and slid his legs onto the floor. *I haven't had a nightmare for months. Why now?* He then remembered the meeting with the President, the questions Washburn raised about the fatal accident. "I thought that chapter was closed," he muttered as he walked into the bathroom.

Placing his hands on the rim of the sink, Scott stared at the face of a 38-year-old man still having nightmares. At six foot four, firm-chested, and with broad shoulders, he was still a one-time SEAL in fighting trim. He maintained a rigid exercise program, a lasting remnant of his training.

A hot shower helped relieve the tension in his neck. After toweling down, he slipped into his blue and gold Naval Academy running garb, grabbed his backpack, and left the apartment.

In the brisk Washington air, Scott put the backpack containing his uniform over his shoulders, started his stopwatch, and sprinted down North Nelly Curtis Drive. *If my timing is right, I should make it through at least 10 lights without stopping.*

As he ran, Scott replayed the meeting with the President. *What was Washburn looking for those probing questions? Are they reopening the case?* Whatever it is they want, I'm ready, he thought, as he pushed himself harder than ever to complete his jog in record time. He wondered if this would be the final time he'd be jogging to this office.

Washington, DC; The Pentagon –
Four minutes, 26 seconds later, breathing hard, Scott was outside the south entrance to the Pentagon. Pulling his military ID card from his pocket, he swiped the card through the reader and handed it to the marine sentry.

Saluting, the sergeant said, "Good morning, Sir," as he scanned the picture. "In-kind of early today, Sir?"

"Good morning, Sergeant," Scott replied. He retrieved his ID and headed down the long corridors to his office. "Another day of endless paperwork," he grumbled.

After showering and changing into his khaki uniform, Scott returned to his closet-sized office, dull gray walls adding to his sullen mood. He surveyed the floor, stacked with boxes of files and shook his head at the mildew smell.

Scott's mind returned to yesterday's uncomfortable interview with the President. What precipitated that? He thumbed through the stack of envelopes a messenger dropped in his basket yesterday. He laughed when he saw the date stamped on the top left corner of each folder was over two months old. "This is crap," he exclaimed and disgusted, left the room with the papers unread. "Just busy-work."

Scott raced up four flights of stairs to the mess hall, feeling trapped, being so far from the sea. There's nothing I can do about this, he thought, seeing there was no one to whom to vent. Resigned to getting back to his office, he poured a mug of coffee and headed back.

Once in his office, Scott placed the steaming mug on his desk and reached for a file marked, 'Routine.' Flipping open the cover, Scott began reading a message from Commander Justin, CO of the USS Jimmy Carter, SSN-23. He was surprised to read that the CO had complained to Commander Submarine Development Squadron (COMSUBDEVRON), 5, and the United States Government Survey office, of inaccurate charts delivered to him the previous year. "What's this," he asked as he read that the CO accused that the map ordered for the Holystone clandestine operation was incorrect and caused a collision with...a seamount.

Scott reread the letter then flipped the cover closed. *Why the hell didn't anyone do anything after this report?* Another ship could have been lost before my incident, and nobody did anything about it?

Grabbing the next folder in the packet, Scott was dismayed to discover the CO of the USS Providence, SSN-719, had sent a similar message four months later. He also complained about charts sent to him by the Government Survey office.

"They say three's the charm," Scott muttered bitterly, pulling the folder open. "Damn it! USS Virginia SSN-774 issued an alert, three months before my boat slammed into the seamount!" He closed his eyes. "How many more COs need to suffer this humiliation? Or even worse, blame themselves for the destruction of their ship and the possible loss of a crew?" He slammed the folder on his desk. He angrily remembered the letter of reprimand from the Board of Inquiry. The words of that reprimand were burned in his memory: "Several critical navigational and voyage planning procedures are determined to have caused the near sinking of his boat; the death of one crew member; and injury to several dozen men under Scott's command."

They blamed me, Scott thought, feeling betrayed by the Navy he loved. *Where in these judgments did it state that the Government Survey Office was incompetent? Nowhere. They took the easy way out and dropped me here, hoping I'd disappear. That's not going to happen.* He picked up the files, eager to see if there were any more complaints against the Government Survey Office.

There was a knock at the door.

Annoyed by his discovery, Scott barked. "Yes, what is it?"

The door opened. "Commander Joseph Scott?"

Scott glanced into the eyes of a woman in a khaki uniform. Silver lieutenant bars were visible on her collar. The National Defense Ribbon and a Surface Warfare Officer Pin were on her blouse. "What can I do for you, Lieutenant? "he asked, irritated at being interrupted.

"Sir, I'm to escort you to the video conference room. Admiral Armstrong is waiting."

"Admiral Armstrong? As in Commander Submarine Group 7?"

"Yes, Sir. Please hurry. We don't want to keep him waiting."

Scott jumped up from his desk, grabbed his cover, and

followed her into the corridor. As they hurried down the hallway, he asked, "Do you know what the Admiral wants to see me about, Lieutenant?"

"No, Sir, Commander. I'm just the messenger, but whatever it is, it must be important for him to be calling for a video conference at midnight, his time."

Scott, contemplating what the Admiral might want, followed her into a classified room.

An information Systems Technician verified Scott's identity and initiated the teleconference.

Admiral Armstrong, sitting at his desk, appeared on a 60-inch monitor.

The Lieutenant and the technician retreated, leaving Scott alone facing the stern-looking Admiral. *Did the meeting with the President and the Secretary of the Navy prompt this interview? Are they going to 'scapegoat' me again?* He came to attention, expecting the worst.

Chapter 8

Videoconference Rooms, Yokosuka Japan, and Pentagon. –

Scott hated waiting. He wished the Admiral would say whatever he had on his mind, so he would know how to react. "Sir, Commander Scott, reporting as ordered."

Admiral Armstrong flipped through the papers in front of him, then straightened up. "Good morning, Commander. Do you know why I'm awake in Japan, at this ungodly hour?"

"No, Sir," Scott responded, watching as the Admiral shoved a stack of papers aside. He saw what he believed was his personnel jacket sitting on the desk. Trying to maintain a rock-solid façade, he remained ramrod straight.

"Commander, please sit. I asked for this conference because I've been ordered by the President to give you a command."

Scott wasn't sure he heard right.

The Admiral expected some type of reaction, but, seeing none, continued, "I want you to know your reinstatement goes against the established doctrine this navy has followed for over 200 years." He aimed dark eyes at Scott. "I must accede to the President's order, but I want to understand why he selected you from among a list of fine Naval Submarine officers we have on hand."

"Excuse me, Sir, did you say another command?"

"Yes, Commander. Let's get to it. I reviewed your service record, and noted there is a one year gap before you reported to Prospective Commanding Officer School. What were you doing that year?"

The mention of that sent a chill down Scott's back. He and the crew had signed a non-disclosure agreement to not reveal the nature of Buffalo's operations during that time. *What the hell can I tell him and not violate the NDA?*

"Commander, I don't have all day." The Admiral glared, wondering if the President was aware of this suspicious gap in the disgraced officer's folder.

Scott nodded. "Covert Operations, Admiral. The mission was classified, Sir."

"Where did this operation take place?" Armstrong asked, dismayed he wasn't made aware of the alleged covert operation.

Scott struggled with what he could share. Was this questioning a test of his loyalty? "The Persian Gulf was the location. That's all I'm permitted to reveal, Sir. I'm sorry, I can't be more specific."

"I see, Commander." Admiral Armstrong studied Scott's face. He begrudgingly had to admit he admired the man for not divulging classified information even if it might be risky in his current situation.

"When did the new CO report aboard?"

"When the ship returned to Guam."

"Did I hear you correctly? For four months, you were acting as CO and in your position as XO?"

"Yes, Sir."

Armstrong looked surprised. "I can't recall the Navy ever allowing a ship to go without a CO for that length of time. Were you not concerned you would be the one blamed for the possible failure of your mission? You did take on the entire responsibility."

"I felt I had no choice, Sir. The mission was classified, and I understood its risk. As acting CO, I accepted the orders and was determined to accomplish our objectives as ordered."

"I see. And where did you go afterward?"

"To Prospective Command Officers school, and then to the USS Louisville. Until, as you know, I was relieved of command. Which reminds me, I found on my desk today three folders, one from the USS Providence, USS Virginia, and Jimmy Carter reporting the charts received from the United States Government Survey office were inaccurate."

Armstrong looked up from his notes. "How long ago were the reports filed?"

"It varies, Sir. Jimmy Carter over a year. Providence four months, and the Virginia about six months. All the reports were marked routine, so they didn't get any attention—"

"Thank you, Commander. I'll look into this." *We may have done Scott an injustice.* Armstrong sat back, deep in thought. *Scott is stronger in character than I thought. He just may be the right man for the job, but I don't like it.* "Commander Scott, despite your past and the Navy's verdict... per the President's orders, you're to receive a new command."

Scott didn't believe it. "Yes, Sir," he replied.

Armstrong studied the man's face again. "Very well, Commander. I will be honest with you. I was very resistant to reinstating you. I still am. But the President feels you deserve a second chance. I can't override him."

"Thank you for your honesty, Admiral. I won't let the President down."

The Admiral hoped that was true. "Now, for the task at hand. This mission is urgent. You must report to Captain Whitfield, Commander Submarine Squadron 15 in Guam as soon as possible. Do you require any additional personnel to return with you to the Middle East?"

They're sending me back to the Middle East? Scott was excited but didn't want to show it. He thought quickly. "To expedite prep time, I'd like to work with the staff I've had the honor of commanding previously. I'd like to request—"

"Excuse me." Armstrong picked up his phone. "Lieutenant Morton, in my office, please? Bring your pad."

Scott waited as a blonde Lieutenant entered the room and sat in a chair next to Armstrong.

"Lieutenant Morton, please, record the names Commander Scott provides."

"Yes, Sir,"

"Continue, Commander," Armstrong said.

"Since I am returning to the Gulf, I'd like to request Master Chief Sonar Technician, Jack Norris, Senior Chief Sonar Technician, Paul Richardson, and Senior Chief Fire Control Technician, Jack Russell."

Armstrong turned to the Lieutenant. "Morton, take care of it. Anything else, Commander?"

Scott glanced at the Lieutenant. "Yes, Sir. Dr. Janice Lace, Professor with the Oceanographic Department at the University of Hawaii."

"A civilian? Why Dr. Lace, Commander?"

"Dr. Lace has done extensive studies for the Office of Naval Research on the Persian Gulf. She was instrumental in Buffalo's forays into the shallows in support of the SEALs. Her knowledge of the area is essential."

Armstrong signaled the Lieutenant to jot it down. "Is there anything else?"

"No, Sir. Thank you again for giving me this opportunity." Scott knew Armstrong had no choice since the President made the decision. He sensed the Admiral still harbored doubts and was determined to prove them wrong.

Armstrong glanced at Morton. She had pressed him repeatedly to let her transfer to a sea unit. *She could be my eyes and ears on this operation,* Armstrong thought. "Thank you, Commander." He turned to Lieutenant Morton. "Please issue the orders for these individuals to report to Whitfield, Submarine Squadron, SUBRON 15, at Apra Harbor in Guam by next Tuesday."

Scott addressed the Admiral. "Sir, with your permission, I'd like to go to Hawaii to brief and enlist the services of Dr. Lace."

"Time is of the essence. You need to fly to Guam."

"Understood, but Dr. Lace is essential for the success of this mission. But being a civilian she may resist your orders. Whatever help you can provide to encourage the school to give her a leave of absence will be appreciated." Scott knew he wasn't revealing the whole truth to Armstrong but also knew Janice Lace might be the key to a successful mission.

"Lieutenant, order the Pentagon to cut travel orders for Commander Scott for Guam, with a stop in Hawaii."

"Thank you, Admiral. I'm grateful for your help."

Morton took it as a signal that the meeting was over. "Is that all, Sir?" She asked, waiting for Armstrong to dismiss her.

She's an attractive woman, Scott thought, surprised when he heard the Admiral say, "Lieutenant, you may add your name to the list."

"Excuse me, Sir?" Morton asked, surprised.

Armstrong's voice was paternal. "You've been bugging me for the opportunity to go to sea. Well, you've got it." He let out a rare smile. "Get going before I change my mind."

"Yes, Sir," Morton said and hurried out of the office.

Scott was stunned. *Just what I need, two women on a submarine.* He wanted to protest to the Admiral but that might not be the best thing to do at this moment.

Armstrong guessed what Scott was thinking and laughed inside. "Questions, Commander?"

"No, Sir."

"Good." Armstrong pulled out another folder. "Buffalo just completed her Mission Certification. Her CO was relieved due to illness."

Another problem, Scott thought. "How long has the XO been aboard?"

"Lieutenant Commander Tom Varney came aboard just before the Tactical Readiness Evaluation Inspection. Would you like to select another XO?" Armstrong asked.

"Sir, it would be a mistake to replace the XO after passing certification. Varney will be fine."

"I agree," Armstrong said. "Good luck, Commander."

"Thank you, Sir," Scott said.

The Admiral shrugged his shoulders. "Don't thank me until you know what the mission is, Commander. Godspeed!"

The video image flickered off, leaving Scott staring at a blank monitor. He stood and left the room, hurrying to his office, hoping his new orders wouldn't be rescinded.

Seated at his desk in Yokosuka, drinking the first of what would be many cups of coffee during his long day, Armstrong wondered if he would ever see Joe Scott again. He thought of Morton, who he might be sending her to her death. "It's what she always wanted," he said, already regretting his decision. "At least, I'll have eyes to watch that guy," he said and placed the reports about the inaccurate charts on his last priority tray.

Chapter 9

Shipbuilding & Offshore Industries Complex; Iran

Admiral Al Jujair stared down at the bottom of the massive drydock of the Iran Shipbuilding & Offshore Industries Complex, 34 km west of Bandar-e-Abbas Naval Base. *It won't be long now. The years of sinking replicas of American warships are nearly over.*

"Admiral, ready to descend?" Captain Kazim, the Admiral's chief-of-staff, asked.

"Yes, by all means." Al Jujair, dressed in workers' coveralls, a stained shirt, leather steel-toed black boots, and a hard hat, proceeded down the stone stairs, as he had done countless times. He noted the seemingly unending coils of electrical cables and hoses draped over the massive stone cavity of the drydock. Yard workers were putting the finishing touches on the polished twin bronze screws under the overhang of the stern. The smell of oil mixed with marine paint created a foul odor. He knew it was because of the black ultraviolet knitted cloth covering the drydock and tanker, not to protect the workers from the sun, but to hide what lay beneath them from the prying eyes of American spy satellites. Every precaution had to be taken.

The Admiral's eyes watered from the fumes created by the

workers applying the final red marine paint to prevent algae buildup. The engineers assured him this final coating would increase the tanker's speed by two knots. Every knot was necessary, he thought, passing a stern eye over the workers.

It had taken Admiral Jujair ten years to expand the Iran Shipbuilding Industry's capabilities under the deception of manufacturing mammoth crude tankers. Even The Fars news media was brought into the effort to hide his real intent, reporting that Iran would soon become a significant commercial shipbuilder. It was a brilliant scheme, and he was the mastermind.

"How much longer will you require to complete the inner hull?" Al Jujair asked.

"Sir, I estimate one week to complete the interior communications and your conference rooms," Captain Ebrahimi, a bright young officer, replied. "The technicians are still waiting for the communication consoles and electrical equipment to be delivered. I will then require one week for installation and testing. Sea trials are scheduled to ensue in two weeks."

"There will be no sea trials. Food supplies arrive tomorrow night. Once stored, and the hull seals are tested, I want the tanker out of drydock. You will send her to the refueling station immediately. Do you understand? I won't allow delays any longer. Put her to sea." He knew each day at dock provided the Americans, and their Israeli puppets, the opportunity to learn the truth about the so-called commercial shipbuilding.

Ebrahimi did not wish to anger his superior, but said, "Admiral, with all due respect, we must take the necessary time to pressurize the fuel tanks to ensure no oil leakage."

The Admiral frowned, not relishing the delay, but realizing oil leaking from the fuel tanks would cause problems with other Arab states. "Very well, but you must not fall behind schedule."

"Yes, Sir. It will be ready on time."

"Has the crew been selected?" Al Jujair asked.

"Yes, Sir, the men will board within a week. The intelligence specialists you requested will arrive shortly after."

The Admiral smiled. "Remind the crew they are to conduct themselves as marine merchant sailors."

"Yes, Sir."

"Notify me once the tanker is ready to leave Port," Admiral Al Jujair ordered, wiping his hand on his pant leg.

"You can count on me, Sir."

The Admiral climbed the stairs back up to ground level, excited that his dream of destroying the American fleet was coming to fruition. *They think they know everything because we let them see our sinking of the frigate. They are in for a great surprise.*

Chapter 10

University of Hawaii; Oceanography Lab –

Commander Joseph Scott parked the rental car and headed for the oceanographic research facility. Informed Dr. Lace was giving a lecture to her graduate class in the auditorium, he gazed at the dark blue water of the Pacific Ocean. The lab and lecture hall were perched on a cliff overlooking the jagged volcanic shoreline. The endless noise created by the swells pounding against the hollow of the cliff made his chest tighten as he approached the building. The roar of the waves reminded him in the next minutes he would again be facing the only woman he ever loved.

Scott paused before proceeding inside. He thought long and hard on the monotonous flight from Washington to Honolulu how Janice might react when their eyes met. Would she be hostile at him walking back into her life? I can't blame her, he thought.

Scott checked his uniform. To make this meeting appear official and minimize Janice's embarrassment at what might be an uncomfortable situation, he opted to wear dress whites. Scott hadn't seen her for over a year but kept tabs on her. He wasn't sure why he did that since he was the one to end things.

Scott pulled open the entryway door. It led down a long

hallway. The pungent odor of formaldehyde drifting from the specimen bottles in the laboratories assaulted his nostrils. Reaching the double doors leading into the lecture hall, he entered the darkened auditorium and slid into an aisle seat. He hoped to go unnoticed for a few minutes. Janice was on the stage. She was the most mystifying woman in the world to him. Beautiful, intelligent, an accomplished professor, and a world-recognized expert in her field, she was a puzzle he couldn't solve.

Janice was addressing her students, stalking back and forth across the stage with leopard-like grace in a sleeveless pink sundress. Her brown skin and sun-bleached auburn hair attested to years working outdoors, exploring the world's oceans. At six-feet tall, she carried her slim frame atop muscular, shapely, legs. Watching her direct the red laser along the outline of an undersea trench on a projection map, Scott thought back to the first time he saw her.

The USS Jefferson City, SSN-759 (Jeff City), had just pulled into the Pearl Harbor Naval Shipyard for pre-deployment upkeep. Never having been to Oahu, Scott left the boat early in the morning on shore leave for three days. He checked into the Hale Koa Hotel in Waikiki. Changing into his Naval Academy running gear, he headed down Kalakaua Avenue toward Waikiki beach. It felt wonderful to stretch his legs after being aboard the Jefferson for two months.

Completing his run, Scott was drawn into a bakeshop by the smell of fresh pastry. Standing in front of the glass counter was a beautiful woman in a red and white running outfit, talking with the proprietor. He glanced at her shoes. High-quality. We have something in common, he thought. He moved closer and caught the scent of her coconut shampoo.

She turned suddenly.

Their eyes met.

She smiled.

Scott's eyes followed her when with her tray, she proceeded to a table in the far corner of the shop.

"I'd like a raisin bagel and black coffee," Scott said to the proprietor, stealing another glance at the female jogger. She's nice-looking, he thought. He picked up his order and walked to her table. "May I join you?" He saw a small smile when she raised her head.

"Are you going to sit down or just stand there staring at me?" She asked. But she was smiling.

Scott felt embarrassed but slid into the seat opposite her.

"I'm Janice," she said.

"I'm Scott...I mean, I'm —" She laughed, and he knew he had to get her into his life.

Things didn't quite work out the way he hoped. So now he was sitting in the dark of a lecture hall anxiously waiting to see how the next chapter unfolds.

"Tomorrow," Janice's voice echoed on the microphone, shaking Scott from his memories. "We will discuss the results of The Challenger's recorded dive narrated by Canadian filmmaker James Cameron. Please have your take-home quiz ready to submit next Thursday."

With any luck at all, tomorrow, you'll be in Guam, preparing to get underway with the other members of the team, Scott mused.

A loud buzzer ended the session.

Scott waited silently in the shadows while students filed out before he proceeded to the stage. Janice was collecting her papers, so she didn't see him. The rich brown tan on her skin glowed under the bright stage lamps. Uncertain of how she'd react, he stepped out into the light. "Hello, Janice."

Janice scanned the floor in front of the stage at a voice that sounded familiar. Her eyes widened. She almost called him, Joe, but caught herself. "Commander Scott?"

Scott smiled. "Why so formal? We were on friendlier terms—"

Janice frowned. "That was a long time ago. And if I remember correctly, you ended our relationship."

Scott caught her icy response. "Janice, we can talk about that later—"

"Right." Janice eyed Scott sternly. "You haven't come here to discuss our relationship. So, what do you want?"

Scott didn't want to hurt her any more than he had, but the mission had to come first. "You're right. I'm not here about the past. I'm on my way to Guam, and thought perhaps we could have dinner before we head there tomorrow."

Janice looked shocked. "You said, we?"

"Yes, we."

"And what do you think I would want to see in Guam?"

Scott looked around to be sure nobody was around for the anticipated explosion. "The USS Buffalo. The President requested you to serve as my science advisor—"

"The President? Who are you kidding? When we worked together three years ago, you kept me at-sea for three months. And we know the ending. Please inform the President that Dr. Lace is not interested." She snapped her case closed.

Scott knew this was going to be a hard sell. He weighed his response and was about to speak when Janice's smartphone rang.

"Excuse me, Commander," Janice said, sliding her finger

across the phone's face. "Good afternoon. Dean Dickenson?" She glanced at Scott.

Scott hid his smile.

"Congratulations? For what?" Janice looked puzzled.

Scott kept his eyes on Janice's face. He knew he didn't have to wait long for a reaction.

"But, Sir, I don't remember sending a proposal to the Pentagon to continue mapping the Persian Gulf." She glanced at Scott. "Just a minute, Sir, I need to ask my associate if he knows anything about this so-called award."

Here it comes, Scott thought.

Pressing the phone against her chest, Janice hissed, "What the hell did you do? Why is this school been awarded a million-dollar contract to map the waters of the Persian Gulf?"

"Not guilty." Scott raised his hands in defense.

"You are too, so guilty. I know you. Dammit! Now, spill it before I clobber you with this phone."

Scott lowered his hands. "Okay, the truth. Yesterday, the President ordered the Pentagon to issue orders for me to report to the USS Buffalo as her new CO."

"You're getting a new command? Congratulations! I'm happy for you. You always wanted to return to sea duty. But what does this have to do with me?"

Scott shrugged. "When I realized I was getting reassigned, I asked for several previous crew members—"

"You asked for me? Damn! This is your doing! How could you do something like that to me?" Janice looked furious.

Scott backed away. "Janice, you're the best in the field, but I promise you, I knew nothing about a contract for your school. Think about it! How can a disgraced officer wrangle something like that?"

"I'll deal with you later, Commander Scott." Janice shot him another icy glare and placed the phone back up against her ear. "Dean Dickenson, I forgot about that proposal. I submitted it last year." She listened attentively. "Yes, I'll do what I can to ensure the university gets this grant." She glared at Scott again. "Yes, I'll leave tomorrow."

Scott recognized the look in Janice's eyes and knew he was in deep trouble.

Janice listened a few more seconds and tossed the phone on the table, her face flush with anger. "Damn you. He placed me on a one-year sabbatical. Did it ever occur to you, Commander Scott, I might have a life which does not revolve around you or the United States Navy?"

"I'm sorry. I was asked who I need for this mission and knew it had to be you."

Janice's eyes were murderous. "It must be some damn important mission for you to risk seeing me again."

"I'm not sure exactly what the exact mission is. It must be of critical importance for the Navy to give me another command."

"You roped me into a mission you know nothing about? Are you off your rocker?"

"All I know is the President ordered me back to the Persian Gulf. I need your expertise if I'm to pull off what I suspect the President wants. I need the best, and, like it or not, you're the best."

Janice smiled with venom. "I am the best at a lot of things. But you're not going to find out."

"I understand." He wondered if she meant it.

Janice folded her arms across her chest, her body language all business. "Let me make my position clear, Commander

60

Scott. Our association on this mission will be strictly professional. There is no going back. You will treat me like you would
any other member of your crew. Understood?"

"I wouldn't have it any other way."

Janice shook her head. "I can't believe you're still pulling
my strings. But for a research grant like this for the university,
I have no choice thanks to you. I'll risk it." She slammed the
locks on her briefcase. "Okay, I'll meet you tomorrow at the
airport. Now get out of here. I've got a lot of work to do if I'm
going to catch a morning flight." She glared at him again. "If
I do that."

Scott hesitated for a moment but decided not to press his
luck. He gave her a formal nod, turned, and left the lecture
hall. He thought if he gave Janice some time, she'd simmer
down. At least he hoped so.

Janice leaned against the podium. Despite her anger, she
watched Scott walk up the aisle in his tailored white shirt,
which showed off his muscular physique. She was furious at
being manipulated and had mixed emotions about spending
months in a confined space with her former lover. He'd hurt
her more than she thought possible. It took months for the
pain to subside. She found it incredible that she felt an electric
spark when she saw him again. His eyes reignited her desire
for him. "What the hell am I doing?" she said, wishing Scott
never returned. Whatever she felt, she promised that this time
Dr. Lace would be in control.

Scott didn't feel relaxed after leaving the building. Seeing
Janice again awakened his feelings for her and his doubts. *Was
I wrong to walk out on her? What right do I have to step back into
her life?* He thought of turning around and releasing her from
her obligation. The mission needed her. She made it clear their

time together was going to be professional. He knew that he wanted more. How much more? He wasn't sure. The truth was he wasn't sure of anything other than he had to complete this mission, whatever sacrifice it entailed. But could he sacrifice Janice? Wasn't he doing that in corralling her for what he suspected was about to be a rough ride in dangerous waters?

Chapter 11

Commander Submarine Squadron 15; Naval Base, Apra Harbor Guam –

Commander Scott, Dr. Lace, and Lieutenant Morton sat in Whitfield's outer office.

Lieutenant Morton noticed Dr. Lace glance at Scott when he wasn't looking. I'm guessing this is going to be an 'interesting' assignment, she thought. She sensed something was brewing between them, something from their past.

This waiting is killing me, Scott thought, peering at the nautical clock on the wall.

Whitfield hurried into his outer office, a First-Class Information Technician in tow.

Scott and Morton jumped to attention. Scott noted an envelope marked Top Secret pressed against Whitfield's chest.

"Commander Scott, join me in my office. Dr. Lace and Lieutenant Morton, please, accompany Petty Officer Williams. There's some paperwork to take care of," Whitfield said.

Scott picked up his garrison cap and followed Whitfield.

"Please sit, Commander," Whitfield said.

Scott sat, waiting for Whitfield to initiate the conversation.

Whitfield walked behind his desk, sat, and placed the envelope face down. He glanced at Scott and unsealed it.

Scott waited, wondering what this new mission entailed. His last operation along the Iranian coastal waterways was no picnic.

Whitfield flipped through the pages. Several times he stopped, glanced at Scott, and then resumed reading. Closing the folder, Whitfield leaned back and stared at the ceiling. He appeared to be resolving some inner conflict.

Here it comes, Scott thought, waiting for the hammer to fall.

"Commander," Whitfield began, "I received an intelligence briefing this past hour. It's only fair to inform you Washington's orders reinstating you to command Buffalo are our first move on the chessboard. Our Intel indicates the Iranian diesel submarine fleet has become their most dangerous and reliable underwater weapon. Department of Defense (DOD) feels Iran poses a serious threat to our Carrier Battle Groups. Frankly, we know little about Iran's submarine combat capabilities." He let this sink in and continued, "Your crew will be required to collect intelligence on their submarines while you operate in the Gulf and Straits of Hormuz." He paused. "I think you are astute enough to read between the lines."

Scott nodded. "Buffalo is sailing into what could become a war zone."

"Without getting into specifics, yes. That is a plausible scenario. But, of course, to be avoided." Whitfield's eyes narrowed, and he appeared uneasy. He rose from his chair and walked over to a large gray safe against the wall and removed a folder. He placed it in a leather pouch along with the latest Intel report. "These are your sealed orders. They are marked Top Secret. You are not to open them until you reach the 10-fathom curve and submerge." He handed over the pouch. "Commander, get Buffalo ready for sea as soon as possible."

64

"Sir, when do we receive clearance for departure?"

"In a week. But that could change." Whitfield sighed. "Washington is looking closely at an incident last week involving one of our Guided Missile Destroyers."

"I don't understand," Scott said, not having heard about the incident.

Whitfield stared at a map of the Middle East, hanging on the wall. "Iran launched a torpedo from one of their new Qaaem diesel subs, sinking one of their out-moded Corvettes. The Oscar Austin was closing to investigate when they fired."

"Target practice is routine, Sir." Scott wondered why a routine drill had caused a fuss.

Whitfield nodded. "According to a message from Austin's CO, the weapon they launched obliterated the target ship. There was nothing left after what the CO described was a massive fireball."

"Another new weapon? Sir, it never ends."

Whitfield glanced at the time. "Enough discussion, Commander. My car will take you to your command. Good luck!" He realized he might be sending Scott on a mission that could endanger his life. While he still wasn't sure he trusted him, he damn didn't want to lose any of his men or ships. "Godspeed, Commander."

Scott stood and shook Whitfield's extended hand. "Thank you, Sir." He started for the door.

"Commander."

Scott turned around.

"Good hunting."

Scott sensed some tension in the Captain's voice. "Thank you, Sir." He walked down the long passageway and out into the bright morning sun to an awaiting car. What the hell have

I gotten myself into, he wondered, gripping the leather case. In it were sealed orders that he knew could imperil his crew, Janice, Morton, and himself. Was he capable of accepting this responsibility? Was taking on this mission a mistake? He gripped the case, more determined than ever.

Whitfield stared at his phone and then hit the numbers he needed. "XO, this is Captain Whitfield. Your new CO is on his way. Remember our discussion." He heard the XO's response and replaced the phone. Watching the smooth water through his window, he knew he was deceptive, but felt he had little choice. The Persian Gulf hid its secrets until it wanted to reveal them, often fatally. After reading Scott's file, he knew the Commander had participated in clandestine operations near Iran's naval bases, which made him more qualified than most. But was it enough? After meeting Scott, he suspected the officer's removal from command was a mistake. Scott struck him as one of those rare leaders who place the mission, crew, and ship first, regardless of career considerations. Despite all that, he wondered if Scott was the right man for such a challenging job. The wrong man, one act of recklessness, could start a war that would inflame the entire region. Was war what Iran wanted?

Sitting in an empty room, several doors from Whitfield's office, Janice Lace and Patricia Morton, were filling out paper-work.

"Your credentials are impressive," Morton said, breaking an awkward silence.

"Thank you." Janice glanced at Morton. "I received my Ph.D. in Oceanography and a Master of Marine Affairs from the University of Hawaii." Realizing she sounded snobbish, she added. "But you know that already. Please call me Janice, Lieutenant."

"Call me, Pat."

Janice nodded. "You know about me, but what's your background, Pat?"

"I received my Masters of Oceanography with a minor in computer science from the University of Rhode Island. I intended to enroll in the Ph.D. program, but funding was a problem. So, I joined the Navy. Once I've completed my service, I plan to finish."

"Good for you." Janice was a little shaken. She had thought of Patricia as an all-Navy and not a fellow academic. "Impressive. How did you get assigned to this mission?"

Pat shrugged. "To be honest, I'm not sure. I requested assignment to a submarine, or any sea billet, too many times to count. I guess Admiral Armstrong, for whom I was clerking, saw an opportunity to get rid of me." She laughed.

Janice smiled but was deep in thought. *Why do I feel jealous? Joe always said he was attracted to my intelligence, but this one is a match and pretty attractive.* "I think you'll find Joe, uh, Commander Scott, to be a demanding but excellent mentor." She picked her words carefully.

Morton caught the first name slip. "I understand you worked with the Commander before?"

"Yes, I was assigned to the USS Buffalo in support of a classified operation in the Persian Gulf three years ago. Commander Scott was XO then, but due to the CO's failing health, assumed command and successfully carried out the mission."

"That explains why you're here." Morton suspected there was more.

Janice replied, "I don't think you being here is an accident. I believe Admiral Armstrong saw an opportunity for you to assist me."

Who is assisting who, Morton thought but kept up her smile.

"Well, now that I know your field of expertise, I'll ask Commander Scott to assign you to work with me. There's a lot to do, and based on your background, you're just what the doctor ordered. No pun intended." Janice laughed.

Patricia was used to taking orders from superior officers, but this was stretching things a bit. On the other hand, it would allow her to see what Janice Lace was all about. "I look forward to it," she replied.

"Good. I think we'll make a great team."

"I do too," Morton said, wondering how Scott would greet this development.

Janice returned her smile but was wary. "Once we're done with this paperwork, we should head to the Navy Exchange and pick up Poopie Suits—"

"What did you say?" Patricia asked.

Janice grinned. "While onboard, you and I need to wear the blue coveralls issued to all crew members. For reasons shrouded in the mists of Navy lore, they're called Poopie Suits."

"I never heard them called that," Morton said, not relishing the idea of wearing something with that name.

Janice loved the reaction. "It'll cut down on the number of clothes we need. I'm sure you know there's limited space to stow personal effects." She realized Morton hadn't been on a sub before. "Also, they're polyester, so there's no lint to cause dryer fires."

Morton pictured herself in the shapeless suit with the disgusting name. She sensed Janice was enjoying her little game.

Janice laughed inwardly at the look on Morton's face. "We could wait until we board and take our chances. But, if you didn't pack sneakers, we also need to purchase those. And the poopies."

"Sneakers?"

"Sure. Sneakers cut down the noise and are easier on the feet on a metal deck plate." I'll bet she loves that, Janice thought, knowing she'd leveled the playing field. No more sexy sundresses and high heels for this Southern belle. "I'll be happy to help outfit you," she cooed.

"Any other suggestions?" Morton asked, annoyed at her self-appointed mentor's enjoyment.

"Oh, yes, I almost forgot. You need to stop using sweet-smelling shampoo. And that perfume you wear. The crew will be excited enough at females being aboard without us smelling like we're in Paris," Janice said.

Not one to give up easily, Morton rose from the table. "As I said, I'm looking forward to serving under Commander Scott." She headed for the elevator hiding a broad smile.

Janice knew that last 'salvo' was deliberate, and simmered as she watched Morton's smooth sashay from the table. She wasn't going to let this Lieutenant be alone with Scott, not until she made up her mind about what she wanted.

Chapter 12

USS Buffalo SSN 715; Naval Base, Apra Harbor Guam –

Scott exited Whitfield's car at the head of the jetty. He paused to survey what he knew to be one of the best attack submarines in the fleet. During the two years, Scott had called Buffalo home; he served as Acting CO and Executive Officer. Today Scott was returning as her CO. He saw the long black predator moored against the far end of the dock and smiled approvingly. If a fight is what the Iranians want, we'll be ready, but only if they provoke it. He assumed this assignment was temporary and expected to be relieved upon returning, mission complete. No matter, he thought. I'm in command now with a chance to prove myself.

Scott walked down the landing and into the hulking shadow of the submarine tender, USS Emory S. Land. Submarine tenders act as floating repair ships for submarines in their squadron, so he was pleased to see the craft nearby. It meant preparations were underway.

The morning was humid. The pungent smell rose from the salty water mixed with diesel fumes. I'm home, he thought, wondering how the crew and officers would react when they found out he'd been relieved for cause from his last command. His thoughts were interrupted when he heard the 2nd Class Petty Officer's voice on a speaker announce, "Buffalo arriving." He felt an adrenalin rush hearing himself announced per Navy tradition. He guessed Tom Varney had provided the topside watches with his picture. It's a good start, he thought.

Lieutenant Commander Tom Varney, Buffalo's Executive Officer, hurried to the bottom of the weapons loading hatch. He glanced down at his wrinkled blue coveralls. The XO knew first impressions were important, but this was a working submarine. He hoped the new Commander would also be a rolled-up sleeve leader.

"Down ladder," Scott ordered.

The tall, African American XO stepped aside.

Scott climbed down, pausing to smell the purified air wafting up through the thirty-foot escape trunk. It was nine months since he inhaled the unique odors of a submarine, and he realized how much he missed it. Stepping into the upper passageway, Scott knew others were observing his every move.

"Captain. Tom Varney, Buffalo's Executive Officer." The XO saluted.

Scott glanced at his XO. *He doesn't mind being a 'hands-on' leader. Good.* He shook Varney's outstretched hand. "Good to meet you, Tom. Please, assemble all officers in the wardroom in 15 minutes."

"Yes, Sir."

"I'll see you then," Scott said and walked through the Control Room. He entered the CO's stateroom, glanced around, and smiled. "Yup. It's good to be home again." He ran his hand over the tan desktop and examined the imitation wood-grained walls. He peered inside the head, the shower behind the door he shared with the XO. "Nothing's changed." He

71

heard a knock on the door. "Come in," he said, closing the bathroom door.

"Captain, the officers, are assembled," Varney said.

"Thanks, XO, I'll be right down."

Scott opened the wall safe and placed the leather case he'd been carrying inside. He locked the safe and checked it. Picking up his notebook, he proceeded to the wardroom.

The officers jumped to attention when Scott entered. He made a cursory look around, detecting several curious glances. "Be seated, please," he said, sitting down at the head of the table. "XO, please do the introductions?"

The men, now seated, aimed their eyes at their new CO.

The XO introduced each officer by name, rank, and duty.

Scott acknowledged each man with a nod. He wanted to determine the measure of each of his top staff and recorded their names in his memory. When introductions were complete, he began, "Gentlemen, at this point, I don't know what our specific orders are, and won't know until we leave port. I can say our time here is short." He saw the men glance at each other. "I believe in transparency and am going to tell you what I know. I'm sure you understand this is for your ears only."

The men attended to every word.

"I believe we will be deployed to the Persian Gulf. Most of you are aware of the threats. While our specific mission is not yet known, I'm confident you understand caution must be exercised near the Iranian coastline." He smiled confidently. "I will meet with each of you individually once we leave port. Of course, if there is a need to see me before our meeting, please inform the XO." He hesitated before continuing. "There is one matter I want to clear up. Some of you may be aware that I lost my last command. I see no point in attempting to hide this. It is public record." *This is more difficult than I thought it would be.*

"Sir, it isn't necessary—" Varney said.

"Thank you, XO, but I want this out in the open. I need my officers and crew to trust me." He looked at the men. "Gentlemen, I would not be here if the accident that cost me my command was judged to be my fault. I won't go into details at this time." He passed his eyes over the men and said, "Any officer here who does not have confidence in my ability may request a transfer without penalty or fear of reprisal."

There were some glances and murmurs.

Scott said, "Is there anyone here who would now like a transfer?" He waited for any hands to go up and then smiled. "Good. Thank you. Now that we've settled this issue, my priority is to prepare for deployment as soon as ordered. Secondly, to allow departments to work with the XO to schedule liberty for the crew before we get underway."

There was a buzz of excitement.

Scott continued, "If a man isn't essential at this time, let's give him a bit of R&R. Get them off the boat. Make sure preference is given to men with wives here." He chuckled. "I'm sure you know why."

The officers laughed.

Scott, feeling more relaxed by their vote of confidence, also laughed. "Any questions? No? Then thank you again. Dismissed! XO, will you join me in my stateroom in 30 minutes? I want to take care of some personal items."

"Yes, Sir." Varney felt relieved. *He's not what I expected. He raised everyone's spirits. But Whitfield doesn't trust him. I guess time will tell.*

Commander Scott was at his desk, filling out forms when he heard a knock followed by the XO entering the cabin. "Please take a seat, Tom. Did you receive notification from Submarine Force Pacific, or Northrop Grumman, regarding the installation of the MK 8 prototype Advanced Swimmer Delivery Vehicle, known as ASDV?"

"Yes, Sir. Yesterday, the shipyard attached the couplings. The ASDV is expected to arrive in two days. Do you know if SEALs will be joining us as well?"

"No, I don't. My guess is the SEALs will arrive when we enter the Gulf of Oman. The ASDV will eliminate the need for Buffalo to enter the shallows... if dropping off the SEALs is part of our mission. That's a huge relief."

"Yes, Sir, I have orders for Master Chief, Jack Norris," Varney said.

"I requested the Master Chief to be assigned to Buffalo because of his work with Northrop Grumman. He was Chief of the Boat on the USS. Greenville during ASDV trial runs. No one outside of Northrop Grumman knows this equipment more."

Varney checked his notes. "I also received clearances for two Naval Undersea Warfare Center engineers and Dr. Lace, senior science advisor. Another set of orders transferred Lieutenant Morton from Admiral Armstrong's staff."

The phone's growler interrupted.

Scott replied, "Captain, yes, the XO is here. Fine, bring the message to my stateroom." He turned to Varney. "You mentioned two engineers are coming aboard?"

Varney slid the personnel sheets from his folder. "Dr.

74

Glen Thomas is the project manager for Code 85 Unmanned Underwater Vehicle (UUV). He holds a Ph.D. in Electrical Engineering—"

"Okay. And the other engineer?"

"Dr. Fred Stone, a Ph.D. in Mechanical Engineering. The Defense Advanced Research Project, (DARPA), ordered them aboard to operate the UUV, which was placed in our torpedo room before leaving Hawaii."

Scott's face showed concern. "Do these scientists have any sea experience? We don't have time to babysit on what could be a dangerous assignment."

"The orders came from Washington." Varney handed a copy to Scott.

"Then, there's nothing to discuss. We have to comply with Washington's orders. XO, I don't know what we're heading into but it could get interesting."

"Agreed, Sir," Varney said.

Scott leaned back in his chair. Though he just met Tom Varney, he felt he could trust him. "Here's what I'm thinking. With tensions mounting between Israel and Iran, we may find ourselves in the middle of something messy. Buffalo must be ready for any eventuality, Tom. Once we're underway, schedule a meeting of all departments to set up battle drills. Just in case."

Varney already concluded this wasn't going to be a standard deployment. He was glad the CO appeared genuinely concerned about prepping the crew and building morale.

"Anything else, XO?" Scott asked.

"No, Sir, nothing else." Tom hesitated. "There is one more thing. Dr. Lace, Sir. I understand you requested her presence?"

"I did. Dr. Lace was invaluable during our previous shallow-water incursions. She's a world-class expert in underwater sound propagation and detection. She'll help us identify navigable points along the Iranian coastline, and incursion points, should that become necessary. Also, Admiral Armstrong, himself, ordered Lieutenant Morton here. I haven't had time to review her records. Talk to her and decide how best to utilize her skills."

"Yes, Sir."

"Has their berthing been assigned?"

"Not yet. I'll contact the Chief of the Boat to make the arrangements."

Scott checked his notes. "One final thing, without impacting maintenance schedules, I was serious about giving liberty to anyone you deem not essential for preparations. Make it for two days. I have a feeling they'll need the break." He smiled. "Tom, add your name to the list."

"Sir?"

"I've read your jacket and you deserve to see your family before we head out. Go home, XO. Buffalo will be fine."

Varney wanted to object but appreciated the chance to see his wife and children before sailing into God-knows-what. "Are you sure, Sir?"

"Affirmative. Just remain within reach in the unlikely event I need you. Relay that to the men as well." He closed his clipboard. "Anything else I should know?"

"No, Sir," Varney said. "Thank you, Sir." He stood and left the stateroom. He suspected why Scott had given the men liberty. Some of them might not come back from this mission. As he entered his stateroom, he fingered the gold cross dangling on the chain under his tee-shirt.

Chapter 13

Bandar-e-Abbas; Naval Base, Iran –

A line of dignitaries walked down the long cement pier behind the Iranian President and Admiral Al Jujair. They headed toward the Damavand, the newest Moudge, a Wave class destroyer. She was the second of seven to be commissioned for the Iranian navy. Jamaran, her sister ship, was docked across the wharf. The crew of both vessels, standing at attention, manned the railings on the main deck and upper levels. They were resplendent in crisp white uniforms.

For a destroyer, Admiral Jujair thought, Damavand is well armed with four Qader anti-ship missiles, a Faij-27 naval gun sitting forward of the bridge, an assortment of machine guns, and two triple torpedo tubes. She and her sister ship will do very well against the Americans. He imagined the destroyers supported by Boghammars, the new high-speed stealth attack craft. He visualized a swarm of Boghammars unleashing their firepower on surprised American ships. It won't be long now, he thought, admiring the sleek vessels.

The Admiral's attention shot back to the present when the military band played the Iranian National Anthem. Once the speeches began, he paid scant attention, detesting the pampering of politicians each time he wanted a new vessel.

"Allah, please give me strength," he mumbled.

"Sir?" Captain Kazim, his Chief of Staff, asked.

Jujair waved his hand. "Nothing. Schedule a meeting with Admiral Mokri next week. I want to discuss training exercises." And we have a lot to discuss, he thought, wishing he could be the one to fire a killer torpedo into the guts of an American ship.

Admiral Mokri was seated in the secure conference room reviewing his notes. He was confident his recommendations for training the Moudge crews in the use of their new shipboard sensors would impress Admiral Jujair. Just starting to relax, he heard the door open.

"Good morning, Admiral Mokri," Admiral Jujair said. "Time is of the essence. Let's start."

Admiral Mokri switched on the projector. "Admiral, with the commissioning of the Damavand, I recommend we intensify our anti-submarine readiness training by adding helicopters to the exercises."

Jujair stared at the helicopter on the screen. "Yes. I agree. Our crews must understand the problems associated with detecting and tracking submarines under all conditions. Only then will we be masters of our waters in the Persian Gulf and Straits of Hormuz."

Mokri pointed to a map. "Several of our submarine captains suggest we concentrate our search for enemy submarines at the northern entrance to our shipping lanes. The water is deeper and, therefore, a most likely place for boats to mask their presence using the merchant fleets entering and leaving the Gulf as camouflage."

Jujair studied the map. "Is it not true the detection of underwater objects by sound is nearly impossible in this area due to the noise of commercial traffic?"

"That is correct, Admiral. I propose our navy limits the amount of traffic during key periods, both day and night. Such control will enhance our ability to detect and identify underwater intruders."

"Very good. That will cause considerable disruption to such enemy missions."

Mokri felt encouraged. "May I ask, in the event our ships do detect an enemy submarine, what are the rules of engagement?"

Jujair liked the younger man's eagerness. "My preference would be to attack any submarine violating our waters. But, that would be an act of war which our government does not want to initiate, at least not yet." He smiled at his prodigy. "No, the limits of your actions, at least for the present, are to track and hound any submarine attempting to evade us. We will force them to surface, embarrassing themselves and their country. We will use our superior tactics and equipment to chase them the hell back into international waters."

Mokri looked disappointed.

Jujair gave him a sly look. "On the other hand, I see no reason why we can't order our surface vessels to drop mines on top of suspected invaders. If nothing else, it will inform these over-confident fools that their covert operations in our waters do not go undetected."

Mokri brightened up. "Yes, Sir. They are in for a rude awakening."

Jujair nodded. "Once the Damavand completes her shake-down, I want her ready for sea. I will contact Vice Admiral Salehi and order him to provide you with two submarines for your initial patrol. This experience will help us develop a coordinated plan of training unparalleled in history."

Admiral Mokri visualized an American submarine ravaged by one of his ships. He couldn't wait to see the embarrassment it would cause the hated Satan infidel nation across the ocean. Praise be to Allah that he had been the one chosen for this mission. His life meant nothing if he had the honor to sacrifice it for his country's victory.

Chapter 14

USS Mahan DDG 72, Persian Gulf, Qeshm Island –

Commander Mack Damon was roused from sleep by the 'Whoot' of the growler beside his bunk. "Captain speaking."

Hospital Corpsman, Master Chief, John Danielson, sounded urgent. "Captain, we've got a medical emergency that we're not equipped to handle. Weapons tech, FTG2 Wilson, suffered a stroke. We can't determine where the blockage is without more imaging capability. We need a major medical facility."

"Do what you can for him. I'll get back to you." Damon turned the station selector to the Executive Officer's stateroom and cranked the handle.

"XO," came the response.

"Call the Navigator and Communicator to the wardroom. We've got an emergency."

Commander Damon, XO Lieutenant Commander Bob James, the Navigator, and Communications Officer, Lieutenant Jim Baston, were just sitting down when Danielson rushed in.

"Grab a cup of coffee and have a seat, Bones," Damon said, pointing to an empty chair.

Danielson didn't bother with the coffee. "Sir, I managed to stabilize Wilson, but he has neurological impairment we can't diagnose. It could become fatal. We need an MRI as soon as possible."

"Bob, what's the closest facility?" Damon asked.

"We're closer to Bahrain than anywhere else. Our best bet is to transport him there," the Navigator replied.

Danielson said, "Bahrain's hospital is well equipped."

The Navigator spoke up, "We're about 120 miles northeast of Jebel Ali in Bahrain."

"Okay, XO, you and Nav confer with Doc," Damon said. "Com, contact Fifth Fleet, explain our situation. Tell them we're heading to Jebel Ali."

"Aye, Sir," Baston said, rushing from his seat.

Damon turned back to the Navigator, "Bob, lay in the most direct course to Jebel Ali. Order the OD to make turns for the best speed of advance. I'll brief the officers. We're sailing into dangerous waters, and I want everyone prepared for any Iranian craft."

The men left the CO alone with his thoughts, now focused on the twin issues of the health of his crewman and the safety of the entire ship should enemy gunboats decide to intercept them.

MK VI Patrol Boat MKVI-1, Jebel Ali Naval Station, Bahrain –

"Hey Skipper, we just received this flash traffic direct from Fifth Fleet!"

Fork halfway to his mouth, Master Chief Boatswain's Mate, Rick Jackson, mumbled, "What now?" He scanned the message and quickly called the other crew members to the cramped dining area. "There's a sailor on the USS Mahan who needs immediate medical attention. We are rendezvousing with her per Fifth Fleet's orders." He gave them a grim look. "Hell could be in the form of Iranian high-speed swarms."

"Hell is right," someone said.

Jackson shot him a look. "Our orders are to leave port asap, proceed at top speed to rendezvous, and make radio contact with the Mahan. Once linked up, we'll take the patient aboard and rush him to a medical facility in Bahrain. Guys, this kid is very sick, and we need to transport him back to a hospital, or he won't make it."

No one questioned their captain's resolve to help.

Jackson said, "Right. Saddle up, men. Let's get moving and save this kid."

The others left for their posts.

Captain Jackson called his communications operator. "Bob, Contact Base Operations. Verify they're in the loop. Ensure they are in contact with Lifeline Hospital and ask them to stand by to receive a critical patient. Make damned sure the medical staff gets notified. We'll contact them when we're an hour out. When clear of port, establish coms with USS Mahan. Tell them our call sign will be 'Roadrunner.'"

Jackson studied the Iranian coastline. He knew it was brimming with danger. Roadrunner was the perfect codename.

USS Mahan, Persian Gulf –

"Bones," Damon said, "We're approved to proceed to Jebel Ali. We'll be met on the way by patrol craft, call sign, 'Roadrunner.' Send HM1 Wayne with Wilson, if you can spare her?"

"Sounds like a plan," Doc said. "I just hope we're in time."

"I'll brief the TAO to be ready to Medevac once we rendezvous." It sounds easy, Damon thought, after Danielson left. I only hope the Iranians don't slow us down.

Ninety minutes later, Damon got his answer. The radar operator announced, "Captain, multiple contacts approaching from the southwest, bearing 260 degrees."

TAO Lieutenant Sam Gross reported. "They just appeared. They must have been hugging Greater or Lesser Tunb Islands."

The radar operator pointed to blips on his monitor. "They're fast and headed our way."

"Hell, there must be at least 50," Damon said. "Bridge, can you identify flag?"

"Can't tell, Captain. From the size of the returns on my bridge repeater, I'm guessing Boghammars, maybe a couple of Bladerunners."

"Bridge, sound GQ," Damon ordered. "If they want a fight, We'll give it to them."

The bridge jumped alive as everyone prepared for General Quarters.

Damon picked up the phone and called radio, "Lieutenant Baston, keep us in radio contact with Roadrunner. Alert them to the presence of probable unfriendlies." He paused and added, "Remind them the rules of engagement apply. Don't fire first, but be ready to return fire."

"Aye, Sir."

"Captain, the fore, and aft Mk 40 cannon guns are ready with high explosive incendiary rounds," the TAO reported.

Damon replied, "Those should light 'em up." He listened to the ready reports from the other ship departments. This is one great crew, he thought. Those bastards are in for a surprise if they try anything.

MK VI PB1 'Roadrunner,' South of Greater Tunb Island –

Johnson was staring hard at his screen. **"Master Chief, USS Mahan reports a swarm of high-speed boats approaching their position. I show 50 contacts closing fast on our destroyer."**

"Range," Jackson ordered.

"Ten-thousands yards and closing," Jackson replied. "USS Mahan reports another group of high-speed contacts leaving Abu Musa Island."

"Shit! Sound GQ," Jackson shouted. "Man, port, and starboard 50s. Place chain guns in standby mode. Assign any man not at GQ to the weapon's locker to draw an M-16. Position them on the bow and stern. Fire only if fired upon and on my order."

Chain gun console operator, Second Class, John Cain, called in. "We're manned and ready. Come on, assholes, do we have a surprise for you."

"Be careful what you wish for, Johnny," Jackson was interrupted by radar, "Sir, USS Mahan is in sight and closing. She's almost surrounded."

"Did Mahan reduce speed?" Jackson asked.

"No. Her skipper increased her speed. She's trying to break through their circle."

"Continue to close," Jackson said. "Range to Mahan?"

"Fifty-five hundred yards."

Jackson felt the tension as the range between his vessel and the Boghammars decreased. Would the Iranians risk the wrath of Mahan's formidable weapons? Were they crazed enough to try that?

Jackson's fears were confirmed when radar announced, "The second swarm of Boghammars split in half."

"Range?" Jackson asked, knowing he'd soon have to make a difficult decision.

"One thousand yards and closing."

Jackson looked out his port window. "We've got a second group racing down the portside and circling back." He hesitated only for a second and then gave the orders to maintain course and speed, plowing between two Boghammars. He saw an Iranian sailor get knocked into the water when his ship hit the stern of the Boghammar.

"Who's next?" Jackson shouted, enemy boats racing back in forth in front of him. Grabbing the phone, he announced, "all stations, this is the captain, we're under attack."

As if on cue, Iranians off his bow and stern fired AK-47s into the air.

Jackson knew this was a deliberate provocation to tempt his men to fire on the assault craft. He ordered into his mic, "All stations, hold your fire."

Directing his attention ahead, the Master Chief failed to observe a Boghammar, on the starboard side. He jumped at the sound of gunfire.

Three Iranian Guards fired their guns into the air. One pointed a rocket-propelled grenade launcher at the bridge.

He's going to ram us, Jackson thought. Shit!

The man with the RPG shouted commands at Jackson as more crewman fired into the air.

Jackson shifted the helm hard to port, trying to knock the attackers into the water before the rocket-grenade was fired.

The Boghammar dodged the maneuver and closed to within 400 yards of Jackson's boat.

Jackson saw the Iranian 51-caliber gun swivel toward his craft and open fire. White flashes erupted from the muzzle of the gun seconds before their bullets struck his ship's armor plating. "That's it! Light that asshole up, Johnny," he shouted to his gunner.

Petty Officer Cain pressed the trigger. The portside chain gun locked on the smaller craft. The metallic noise of the Bushmaster's chain drive was followed by the lobbing of ten explosive rounds into the Boghammar's hull. The massive explosion knocked Jackson to the deck.

Getting up, Jackson surveyed the water around his boat. Nothing remained on the surface. "Stupid idiots," he said, hating the waste of life. He turned back to the other ships. What would they do now? Whatever they tried, he was ready.

After the explosion of one of their craft, the rest of the flotilla reversed course and fled. Within a few minutes, little evidence remained of the brief but fatal engagement except debris on the water's surface.

Jackson kept his eyes on the scattering enemy. Was this attack evidence of a more aggressive Iranian official policy, or merely the result of an overeager skipper? Whether it was an accident or a death wish, the enemy captain made a fatally flawed decision. He heard his men cheering their victory and wondered how many more men on both sides would be sacrificed in this deadly game of chicken.

USS Mahan –

Watching the brief skirmish from his bridge, Commander Mack Damon exclaimed, "Holy shit!" as the explosion on the Iranian boat lit the sky. "XO, contact Roadrunner and see if they need assistance," he ordered.

The XO grabbed the phone. "Roadrunner, do you require assistance?"

"Negative," Captain Jackson responded.

"Captain, the hostiles are fleeing north. They've had enough."

"Roger. Remain alert, in case they decide to return."

Still watching for enemy interference, Commander Damon observed as Wilson, tied to a stretcher, was lowered into a rigid inflatable boat.

Hospital Corpsmen Wayne walked across the portable gangway to the inflatable. "Transfers complete," he signaled to the bridge, and the inflatable raced toward the rendezvous point.

Once the inflatable was safely away, Damon readied to proceed. "TAO, standby to resume our current duties. OOD secure from General Quarters. XO, join me in the wardroom. We need to draft our report for Fifth Fleet! Let them know there is one less Iranian Boghammar to attack our boats." He hoped this demonstration of America's naval might would deter the Iranians but had his doubts.

The Office of the President, Washington DC–

"What did you say?" President Washburn roared, staring hard at the Secretary of the Navy.

"Sir," Secretary Richards said again. "One of our patrol boats was attacked by the Iranians...and returned fire."

"Give me the damn details," the President muttered, sitting down on the couch.

"USS Mahan, a destroyer, had a life-threatening medical emergency. The closest medical facility was Lifeline Hospital in Jebel Ali."

"Where is that?" Washburn asked.

"Bahrain, Sir. We maintain a small shore establishment there. We luckily had one of the new high-speed MK VI Patrol Boats, refueling at Jebel Ali Naval Station—"

"Get to the battle," Washburn interrupted, weighing the impact of this incident.

"Yes, Mr. President. Fifth Fleet sent the Mark VI to meet the USS Mahan. The Mark VI was the quickest way to move the Mahan crewman."

"Okay, so what the hell happened?"

"A swarm of high-speed Iranian patrol craft advanced toward the USS Mahan as the Mark VI approached. Several Iranian Boghammars veered off, but one got too close, and, according to the Commander of the USS Mahan, and the Master Chief commanding the Mark VI, the Boghammar opened fire."

"Ah shit. I don't believe it," Washburn said.

"Well, Sir, consistent with our rules of engagement, the

Patrol Boat's skipper returned fire—"

"And?" Washburn sat forward.

"The Iranians are now short one Boghammar. The Mahan's CO says it disintegrated when our chain gun rounds hit their fuel tank. The boat was gone in less than a minute."

Washburn shook his head and asked, "Any survivors?"

"None, Sir."

"I'm sorry to hear that."

"Yes, Sir."

"Okay. Any noise yet from Tehran?"

"Not a peep." Richards slid a folder across the desk. "Sir, we believe this was an over-zealous act by the Iranian skipper. There aren't any indications that their officials ordered this attack."

"Let's hope so." Washburn shook his head. "How's the crewman from the Mahan?"

"He's in guarded condition, Sir, but the Mark VI broke its speed record to get him to hospital." Richards smiled. "Sir, they did a good job."

"Okay. Three things we need to do. First, swear the crew of our boats to secrecy. If Iran doesn't want to make this incident an issue, we won't, either. Second, message Guam to let Commander Scott know we need Buffalo underway now. Third, award the crew of the Mark VI a Presidential Unit Citation. Do it in a private ceremony." He frowned. "Now, if there's no more 'good' news, thank you." He stood and added, "Keep me informed at all times of anything going on with the Iranians. No slip-ups."

"Yes, Mr. President," Richards said, eager to be dismissed.

Washburn gazed out at the well-manicured lawn from his Oval office. He spoke in a soft voice, "If these Iranian cat and mouse games don't stop, I'm afraid we're in for a major confrontation. We know about Iran's threats. I'm worried they'll cripple our entire fleet unless we stop them now." He glanced at his calendar. "Let's retrieve Alias, so we at least know what the hell we're dealing with. Ray, send Buffalo to sea ASAP. No more delays."

After he was again alone in his office, Washburn stared at the painting of Abraham Lincoln, the President he most admired. Like Abe, Washburn would do almost anything to avoid a war, but if Iran pushed too hard, he knew he'd have little choice but to respond with force. "Scott's mission is critical," Washburn said to Lincoln's portrait. "I hope to God I picked the right man for the job."

Chapter 15

USS Buffalo; **Naval Base, Apra Harbor Guam –**

Commander Scott handed the message board to the XO. "How soon can we leave port?"

"Seventy-two hours once the ASDV is locked down, and the pre-checks are complete," Tom Varney replied.

"Gentleman, Whitfield wants us out of here ASAP. Things must be heating up. Prepare for reactor startup at midnight, Monday. I want to depart by 0800 Tuesday," Scott ordered.

Everyone left except for Scott, the XO, Navigator Lieutenant Jeff Obermeier, and Supply Officer LTJG Terry Washington.

"Terry, how far are you in loading our stores?" Scott asked.

Terry Washington looked as if he'd just graduated from high school. He reported aboard a month earlier as the Supply Officer. Onboard repair parts and good food were critical factors in maintaining morale and assuring successful operations. "Buffalo will receive a shipment of dry stores this afternoon. Now that I know we're getting underway, I'll contact the warehouse and request they deliver the perishables I ordered. Once we are loaded, the boat will have enough consumables for five months."

Scott frowned. "Just make sure there is enough TP. I don't want the crew to be without their favorite tissue." He gave a good-natured laugh.

Washington took his duties seriously, so he was relieved the new CO was laughing. "Yes, Sir. I'm on the case."

"Okay. Good job. XO, authorize liberty as we discussed. Give preference to crew with family on-base. Make sure they understand they must remain in communication with the duty watch officer. Thanks, Terry, you're dismissed. Nav, stick around, please."

Jeff, who had stood, sat back down at the table.

Scott began, "Jeff, we need to identify a minimal threat of detection track."

The navigator nodded. "I did this transit several years ago, so I'm aware that between the Pacific and the Indian Ocean, there are a slew of islands, shallow shoals, and other potential problems. You know the area is crawling with shipping too. They've got everything from small fishing boats to super Panamax tankers."

"That does complicate things," Scott said.

"We'll be transiting with the Advanced SEAL Delivery Vehicle, aboard. That means we need to make the trip submerged, with Navigation fixes limited to the occasional satellite pass. With this hump on our back, it will be easy for the Iranians to spot us."

Scott was impressed. "You're right. The water will be too shallow. We'll have little room to maneuver."

The Navigator scratched his head. "Sir, six or seven Straits connect the Pacific and Indian oceans, but most are far too shallow for submerged transit by Buffalo."

Scott made notes of the Nav's concerns. "Tom, make sure we brief the OODs and Diving Officers on the hazard of coming up to periscope depth for navigation fixes under these conditions."

"It would also be a good idea to practice Emergency Deep procedures." Tom Varney suggested.

"I agree." Scott jotted it down and then said, "Tom, go home. Spend a couple of nights with your wife and kids."

"Thank you, Captain." Varney reluctantly got up. "I hate to leave you like this."

"Tom, there is nothing you can do here that I can't. If I run into a problem, I'll call you."

"But—"

"Go home, Tom. That's an order. I don't want you back until 0500 Tuesday."

Tom turned to leave just as the Squawk Box growled. It was Lieutenant Wilkinson, the weapons officer. "The shipyard completed the installation of the ASDV. Master Chief Norris and the corporate techs are verifying electrical connections now. They're also checking potential mechanical issues and preparing for repairs at sea. The Master Chief indicated the work should finish in about five hours."

"Thanks, Steve. we'll leave once the engineering and weapons departments complete pre-deployment checks," Scott said and saw Varney watching from the doorway. "What are you waiting for, Tom? Go home before I change my mind."

Varney left but hoped leaving the new CO with his boat wasn't a mistake.

"Morning, Sir," the XO said, looking refreshed after two days of R&R.

"Good morning, Tom." Scott was genuinely glad to see his XO.

"What's our status?" Varney asked, perusing his charts.

Scott replied, "Normal start. The turbine generators are supplying all loads with shore power disconnected. Don't worry. All are functional." He smiled. "They're rolling the engines to keep them warm. The Engineering Officer on duty reports that he is ready to engage the clutch, and we can cast off when ready."

Varney nodded. "Great job. Any pressing issues I should attend to?"

"Take the muster and prepare to go to sea if everyone's on board," Scott said.

"Yes, Sir." Varney left.

Absorbed in examining the crew records, Scott didn't realize an hour passed until the XO called, "Ready to depart, Captain."

"Do we have a full muster? Are Dr. Lace and Lieutenant Morton aboard?" Scott asked.

"Yes, Sir. The ladies checked in at 0530. They're in the wardroom waiting for the Chief of the Boat to show them to their quarters."

"I'll be right there." Grabbing his cap, Scott headed for Control. Moving to the ladder, extending three stories up to the bridge, he shouted, "Up Ladder." Once in position, he said, "XO, get us underway."

"Aye, Sir," Varney said.

Scott was eager to test the mettle of the ship and crew. He realized that this wasn't a game. There was real danger ahead, and all their lives depended on him.

The Office of the President; Washington, DC –

President Washburn summoned the Secretary of the Navy and CIA Director, as well his Chief-of-Staff, Ian Williams. "How much longer before Buffalo is at sea?" He asked, frustrated at not receiving a report about the sub deploying from the base.

"Buffalo will be leaving port within two hours," Richards responded. "They had to wait for the Advance SEAL Delivery Vehicle. It's now attached to the submarine's hull, so they're ready to go."

Washburn looked annoyed. "And the SEALs, when are they due to arrive?"

"In two weeks," Richards replied. "Once Buffalo arrives in the Gulf of Oman. If there aren't any more delays—"

Washburn stared at them with hard eyes. "Gentlemen, let's put this straight right now. There is no if. And no more delays. Do you understand me?"

"Yes, Sir," Richards said.

"Sir, we have an update on the Iranian Damavand class destroyer," Ure said, pulling the report from his case.

"You look worried," Washburn said

Richards jumped in. "Mr. President, Iran's newest Frigates are reported to be equipped with the most advanced surface and subsurface combat weapon suites—"

"What does that mean in English?" Washburn asked, increasingly worried by all the Intel about Iran's new capabilities.

Richards recognized the President's impatience. "Sir, Buffalo will be hard-pressed to remain undetected if these destroyers start hunting her."

The President glared at Richards. "Are you having second thoughts about Scott?"

"No, Mr. President. Dr. Ure and I believe Scott is the correct choice—"

"Good! Now no more delays. Notify me when Buffalo leaves port." Washburn returned to his seat. "Good day, Gentlemen."

"He's in a foul mood this morning," Ure said, once outside the door. "Let me know as soon as Buffalo leaves port." He stopped in mid-stride. "Ray, what are you not telling the President and me? What's eating you?"

Richards searched the hall to be sure nobody was listening. "Although I acceded to reinstate Scott, I have reservations on his ability to execute this mission—"

"It's kind of late to raise that now," Ure snapped.

"I understand. But if Scott screws up and Buffalo is discovered by Iran...hell, our careers are over." He shook his head. "More important, the world will know this administration failed to stop Iran. Imagine the repercussions of that."

"Imagine the repercussions if we do nothing," Ure replied. "We just better hope Scott is the right man for this job."

Richards nodded and said a silent prayer.

Chapter 16

USS Buffalo; Transit –

Scott opened the stateroom safe and pulled out a thick 10 by 13-inch manila envelope marked 'TOP SECRET.' He noted his name in the upper right-hand corner. Turning the classified package over, Scott sat down, broke the seal, and withdrew the orders and communication codes.

Vice Admiral Submarine Force
U.S. Fifth Fleet

To: Commander Joseph L. Scott, Commanding Officer, USS Buffalo SSN-715

From: Vice Admiral Charles W. Clarke, Submarine Force U.S. Fifth Fleet.

Subject: Operation 'Tip Toe'

Appendix: Communication between Commander U.S. Naval Forces Central/ U.S. Fifth Fleet and Buffalo.

USS Buffalo is hereby ordered to proceed at best speed, to the

Straits of Hormuz and initiate operation 'Tip Toe' as outlined below:

1. Embark SEAL Team 6 at coordinates 25°09'51.87 N; 57°29'15.04'E. Should changes to the rendezvous point be required, Fifth Fleet will issue a separate message.
2. Assist Naval Underwater Warfare Center engineers in conducting underwater mapping.
3. Initiate 'Clean Sweep.' Survey all shipping corridors in the Straits of Hormuz for mines. Record type and location.
4. Monitor Iranian naval activity around Bandar-e-Abbas Naval Base and Straits of Hormuz.
5. Maintain track on Iranian submarines in the Straits of Hormuz and the Gulf of Oman.
6. Rules of Engagement: Buffalo is not authorized to engage hostile units unless first fired upon.

Scott sat back. The orders were similar to previous ones but more complex because of the significant threat from Iran. He was confident he had a good crew but wondered if they were up to everything Washington was demanding. Was he?

Varney knocked and entered.

Scott handed the orders to his XO.

Varney's face remained expressionless as he read the document.

"What do you think, Tom?" Scott asked.

"It's a lot," Varney said.

"Tom, although I am confident this crew can stand up to what awaits us, for their sake, we must drill them hard. I suspect Iran will try and stop us with everything they've got. Some of which we may not even know about."

"Buffalo has the stealth to operate undetected in the Gulf," Varney said.

"I know, and our science advisor will help locate the penetration points for the SEALs to land, even in the shallows. I believe we have the best assets available but let's not fool ourselves. This mission won't be a walk in the park."

"We're ready, Sir. What are your orders?"

Scott had already set his priorities. "First, let's drill the crew on maintaining ultra-quiet operations. Second, train all diving officers on precise depth control. We can't afford Buffalo being seen in shallow water."

"I understand," Varney said, taking notes.

"Third, impress upon the OODs that they must remain vigilant at all times. There likely will be much smaller craft patrolling, especially near the naval base and in the channels." He stopped to think. "We'll limit our periscope depth excursions as much as possible during the day."

"Anything else, Sir?"

Scott hesitated. "Yes. Let's ensure the ASDV is ready for deployment at a moment's notice. I'm hoping by using it. we can limit the time Buffalo needs to operate in shallow water."

"I'll check that right away," Varney said.

Scott smiled. "Tom, I know we're ready. But you know Washington. Our boys back there may not be telling us everything."

Varney nodded.

Scott felt comfortable confiding in his XO. "There are a lot of things I don't understand right now."

Varney smiled. "With permission, Sir. I think you are the

right man for this job."

"There's more. The specialists and crew members I requested were transferred in record time. No questions asked. The Defense Advanced Research Projects Agency, in conjunction with the Naval Undersea Warfare Center placed an advanced prototype aboard and civilian engineers to operate the damn unit. There is a reason this vehicle was placed aboard our ship. Talk to those engineers and find out what their orders are."

"Yes, Sir."

"Tom put a training plan together, and I will approve it, but first, I want you to review this document." He opened his safe and withdrew a file marked 'Top Secret' emblazoned across it in red block letters. "You'll find this interesting reading." He handed it to the XO."

Varney read the title, 'Mine Deployment in the Persian Gulf' and nodded. "You're right. It will be interesting reading." He handed the file back to Scott who locked it in his safe. "Have you eaten yet?"

"No, Sir. I was heading down to the wardroom after our meeting."

Stopping in Control, Scott announced to the crew over the 1MC system, "All hands, this is the Captain. I have read our orders. What I can tell you is that Buffalo is ordered to the Persian Gulf. The rest will be relayed to you shortly." From the look on his XO's face, he knew the man he was trusting understood the risks of this top-secret mission and was ready to do what he could to help Buffalo succeed.

Scott and Varney entered the wardroom as the second sitting started.

"May we join you?" Scott asked heading to his sit at the head of the table.

The men and women at the table nodded.

Scott spotted Drs. Stone and Thomas. Janice Lace and Lieutenant Morton were sitting toward the end of the table with the two civilian engineers. He thought he caught Janice shooting glances at him during her conversation.

Janice thought Scott was deliberately avoiding her. She was confused. They'd been at sea for eight hours, and he'd made no effort to meet with her alone. She knew she shouldn't care, feel relieved. But seeing him again, rekindled the attraction. Was it only her physical longing? She should hate him, but somehow that wasn't possible. How the hell am I going to survive this trip, she thought, aware Morton was observing her. Lieutenant Morton—another problem. Damn Scott and the Navy, she groaned, but knew she didn't mean it.

"Dr. Stone. Welcome aboard Buffalo. I understand you hold a Ph.D. from MIT?"

"Yes, Sir. My brother Glen and I received our degrees while working at NUWC. We were selected for their doctorate program."

Janice tried not to show she was annoyed that Scott was ignoring her. She pretended to listen to the conversation but felt distracted. Dr. Stone has a handsome face, high cheekbones, and broad shoulders. Why can't I be interested in someone like him and not Joe Scott?

Scott studied the two engineers. "I had no idea you two are brothers. Why are your surnames different?" He cast a quick glance at Janice, who appeared to be staring at Dr. Thomas.

Morton was looking at Scott.

Dr. Stone replied, "My father died two years after I was born. Our mom remarried, hence the different surnames."

Janice was simmering. Scott was still ignoring her. Being manipulated by Scott into this situation was a huge mistake.

"Dr. Lace, Lieutenant Morton, welcome aboard."

"Thank you, Sir," Morton said, smiling.

Janice nodded.

Scott took note of Janice's lack of warmth but had important matters to discuss. "Dr. Lace, with your knowledge of the acoustic environment, would you, when time permits, hold classes for the men on the acoustics of the coastal areas we'll be working in?"

Janice tried to smile. "Thank you, Sir, for the warm welcome. Lieutenant Morton, and I will be happy to instruct your crew as you require." She turned to Morton, who nodded her agreement.

Scott said, "That will be a big help." So far, so good, he thought.

Janice continued, "Lieutenant Morton and I discussed this earlier. A good place to start would be with your acoustic library and the sound velocity profiles we anticipate in the Gulf and Straits of Hormuz. I'm sure your database will need updating with current measurements, for greater counter-detection accuracy."

"I don't understand," Lieutenant Wilkinson, Weapons Officer, asked. "Are these updates critical?"

Janice smiled at the Weapons Officer. "The information stored in your acoustic library is based on algorithms NUWC used to calculate water conditions. It is not up to date."

"Don't we obtain the current temperature profile and sound

velocity data when we launch a probe?" Lieutenant Wilkinson asked, surprised to learn Buffalo had depended on outdated information.

"Yes. You can launch a probe to get the current water conditions, but most sonar teams rely on the data provided by the ship acoustic software library."

Varney stepped in. "How do we assure that we're using the best information?"

"Based on our briefing about the UUV, I propose to load the latest acoustic data files into an algorithm Lieutenant Morton, and I are working on. We'll feed your memory banks real-time acoustic data to replace your outdated files," Janice said.

"Sounds like you have your work cut out for you," Varney remarked, impressed with Dr. Lace's expertise.

Scott said, "They do."

Morton's eyes met Scott's. "I want to thank you for allowing me to assist Dr. Lace." She gave him a warm smile.

Janice bristled at the southern sweetness.

Scott returned the smile. "With your background, Lieutenant, I know you and Dr. Lace will make the perfect team."

"When will you be able to provide a demonstration of the new system?" Varney asked.

"We'll develop a model and test it within the next week," Lieutenant Morton replied. "My goal is to be able to filter out the background noise and increase our operators' recognition of potential targets."

Janice restrained herself from correcting her with, 'Our goal.' Now was not the right time, not in front of Scott.

"This is vital work," Scott said. "We'll be operating close to many different classes of Iranian vessels. Distinguishing between background noise and the noise of their craft is paramount for the safety of this ship. It will enhance the de-tection of surface and subsurface friendlies and hostiles." He turned to Wilkinson, "Steve, contact Senior Chief Richardson and draft a plan to conduct an acoustic survey using the towed array sensor."

"Yes, Sir."

"Great!" Scott replied. "What is the status of our propulsion plant?"

"Everything aft is fine. The only issues are with the oxygen generator and number two high-pressure air compressor. The compressor is a straightforward fix, just a third-stage gasket leak, already being repaired. Auxiliary division is still troubleshooting the O2 Generator," the Engineer replied.

"Inform me when the Generator issue is resolved."

"Yes, Sir," Wilkinson said.

Varney leaned toward Scott. "I can see why you brought Dr. Lace and Lieutenant Morton aboard. If they can help filter out the background noise of the ships in the Gulf, it will be a huge advantage at being able to spot enemy vessels."

And surviving this mission, Scott thought, admiring Janice's ability to put their past aside and work for the benefit of the crew. The ship's safety depended on every member doing their job without distraction, so why am I thinking of her?

Chapter 17

USS Buffalo; Underway –

"Let's go, it's time for our meeting," Fred Stone urged his brother who was final-checking the UUV. Picking up his black leather work bag, he walked between the rows of torpedoes.

"Please take a seat," Scott said. "I've reviewed the messages sent by the Defense Advanced Research Projects Agency (DARPA). They authorized the Unmanned Underwater Vehicle, but what your task is still a mystery to me." He stared at their silent faces. "I'm not sure I like the idea your equipment is taking up two spaces that we could use for additional torpedoes."

Dr. Stone realized this might not be an easy sell. Scott's support was needed if they were going to accomplish their orders. He would risk whatever it took to achieve his goals.

"Captain," Dr. Thomas said. "We're authorized to—"

A knock at the door interrupted the meeting.

"Enter," the XO said.

Dr. Lace and Lieutenant Morton were in the doorway.

Scott smiled. "Dr. Lace, Lieutenant Morton, please, join us. This discussion about the UUV will interest you."

"Thank you," Morton replied.

She and Janice took seats.

Scott's eyes lingered a little longer on Janice. "Dr. Thomas, continue."

Thomas glanced at his brother and said, "May I ask a question first?"

"Sure, what is it?"

"What's a baffle?" The young Ph.D. asked.

Scott smiled. "Good question, Dr. Thomas. I hope all of you feel free to ask about anything you don't understand. A baffle is an area behind a submarine where its sonar is unable to pick up sounds of other craft because the sensors are mounted on the hull. It's difficult to hear a boat in the baffle behind you when your propeller is making noise there." He saw the look of confusion. "We use the term 'baffle clear' to describe what we do before coming to periscope depth. We turn 90 degrees to one side until we can hear what is in the region astern of us. We then return to the original course and turn 90 degrees to the other side. Have I answered your question?"

"Yes, Sir. Thank you." Thomas said. He removed the double wrap binding from his test plans marked 'Classified.' He distributed a copy to each person at the table. "Over three years, Code 85, in partnership with DARPA, developed several UUV prototypes. Last year, we tested an electric motor driven vehicle designed to swim from a host submarine. We call the vehicle, Hunter."

"Good name," Scott said, taking notes.

"Hunter is capable of surveying the sea bottom in preparation for SEAL incursions, or assaults on enemy submarines." He let this sink in. "Due to its success in preliminary testing, we expanded the program to include locating and mapping harbor entryways and pinpointing mines with an advanced-type scanner in the UUV's nose."

Scott interrupted. "Has Hunter been used to search for mines?"

Stone replied, "Sir, this is the first time Hunter will be deployed from a submarine for locating subsurface mines, but we're confident—"

"Are you kidding me? Let me see if I understand what you said. Your craft has never been launched from a submarine nor tested in shallow water? Dr. Thomas, do you understand this ship and crew's survival could depend on your vehicle's untested capability?"

Thomas was taken off-guard by the Captain's skepticism. "I understand your concern, Sir, but Dr. Stone and I conducted six months of extensive testing at the Atlantic Undersea Test and Evaluation Center in the Bahamas, and the shallow waters of Narragansett Bay. The UUV operated as designed. DARPA would not order the unit onto your ship if it was not ready."

Scott wasn't convinced. He stared at Thomas, suspecting the scientist knew a lot more than he was sharing.

Stone continued, "We've taken great pains to make the UUV undetectable by an enemy."

"Can you go into detail on how that's accomplished?" Janice asked.

"Yes, of course. Hunter is cylindrical in shape and the same size as the old MK 37 electric torpedo. It's only 19 inches in diameter, so it can 'swim out' from a standard 21-inch torpedo tube under its own power, but without the usual torpedo launching noise. That's a considerable advantage—"

"Okay. You're saying we can launch the unit without our ship being detected?" Scott interrupted again.

"Yes, Sir. It is smaller and 1,100 pounds lighter than a Mk 48 ADCAP torpedo," Stone replied.

"Okay, assuming it is undetectable, how does it complete its mission?" Scott was still skeptical.

"The UUV is mounted with forward-looking and side-scanning sonar to form a visual image. The wire guidance system is up-graded with Teflon coated shielded fiber optical strands. This allows a massive amount of data to be passed between the UUV and its computer contact. Its tether provides external power from the host submarine—"

"What if the tether breaks?" Scott interrupted.

"The UUV houses an electric motor and batteries that provide power if the tether breaks," Thomas answered.

"And how long can it last on those batteries?" Varney asked.

"Hunter can be free of the host submarine up to 72 hours. This, of course, is speed dependent. The operator can even program the UUV to drop into hibernation mode, then resume searching along pre-established way-points."

"What about counter-detection?" Steve Wilkinson asked. "We might be required to maintain ultra-quiet conditions."

"Noise is almost nil," Stone replied. "The electrical motor has been tested, and no sound radiates through the vehicle's hull."

Scott had been reading the stats. "Dr. Thomas, once Hunter is deployed, I want you to place it in a stationary position above the seafloor. We'll conduct a sound survey on the UUV," he said, still not willing to trust the experts, who might have a vested interest in its success.

"Sir. That's fine but I already told you Hunter is virtually noiseless."

"I still want it done." Scott shook his head. "If I understand you, Hunter will provide real-time video of what it sees?"

"Yes, Sir. All visual tapes will be sent to my computer in

real-time," Stone replied.

Scott thumbed through the tech manual. "Anything else we should know?" He asked, "I know you said it's impossible, but what if an enemy craft catches Hunter?"

"In this most unlikely event, Hunter can self-destruct. It can become a lethal weapon against its captor," Dr. Thomas said.

Lieutenant Wilkinson exploded, "Friggin' wonderful! As if I don't have enough to be concerned about. Here's a 'bomb' capable of destroying us housed in my torpedo room."

"Is Lieutenant Wilkinson's concern justified?" Scott asked.

Thomas shook his head. "No, Sir. We've taken safeguards to prevent an accident—"

"But accidental ignition is possible. Is there any chance Hunter could trigger mines?"

"No, Sir," Stone responded. "Hunter's hull is made of a composite material. The magnetic field produced from the electric motor is insulated to eliminate detonation."

Thomas chimed in, sensing the project was on thin ice with the skeptical Captain, "Our engineers placed the UUV within one foot of every known mine without triggering any detonators. Sir, we worked hard on safety issues."

Scott closed the file. "Thank you, gentlemen. I will study your manual and note additional concerns." He turned to Janice. "Dr. Lace, what do you anticipate visibility will be in the channels?"

Janice replied in her most professional tone, "Less than 32 feet. If there is a lot of channel traffic or storms in the area, more like 10 to 15 feet."

Dr. Thomas, sensing an opening, interrupted, "Captain, Hunter's sonar will detect and alert us of the presence of any object floating above the seafloor or on the bottom at a distance greater than 30 feet."

Scott frowned. "It appears there are a lot of unanswered questions at present, Dr. Thomas. How do we retrieve Hunter, for instance?"

"Once her mission is complete, the vehicle will return to the mother ship and enter stern first into the torpedo tube."

"What about the tether," Scott asked.

Stone pointed to a slide showing the wire anchoring the UUV to Buffalo. "Before reentering, Hunter will, on command, sever the remaining wire."

Wilkinson shook his head. "What about the tracking device attached to the torpedo door. Won't that be detectable by other ships' sonar?"

"No, Sir. This device is only detectable within 100 feet of the torpedo. It uses a very low frequency outside the detection range of all passive sonars.."

Scott turned to Doctors Stone and Thomas. "Doctors, I want Hunter to use the stealth option out of the torpedo tube. Understood?"

"Yes, Sir," Thomas said.

"XO, make sure the officers on duty in Control understand Buffalo must remain at slow speed when Hunter is deployed. Steve, notify Chief Juststone about this igniter. I want him to monitor the vehicle while the unit is on board. I also want him involved with Hunter's operations."

"Yes, Sir."

"I will be running a diagnostic on the system after this meeting if you care to join us, Dr. Lace," Thomas said.

Scott shot him a glance. "Dr. Lace, show Lt. Pearson, where the SEALs incursion point was during our last mission here."

Janice pointed her laser at the Bandar-e-Abbas Naval Base. "This is the precise site."

"Excellent," Scott said. "Video pictures of the mines and shallows will be a huge help during this operation." He glanced at Thomas. "Hunter might be a godsend if everything you state is correct. Thank you, gentlemen, and Dr. Lace."

There was a knock on the wardroom door, and IT Weathers handed Scott the message board.

Lifting the lid, Scott read the message and said, "Would all but the officers, please leave the wardroom."

Drs. Lace, Stone, Thomas, and Morton hurried out.

"What was that all about?" Stone asked, once outside.

"Nothing good, I'm guessing," Thomas said. "He's a cynical bastard."

Stone laughed, "You would be too if you had this ship and all the crew in your hands."

Janice sighed. She was beginning to think nothing good was coming from this mission. She only hoped her work would keep her too busy to allow her to show her frustration with Scott.

"Good meeting," Morton said, the sweet smile burning holes in Janice's brain.

"Let's hit the books," Janice replied, wondering if Morton was ever going to show her true self.

Back in the wardroom, Scott handed the message board to the XO. "Gentlemen, Fifth Fleet issued a warning to all naval units of increased Iranian threats to our ships. According to this message, USS Mahan and PB 1 were attacked by Iranian boats. This occurred while they were transporting an injured sailor." He let this sink in and continued, "Our patrol boat returned fire and destroyed the attacking vessel, a Boghammar."

The officers were silently mulling the implications of this new information.

Scott frowned. "I'm sure you know what this incident means, so let's be prepared for all eventualities. Thank you."

The officers rose and left the room.

Varney remained behind. "We're heading into deep shit," he said.

Scott nodded. "I only hope this UUV is as good as they say it is." He wished he had left Janice in Hawaii. This latest news made him realize he had placed her in great danger.

Chapter 18

USS Buffalo; Gulf of Oman –

Scott was signing the Night Orders when Varney knocked and entered his stateroom. "I reviewed the Eight O'clock Reports and the updated satellite navigation. All conditions are normal; Buffalo is on track and on time. There was one issue. Maneuvering reported a high chloride alarm from one of the condensate system salinity cells."

"Status?" Scott asked, still preoccupied with his thoughts about the UUV.

Varney smiled. "Initial and backup chemical analyses were negative."

"Good. You performed cleaning?"

"Yes, Sir. The sensor is functioning again, so all is well in engineering."

Scott nodded. "In eight hours, we're scheduled to rendezvous with SEAL Team 6. I want to sit down with their commander and discuss their orders." He looked up. "The OOD's must continue depth control drills."

"I had the duty officer drill each section. I think you'll be pleased with the results."

"I'm sure I will. I want to meet with Lieutenant Morton and Dr. Lace for an update on the acoustic algorithms they're developing. We need to be prepared before we enter the Gulf."

Varney understood there was no telling what Iran had in its inventory of weapons. Jet skis weren't far-fetched.

Scott continued, "I don't want the Iranians testing their increased capabilities on us. The key is to continue upgrading our understanding of the operating environment. Hunter and the expertise of Dr. Lace, Lieutenant Morton, and the two engineers will increase our abilities a great deal, assuming the UUV performs up to their expectations."

"I concur, Captain. The sooner we can record hard acoustic data on this new type of high speed, low noise, Iranian threat, the better it will be for the entire fleet."

"Yep. I want Hunter in the water as soon and as often as possible. It won't do us one damned bit of good sitting in the torpedo room. We need to gather all the Intel on their underwater defenses."

"Agree, but the engineers stated they only arrived with ten tether canisters."

Scott handed Varney a requisition order. "I instructed Dr. Stone to order 15 more canisters to be delivered to the SEALs in Fifth Fleet. Forward a copy of the Operations Order to Weps, Nav, and the engineers."

"Aye, Sir," Varney said, impressed again with the CO's knowledge.

Scott picked up the phone, spun the growler. "OOD, when do we update our navigational status?"

"The next NAVSAT will be in 30 minutes," Wilkinson replied.

"Very well, Steve, when you raise the transit mast for a NAVSAT update, extend the communication and navigation antennas. Also, let's look at the surface picture for un-friendlies before transmitting our message traffic." He looked at Varney. "Tom, continue to limit coming to periscope depth until after dark. I don't want to chance us being spotted. I'll be in my stateroom if anything comes up."

Varney hoped nothing would happen.

USS Buffalo –

A broad smile crossed Scott's face visualizing standing against a fireplace in the living room he and Janice had shared in New London, Connecticut. The smell of the century-old colonial house, the wide-planked, yellow, pine floors, and fluted window and door trim with rosettes at each corner brought back fond memories of their time together.

The crackling of the burning logs he saw in his mind replaced the hum from the fan in his stateroom. Eager to wrap his arms around Janice after returning from months at sea, he had stared into her eyes as she undressed before him. In a strange, out-of-body fantasy, he saw himself moving close to her. He smelled the fragrance from the perfume he'd given her. The passion radiating from her body was palpable. Her breath brushed against his face. Unable to control his desire, he pulled her into his arms, pressing his body against her. His initial kiss was rough and eager, long and hard.

Janice broke from his lips and gently pushed him away.

He wondered what was wrong.

Taking his hand, Janice led him into the bedroom. She stopped at the foot of the bed.

He pulled her into his arms. They kissed again, each fueling the other's desire. He whispered, "I love you, Janice," as he lowered her onto the bed.

The high-pitched shriek of the growler shattered Scott's dream. His duties left him no more time to think about the past.

"Captain, all message traffic has been sent. Returning to ordered course and speed," the OOD reported.

"Thank you," Scott said, looking at the clock and realizing he'd been asleep for only an hour. Not enough. He shut his eyes again, trying to recapture the dream. No good. He lay awake, thoughts fighting for prominence in his brain.

Buffalo started her descent back to transit depth. The slight vibration when the sub's speed increased reminded Scott that she was heading toward the Gulf of Oman. Sleep was impossible.

Israeli Naval Submarine Tannin (Israeli SSK Dolphin-2 Class); Gulf of Oman –

Sigen Aluf Lev Zak, age 36, considered himself one of the luckiest men in the Israeli Defense Forces (IDF). At a rank equivalent to an American Lieutenant Colonel, he was given command of the INS Tannin. She was one of two Israeli Dolphin-class II submarines, with German engineering, boasting the Seimens Air Independent Propulsion system. This made Tannin capable of remaining underwater for 30 days under normal operating conditions with a maximum speed of 25 knots without charging her batteries.

Zak gazed around Tannin's Combat Information Center. Space was tight, crammed with electronic equipment making her a formidable weapon. Measuring 225 feet in length with a 22-foot beam, she had state-of-the-art automatic sensor management, fire control, navigation, and operations systems. She was bristling with the latest anti-submarine armament, including 16 DM2A4 Seehecht wire-guided torpedoes. She can also carried a nuclear-tipped 'Popeye' turbo cruise missile, and the U.S. supplied Harpoon ship-to-ship missiles. He felt confident she was ready for any event.

Tannin's Suez transit involved sailing through hostile territory, from the northern entrance at Port Said, through the canal to the Great Bitter Lake, and down the narrow channel to Suez and into the Red Sea. Every navy in the world conjectured what Israel's objectives in the region were. They worried any incursion into Iran's territory by an Israeli craft would spark a major confrontation.

The Haifa Naval Base pre-cruise briefing with Zak and Lieutenant Colonel Pfeffer, his XO, resulted in Tannin being ordered to idle at the mouth of the Persian Gulf to obtain acoustic and other Intel about submarine operations in the region.

Zak knew the risks. He was kept abreast of any movements by Iranian or other vessels in the area by Israeli Central Command. He and his crew remained at constant alert.

Arriving at the Gulf of Oman, Tannin's Sonar technician reported a faint, intermittent contact, on the 60 Hz band. His tentative classification was a 688-class submarine's reactor coolant pumps.

"Is your classification definite?" Zak asked, walking over to the sonar station aft of the periscopes.

"No, Sir," Petty Officer Dan Kahan said, listening for better contacts. "Not 100 percent."

Zak knew the Rafael sonar was the first system Israel possessed that could discriminate weak contacts from background noises. A new system, there was nothing to compare it to in the Israeli acoustic library. "Let's play it safe for now. Stay in her baffles while we run sound cuts. What's her course?"

"Looks like she's headed towards the Straits, Sir," the Electronic Technician Navigator, Petty Officer Abelman, reported.

"Distance to the Straits, XO?"

"Three Hundred nautical miles."

Zak was deep in thought. "If an American, she's not a threat, but we can't be sure. Run sound cuts for our data bank, but stay alert. Unless she makes an unexpected course change, let's just wish her safe travel and good hunting. She'll need it where she's headed." He turned to his XO and smiled. "Let her arrive first, and we'll wait and see if all hell breaks loose."

USS Buffalo –

"Chief," Sonar Technician Submarines, (STS1), Sorenson piped up, "I noted a slight echo when we cleared baffles just now. I think someone behind us slowed, possibly to avoid detection. Presently, I detect no machine noise and no cavitation."

Richardson studied the waterfall display in front of Sorenson's station, then checked the trace on the strip chart. The latter showed only several tiny but discrete noise spikes.

"Yep, it isn't much, but we see the spike. Nice catch, Sorenson."

"Conn, we detected a possible transient contact. Very faint, bearing 160 degrees. Difficult to track."

"Captain's on his way," the OOD said.

"Chief, what have you got?" Scott asked upon entering.

"Well, Sir, it's either nothing or a quiet diesel boat keeping pace with us at 10 knots," Richardson said.

"You're not sure?" Scott asked.

"Petty Officer Sorenson thought he heard, and the trace confirms, a slight tonal when we cleared baffles last. It was so brief we weren't sure there had been any transient until we checked the printout." He showed Scott the strip chart. "It slowed when we cleared baffles."

Scott studied the printout. "If she's on the same course we are, she could be intending to enter the Straits." He peered at the monitor. "It seems unlikely there are any Iranian boats this far outside the Straits of Hormuz." He studied the chart again. "Very well, Chief, let's go with your assumption for now, but keep your ears open and let Conn know if you pick up this unidentified boat again." He put down the chart. "I don't want to take any chances we've got a hostile on our tail." Scott turned to Varney and motioned him to follow him to his stateroom. Once the door was closed, he indicated a chair. "Tom, do you recall all the kerfuffle about a week ago regarding an Israeli boat transiting the Suez?"

"Yes, Sir. It made me recall Psalm 23, the 'Valley of the Shadow of Death' part. Egypt and Sudan on the right, Saudis and Yemen on the left, and they all want your country dead."

Scott nodded. "Well, the sonar contact we just detected could have been an Israeli boat running submerged under ultra-quiet conditions. Tracking us at ten knots implies it must be using fuel cell Air-Independent Propulsion or some variant. My guess is it could be a Dolphin."

"That could be trouble," Varney said.

Scott leaned forward. "If she's in the region outside the Straits of Hormuz, no big deal, but, if we're both going where wise men fear to tread, you're right, it could be interesting."

Chapter 19

National Geospatial-Intelligence Agency; **Dahlgren, VA -**

Colonel Bill Johnson was sitting at his desk when Technical Sergeant Wallace knocked on his door. "Colonel, I just analyzed the new pictures from the KH-4B Corona strategic reconnaissance satellite."

Johnson accepted the pictures and listened to Wallace's analysis of the images displayed in the Straits of Hormuz, near the Bandar-e-Abbas Naval Base.

Wallace pointed to the first photo with the tip of his pencil. "The picture shows a destroyer north of the Musandam, between the three islands in the middle of the Straits. Astern of the destroyer, there are white spots. I count six in various shapes, depending on their distance from the destroyer."

"Can we identify any of them?" Johnson asked.

"I was able to distinguish personnel on the fantail, possibly dropping objects over the side. I'm guessing bombs or grenades."

"Any more prints?" Johnson asked, staring hard at the image.

"Yes, Sir." Wallace placed several photos on the desk.

"What I'm I looking at?" Johnson asked.

"The destroyers appear to be searching between the channels. They may be tracking a submerged contact."

"Are any of our subs in the vicinity?"

"I don't know," Wallace responded. "I doubt if the intelligence agency would inform us if they knew. They could be working exercises with their submarines, to test their anti-submarine warfare capabilities."

"Sounds reasonable, Anything else?"

"Before the Iranian destroyers entered the commercial shipping lanes, they blocked commercial shipping. They issued warnings not to enter the north and south channels. You can see a large number of ships waiting to enter."

"Okay, you're on a roll, Sergeant. now for the hard part, why?"

"I'm not sure, but the satellite pictures show an Iranian Kilo-class sub on the surface several thousand yards astern of one of their destroyers. A photo fifteen minutes later shows the submarine pulled the plug."

"I don't understand."

"Based on the position of the destroyers and the white circles, I believe these spots were caused by small explosions. Their navy may be conducting training operations."

"Nothing new there. The Iranians are always doing that," Johnson said.

"Yes, but this exercise lasted over 24 hours. Once completed, the blockade was lifted, and commercial traffic resumed."

Johnson listened to Wallace's report with great interest. In the short period he'd worked with his subordinate, he found him to be a meticulous analyst. "Anything else I should know?" He asked.

"I counted 20 high-speed boats. Most likely, Bladerunners, racing toward the commercial ships in the Persian Gulf."

"Bladerunners?"

"We have Intel that Iran purchased a South African version of the British Bradstone Challenger, their new ultra-high-speed boats," Wallace said. "The NATO designation is 'Bladerunner.' From the satellite pictures, I'd guess the Iranians are testing their 'Bladerunner' clones to use in the future against merchant ships."

"How fast are these boats?" Johnson asked.

"USS Gray, reported clocking one at 75 knots."

"Okay. I've heard enough. Put your findings in a report with the accompanying photos and bring it for my signature. I'll forward your work up the chain. Great job, Sergeant! Well done! I wonder if our submarines operating in these waters are aware of this new threat?"

Wallace wondered the same thing.

Chapter 20

USS Buffalo; Gulf of Oman –

Janice Lace sat with Patricia Morton in the wardroom. She was still fuming at how Scott had the government manipulate the university with a million-dollar grant. *Oh, he said he had nothing to do with that ploy. He is so guilty.* Her thoughts were interrupted when Drs. Thomas and Stone entered, followed by the XO, department heads, Master Chief Jack Norris, and Commander Scott.

Scott showed immediately he was all business. "Except for our civilians, have all of you read the Operation Orders?"

"Yes," the officers responded.

"Then you understand, Buffalo will conduct clandestine operations near the Bandar-e-Abbas Naval Base. We'll be searching littoral (shallow) waters but will be limited by our need to maintain a stealth posture. It won't be easy due to the cluttered and noisy environment." He surveyed their faces. "Dr. Lace, Lieutenant Morton, Drs. Thomas and Stone, I need the four of you to develop plans for conducting surveillance operations along the coastline. The objectives are to locate and identify any mines in the area. Please, submit your plans to the XO by 2200 tonight. I'm sorry about the rush. Any questions?"

There were none.

"Lieutenant Obermeier, continue," Scott said.

The Navigator went to the front of the table. He removed the cover over a chart of the Straits of Hormuz. "Team 6, when ordered to infiltrate the naval base, will disembark from the ASDV at a predetermined point between Qeshm Island and here." He pointed to the island of Jazireh-ye Hormuz. "The depth between the two landmasses is 55 meters, 180 feet at mean low water. The distance to the harbor is 15 nautical miles. If the ASDV can maintain a max speed of eight knots, it will take them 90 minutes to reach the point of debarkation near the harbor. Once the vehicle is deployed, we will remain at the drop zone and wait for the SEALs return."

Scott took over. "Thank you, Nav. Well done. Dr. Lace?"

"Captain, when we surveyed this area three years ago, the SEAL Team reported strong currents between these land points and up into the channel. The submersible may be hard-pressed to maintain an eight-knot speed against those currents. Three to five knots would appear more realistic."

"What's your recommendation, Dr. Lace?"

"I recommend they ingress and egress with the tide. It should give the ASDV a knot or two."

"That seems sound," Scott said. Thank you." He aimed his eyes at the engineers. "Dr. Thomas, I want Hunter to test the route before the SEALs are on board."

"I agree," Master Chief Norris jumped in. "Hunter can also provide us the contour of the bottom, hazards, and updates on currents."

Dr. Stone replied, "Hunter's data will be downloaded into the SEAL's vehicle navigational system, preventing them from running into obstructions when entering the harbor."

Scott asked, "Dr. Stone, can you directly input the data into

Buffalo's Combat Control Systems at the same time?"

Stone looked thoughtful. "I don't see any reason, why not. Our data collection equipment is from the tether wire. Nav data is Nav data, and your Combat Control System should be able to use Hunter's. I'll send a message to NUWC to confirm this."

"Good. You and the XO draft a message for our next communications pass," Scott said. "As you know, our communications must be limited to avoid detection. Good. We won't be blind. Weps, place Hunter into tube one tomorrow. Dr. Stone, how much time is needed to do your pre-launch checks?"

"Thirty minutes," Dr. Thomas answered.

"And what is the turn-around time between missions?" The Weapons Officer asked.

"That depends if Hunter remains on ship's power, two hours. If power is lost, it takes at least five hours to cool down and recharge the lithium batteries," Stone responded.

The entrance of IT Weathers followed a knock on the door. "I'm sorry to disturb you, Sir. We just received these photos."

The expression on Weathers' face told Scott whatever was in these photos demanded his prompt attention.

Chapter 21

USS Buffalo; Gulf of Oman –

Scott opened the package. "I thought things were going too smoothly," he muttered, handing the pictures to the XO.

Tom Varney looked at the grainy black and white photographs. He then passed them down the table.

Scott read the message attached to the package. "Langley is reporting a sharp increase in Iranian naval activity in the Straits of Hormuz. A large number of pallets on the pier are convincing evidence that preparations are underway to put another Iranian Qaaem Class boat to sea. They also report two Iranian Kilo submarines pier-side are being loaded with mines."

The room was silent as the officers examined the photos.

Janice Lace broke the silence. "Did anyone else see the drums stacked on the barges in this photo? Could they conceal the mines?"

The XO examined the photo. "Did we receive a text file with these satellite pictures?"

Scott thumbed through the papers. "Not that I see. Intel did mention armed Boghammars and Bladerunners sitting in the cove, and three Kaman Class Missile ships tied to the pier."

"Excuse me, Captain, what is a Boghammar?" Dr. Stone

asked.

"They're high-speed patrol boats," Varney answered. "We believe they were built by a Swedish company. Most are fitted with 107 mm multiple rocket launchers and large-caliber recoilless rifles. They can be lethal in swarms."

Stone sighed. "I'm sorry, I asked."

Scott pulled out a photo of the Missile boats. "We can't out-run them if they spot us. They're damn fast. The Revolutionary Guard maintains over 1,000 small boats, in packs of 100, strung out in key positions along the coastline. Included in the mix are the new Bladerunners and Boghammars." He turned to Varney. "XO, make sure all officers and lookouts receive instruction on all known types of vessels in our operational area. We don't want to be surprised by these buggers."

"A list of Iranian surface and submarine units, plus tactical publications, were included with the Night Orders," Varney replied.

Scott nodded approval. "Anything else? Anyone?" He cast his eyes at each of the people in the room, avoiding eye contact with Janice.

"It would appear," Dr. Thomas said, "with the Israelis pushing Washington to attack Iran's nuclear facilities, the Ayatollah may be getting ready to follow through on his threat to close the Straits."

"You may be right," Scott said. "Buffalo could find itself in the middle of a war."

"How does all this affect the SEALs' mission?" Janice asked, looking at Scott.

"Their orders won't be known to us until they're aboard, so I can't as yet respond to that. But speaking of Team 6, are we prepared to rendezvous tonight, XO?"

"Yes, Sir. We'll be taking on one officer and five enlistees."

"Captain," Janice said, studying several photos under a magnifying glass. "Look at this picture of the harbor entrance. Now, look at this one. The same tug, 10 minutes later, appears to be dragging a string of floats behind it."

Scott looked over her shoulder at the two grainy pictures. "I've seen floats like this before. I bet the tug is closing the entrance to the harbor using a torpedo net." He straightened up. "What is the distance from the breakwater to the landing?"

"Less than a mile," Janice supplied, still studying the image. "You must travel another two miles in shallow water to the harbor entrance. That's assuming the ASDV can discharge the SEALs near that location."

Scott gazed at the map. "Thank you, Dr. Lace. XO, Let's see what additional information we receive over the next 24 hours on this tug." He gave Janice a slight smile.

Janice caught the smile but relegated it to his approval of her work and nothing more. She focused her eyes back on the photos. "Wait," she said. "Please hand me the magnifying glass again?" She peered through the glass. "XO, may I see the first picture of the harbor entrance again?" She switched back and forth between the two pictures, then looked up.

"What is it?" Scott asked, "Have you noticed something else?"

Janice handed him the photos. "If you look close, you can just make out a long thin tubular shape in front of the net." She looked into his eyes. I guess that it's a mini-submarine."

Varney looked through the glass. "I think Dr. Lace is right. With this configuration, two divers could fit."

"Entering the harbor just got harder," Janice said. "The SEALs could face real danger if that sub is there."

"We'll warn the SEALs of the possibility of running into Iranian divers and that mini," Scott said. "Dr. Lace, is something else troubling you?"

Janice nodded. "Anyone else troubled as to why the Iranians would choose to load mines on their submarines and surface craft in broad daylight?"

"What are you driving at?" Scott asked, impressed with her contributions, affirming his decision to recruit her.

Janice aimed her eyes at Scott. "They know we can see them. I think it's intentional. Iran wants us to know they're preparing to mine the Straits." She looked intently into Scotts eyes. "Why would they want us to know that?"

"Good question," Scott said.

"At least they can't shoot at us with a boatload of mines," the Weapons officer muttered.

"I wouldn't go so far, Steve," Scott said. "We don't know how many or what types of mines they've got." He searched his documents. "This Intel report says Iran purchased several hundred EM-52 rising mines from China recently. This could be them."

Dr. Stone asked, "What is rising mines?"

Wilkinson explained, "They can be deployed from a submarine and sit on the bottom until the mine senses a target."

Scott nodded. "Once activated by a near-enough contact, a rocket-propelled charge fires and it homes in on that target with its guidance system. They're like a torpedo waiting to be triggered by a near contact. One mine can cripple or destroy a ship."

"Can we go deeper than these mines? Can we run under them?" Dr. Thomas asked, disturbed by this new threat to his beloved UUV.

Wilkinson shrugged. "Nobody knows for sure. The Revolutionary Guard keep their tech data about weapons under tight control."

Scott located the heading in his reports. "Intel states the mines can be placed in shallows or at a depth of up to 656 feet. The general opinion is this mine is more effective placed in deeper water." He looked up. "This is one reason why Buffalo was ordered to search the Persian waters. Using Hunter, we need to determine what type of mines, if any, Iran is placing, especially in the littorals and the entrance to the Straits." He aimed his eyes at Janice. "I agree with Dr. Lace. I think we have discovered a major concern and must be cautious. Great job."

Janice nodded.

Scott turned to Stone. "Dr. Stone, what are Hunter's depth limitations? Can she go under these mines."

"We've tested Hunter to 600 feet," Stone replied. "I don't think the mines will become an issue."

"Not unless we're forced to defuse them," Weps said.

"Or if our radiated noise triggers them," Varney muttered.

Scott made a note on his pad. "Very well, XO, alert all departments to maintain ultra-quiet conditions. I want all non-duty personnel confined to their bunks when an alert sounds. Engineer, any problems with shutting down one of the turbine generators to lower our sound profile?"

"No, Sir. I'd recommend we shut down one of our engines aft and place our circulation pumps on slow speed to minimize sound."

"Good ideas." Scott jotted it down. "It looks like you're all on a roll. Anything else? Feel free. Every idea helps."

"Set the ventilation fans to slow speed," Varney suggested.

"Senior Chief, comment?" Scott asked.

"Yes, Sir. Use sound powered phones."

Senior Chief Richardson, what is the status of sonar?"

"Calibrated, tested, and operational, Sir. We've also conducted training on shallow water operations utilizing the acoustic library. Dr. Lace and Lieutenant Morton attended the sessions to assist my men in identifying hostile submarines and surface ships." He smiled at Janice. "Very helpful, Sir."

"Thank you. Chief, can our sensors detect water lapping against a small idling boat?" Scott asked.

Dr. Lace answered before the Chief could respond. "Buffalo would have to be sitting in a pure environment devoid of any background noise to detect that kind of almost inaudible sound."

Scott studied her face and said, "Okay. I want you to work on any way we can sharpen our ability to pick out even these nearly inaudible sounds. We need to consider any moving object, any idling motor, as a threat until we get a clearer picture of what Iran possesses in their arsenal." He stood. "Thank you, everyone, for a very productive meeting."

Janice stood with the others when Scott left the room. She stared at his back, admiring how he had already gotten the respect of this crew. His presence and his organizational thoroughness had won them over, she thought. The problem was, he was winning her over as well. That can't happen, she promised herself. "Morton," she said, "Let's hang here and start working on the data we've collected so far."

Morton had also been observing Scott. She saw Janice's eyes were focused on him whenever he spoke. While she admired Scott, was attracted to him, she suspected Janice had unfinished business. She knew any move she made would hurt her. She had no desire to cause a problem. A wrong step before their relationship came to an end, would risk her losing her chance at Scott as well. She could afford to wait and see how things played out.

Varney, busy with paperwork, listened with interest as the two women worked. Their knowledge and dedication were impressive, but he sensed some rivalry between them that might be disruptive if not kept in check. He had a suspicion it had something to do with the new CO, but Scott had shown no sign of interest in either of these two bright and educated experts. So what was the problem? He made up his mind to stay alert and observe their behavior just in case.

Laying a chart of the Persian Gulf on the table, Janice pointed out the characteristics of the currents, shoreline, and wind patterns of the area to Morton. "Although it's been three years since I collected environmental and acoustic data here, very little has changed in the region. The water flows in along the northern shoreline, and the outflow is along the southern coastline."

"How will this affect the operation of the UUV?" Morton asked.

"Once it moves into the shallows, the UUV must remain close to the bottom...to reduce the impact of the currents. They haven't tested Hunter in this type of environment. We'll have to wait until she's deployed to answer your question."

Morton pointed to an elevation ring on the map. "It looks like Buffalo and the ASDV will have less than 140 feet of depth along the coast and parts of the Straits. That doesn't leave a hell of a lot of room for a sub."

Janice nodded. "Tell me about it."

Morton looked puzzled. "Does depth change that much?"

"A great question. Surface conditions, local temperature, and salinity of the water can affect transit. An unexpected warm layer could make Buffalo sink like a stone, while a cold one would make her more buoyant."

Varney, who had been listening, spoke up, "All that can also give our sonar operators a headache in distinguishing sound signatures of various craft."

Janice added, "The more we understand the environment, the better we will be able to assist in the detection of Iranian submarines and other vessels."

Varney replied, "I have a gut feeling their diesel subs, running submerged, will be our biggest headache."

Janice nodded.

"And don't forget the possibility of an Israeli Dolphin II conducting covert operations in the same waters we're in," the XO added. "Any help you can give us in picking that one out will be huge."

Janice was beginning to understand why Scott had opted to keep Tom Varney as XO. He would be a great asset in any emergency. Whatever her feelings about Scott and Morton, she was determined to do whatever was required to ensure the safety of the crew. She understood they were heading into hazardous waters. She knew it was dangerous in more ways than one.

Chapter 22

Iranian Kilo K-901; Gulf of Oman –

Captain Atash Karini, commanding Iranian diesel submarine Kilo 901, ascended the periscope stand and pressed his eye against the rubber buffer surrounding the scope's ocular. He placed both hands on the handle grips and rotated the right grip to increase the magnification. "Bearing. Mark."

Second, in command, Lieutenant Commander Mohsen Pejman responded, "Bearing 320."

"Look, XO!" Karini stepped aside.

Mohsen Pejman peered into the eyepiece. "I don't believe this," he said, looking at the Captain.

"Range," Karini shouted, aiming his periscope at the new contact.

"Two thousand meters."

Detecting the unmistakable signature of the 8-meter diameter screws an hour earlier, Karini ordered Kilo-901 to rise to periscope depth astern of an Iranian supertanker. At 1,056 feet in length with a beam of 180 feet, the supertanker dwarfed the 210-foot-long submarine. Registered to the National Iranian Oil Company, the tanker left the shipyard five days earlier enroute to Argentina, or so the shipping manifest reported. The Captain wondered why the secrecy about a supertanker.

Pejman looked puzzled. "Captain, Tanker's Ship Master, Dakir Sassani, reports his heading is 180 degrees, speed five knots. The transponder is activated. He wants us to submerge and continue under the hull and then surface in the open cavity."

"Did you say surface under the tanker?" Karini asked.

"Yes," the XO replied, still looking confused. "Sassani says, this is an order."

Karini sighed. "OOD, inform him I'm starting my approach. Make your depth 45 meters ahead, two-thirds."

Sonar Specialist, Shahr Am Pahlavi, replied, "Control, hold a faint broadband noise bearing 090 degrees on the monitor. The contact is closing."

"Do we hold a surface contact on the bearing?" Karini asked.

"No, Sir," replied the OOD checking the radar scope.

Karini hurried to sonar. "Where is it?"

The sonar operator pointed to the broadband lines on the bearing time recorder. "Based on the increased signal to noise, I estimate the submarine is doing 20 plus knots."

"Is it an American nuclear sub?" Karini asked.

"I am unable to determine if it is an American, German, or an Israeli, Sir," Pahlavi replied. "There are no distinguishing narrowband lines on the bearing."

"Were we detected?" Karini asked.

"I believe not, Sir. The flow noise across their hydrophones masks any counter-detection."

"Report if the sub slows. OOD, contact the tanker and inform him we intend to maintain our current position until a submarine detected moments ago opens from us," Karini said.

"Control, Sonar. Detected a 50Hz broadband line on the

starboard side," the sonar specialist reported. "Sir, it's a diesel submarine."

"It can't be one of ours," Karini muttered to his XO. "None of our boats can reach that speed submerged."

"So, it could be an American submarine, being shadowed by an Israeli." The XO laughed. "I wonder if the American knows the Israeli is following him?"

Karini nodded thoughtfully. "Based on recent Intel, it could be an Israeli Dolphin. XO. Send a message alerting Vice Admiral Salehi we detected what appear to be American and Israeli submarines, north, in the Arabian Sea. Ask for orders." He smiled at his XO. "We could be in for some fun here."

The XO was disappointed by the reply: "Maintain your orders. Now is not the time to challenge enemy submarines."

Twenty minutes later, Karini, deeply disappointed, headed the Kilo-901 toward the stern of the W/T Seed. The propeller wash of the supertanker's two counter-rotating screws made the submarine quiver. Moving closer to the tanker, she shook more violently. Compartment lights flickered, cups and dishes fell and shattered on the galley deck. The crew held on to whatever they could as the violent shaking continued.

"Drop five revolutions," Karini ordered. "Steady," he said, struggling to maintain his balance as the boat rolled from side to side. He peered through the periscope as his ship advanced farther under the supertanker.

When the stern cleared the tanker's screws, the violent rolling and shaking stopped.

"Drop ten turns," Karini ordered. "XO, take a look!"

Pejman stepped back on the stand and peered into the eyepiece. A bright red hull filled the lens. He rotated the right handle, decreasing the magnification. "I don't believe this,

Captain. I would not have thought it was possible to place a submarine inside a supertanker."

Karini pressed his eye against the lens. "Add five turns. XO. Prepare to broach." He felt the submarine rise into the tanker's cavity. He saw flashing red beacons along the port and starboard walls of the opening. "XO, surface, and drop three turns." Keeping his eye on the scope as his submarine lifted into the tanker, he felt a slight shudder when the low-pressure blower started on the ballast tanks. The brightness from the tanker's lamps blinded him until he flipped the filter over the periscope viewers. "Impressive," he murmured and relaxed his grip on the handles. "Most impressive."

Line handlers from the tanker's crew were forward, leaning against the railing, preparing to secure K-901.

"OOD," Karini ordered. "Shift duty personnel to the bridge. Send line handlers on deck to help secure the boat." He heard the boat's low-pressure blower continuing to force water out of the ballast tank.

"K-901, we are extending clamping claws now," announced a deep voice from the overhead speakers.

Karini hurried up to the conning tower leading to the bridge. He was stunned by the size of the four massive white claws lowering down along the hull of his submarine. "OOD, all stop," he shouted down the hatch.

There was a loud grinding sound of the hydraulic motors overhead as the enormous clamping jaws continued to drop down along the sides of the much smaller submarine.

Karini watched, silently, fascinated by how the descending arms were cradling his boat.

"Captain," a hoarse voice from above interrupted. a portly, middle-aged officer leaned over the railing. "I'm Captain

139

Sassani. Please hurry? Commodore Yazdi is waiting."

"Commodore Yazdi is here?" Karini was surprised.

"Yes. The Commodore arrived about an hour ago with the others."

"Others?"

"Your questions will be answered soon," Sassani replied. "My supply chief will meet with your XO and provide details of the work schedule for your boat."

Karini turned to his XO, who had just stepped on the bridge. "I leave this in your able hands, XO."

Karini climbed down the ladder, annoyed at the volley of commands and puzzled by why he was summoned for a meeting with Commodore Yazdi. He stepped out onto the deck, proceeded across the gangway, and climbed up the aluminum ladder to the tanker's catwalk. Once he reached the top, the ship's master, Captain Dakir Sassani, greeted him. Unimpressed by the Sassani's squat appearance but, considering the command responsibility he shouldered with this massive tanker, he guessed there was more to Sassani than met the eye.

Sassani extended his hand. "Welcome aboard, Captain."

Karini hesitated. He looked down at his submarine, now held hostage in the arms of four massive white claws. He shook Sassani's hand, wondering what all this was about.

"Impressive, is it not?" Sassani asked, waving his hand to emphasize the enormous size of his ship.

Karini looked down again. His submarine appeared small in the pool of water within the tanker's hull. A catwalk had been attached to the outer bulkhead and extended around the ship. He saw the forward weapons hatch open. Several sailors stepped out on the deck. They were removing the deck cover and extracting the weapon loading tracks from between the floor and the outer hull of the submarine.

Sassani smiled. "Your questions will be answered soon. Please follow me now. I assure you your men and sub will be fine."

Karini reluctantly left his ship captive in the giant claws. As he followed Sassani, he wondered about his fate and the future of his ship and crew.

Captain Sassani, the tanker's master, led Karini through an open door, and down a lit passageway. The pale green walls and tiled deck gave the vessel's interior an austere, even Spartan, atmosphere. The faint, unmistakable odor of diesel fuel was evident even in the personnel areas. They continued to the end of another passageway, turned left, and walked through a gray watertight door onto a platform. Climbing down a steel ladder, they stopped in front of a door with a stainless-steel plate coded by the red letter 'E' for Engineering.

What am I doing here, Karini wondered, as Sassani pulled up on the long steel handle, releasing the multi-dog fitting. "After you, Captain."

What the hell is going on? Karini thought. Yazdi was the last person he'd expect to see on a tanker in which his sub was now a captive.

Chapter 23

W/S Seed; Gulf of Oman –

Captain Karini felt anxious as he stepped over the sill. The airconditioned chamber was a welcome relief from the humidity of the tanker's open hull. It was difficult to see the full extent of the compartment in the dim light of the overhead red night lamps. He saw several men hunched over monitors. To the left, he saw a large light table. There were several men in the middle of a discussion. He recognized Commodore Yazdi.

Yazdi looked up. "Captain Karini, it's a pleasure to see you again. I hope you had no difficulty maneuvering into our tanker."

Karini was relieved at the Commodore's tone. "Sir, I was not sure what to expect when I was ordered to maneuver under this supertanker. This is a well-kept secret."

Commodore Yazdi nodded to a man in a civilian suit.

The man didn't nod back. His eyes were studying Karini.

Karini didn't recognize this man, but there was something about this civilian that made him uneasy. He guessed the stranger with his rigid posture and lack of visible reaction was from one of the intelligence services, perhaps the Islamic Revolutionary Guards Corps, or the Ministry of Intelligence and Security. He had an inherent distrust of these agencies.

Commodore Yazdi continued, "Karini, as you can see, this tanker was configured to transport submarines undetected by our enemy. Not only does she conceal your location, but provides food, spare parts, fuel, mines, and even torpedoes. We are equipped with the latest intelligence suite to provide our vessels with the information they need to carry out assigned missions. This tanker is a base on the sea."

Karini said, "It's impressive. Quite ingenious, Sir."

Yazdi smiled. "I agree. You should feel honored. Your submarine is the first to use this new vessel. This must remain a secret."

"Your trust honors me," Karini replied. "From this tanker, I will be deadly against the Americans. They will never suspect this."

"You may not be so euphoric once you receive your new orders. But I'm getting ahead of the purpose of this meeting. Please, follow me."

Karini wondered what other surprises the Commodore had for the American enemy. He followed Commodore Yazdi into a room filled with cigarette smoke. There were three large LED monitors attached to the wall where sailors were busily entering data. A rectangular table covered with green felt filled the middle of the room. In front of the four men seated at the table were an ashtray, a carafe of hot mint tea, and the traditional small dish holding lumps of rock sugar.

It was a strange environment for a tea party, Karini thought as he gazed at the men's faces.

The civilian he'd seen earlier was seated at the far end of the table. He did not smile as Karini approached.

A chill ran through Karini's body. *This guy reminds me of one of Hitler's SS. He's not to be trusted.*

Yazdi waved his arm. "Captain Karini, I believe you know Captain's Giv Alizadeh, of K-903; Ardeshir Naceri, Q-100 and Mortez A Kashani of Q-104. They were brought here by helicopter."

Karini nodded. "It is great to see all of these fine Captains."

Yazdi sat and pointed to a vacant chair. "Please, Captain, take your seat with us."

Karini sat, noting there was no paper or pen to take notes.

Yazdi made a tent with his fingers. "I asked each of you here to discuss our mission." He surveyed their faces. "We are going to mine the Straits of Hormuz."

"Mining the Straits?" Kashani asked.

Yazdi nodded. "Correct. Each of you has been chosen because you've demonstrated loyalty, tactical astuteness, and leadership conducting simulated attacks in our training exercises. Congratulations."

Karini saw the other officers straightened at these compliments. He felt proud and eager to learn more.

Yazdi continued, "You can see each monitor has been given a name: Sector 'Yazdah' will be patrolled by Kashani in Q-104. When ordered, you will lay a barrier across the western entrance of the Straits."

Kashani didn't hesitate. "Yes, Sir. It shall be done."

Yazdi continued, "K-903's sector is designated 'Davaazdah.' Captain Alizadeh, your orders are to remain north of K-901's sector. Once you lay your mines, you will return to Bandar-e-Abbas Naval Base and rearm."

Alizadeh nodded. "I consider it an honor."

Yazdi pointed to the third screen. "Captain Naceri, Q-100, is assigned to Sector 'Sizdah.' You will plant your mines along the line indicated on the monitor."

"Your plan will defeat the infidels," Naceri replied.

Yazdi let out a brief smile. "Each of you will receive updated orders once you are in your sector. Karini, once your torpedoes are replaced with mines, you will proceed north. You will set-up a barrier between Wadi Bih, off the Musandam Peninsula, and Jask, designated, 'Chahaarda.'"

Karini estimated the distance he would have to travel to accomplish this second mission. "It shall be done," he said, still unsure of how long it would take to traverse from the first location to the second.

Yazdi aimed his dark eyes at the men at the table. "The exact placement of the mines I leave to each of you to determine. Your boats will be filled with various types of our most advanced mines. It is paramount the precise coordinates of each mine be recorded and forwarded to my office so we may relay their location to our great nation's ships and submarines." He raised his arms. "With Allah's help, we will teach the infidels a lesson they will not forget. Any questions?"

Naceri cleared his throat. "Sir, I read Admiral Jujair's report. He believes the Israeli enemy is preparing to attack our nuclear facilities—"

Yazdi interrupted, glaring at the officer. "I will say this, the Admiral believes delaying the International Atomic Energy Agency from inspecting our enrichment plants will initiate an attack by the Israeli enemy. Cowards that they are, they will, of course, enlist the aid of the United States. If this happens, our government will follow through on its promise and close the Straits." He leaned forward, his eyes intense. "Securing the Straits of Hormuz and locking the American Battle Group in the Persian Gulf, while prohibiting others from entering, is our top priority. Our actions will send a clear message Iran will no longer tolerate interference from the United States or members of the UN Security Council. Any more questions?"

Karini raised his hand. "I reported alien ships within our waters. Has this been verified?"

"Based on your report, Karini, there is a strong possibility an American, German, or Israeli submarine entered the Persian Gulf. Each of you must remain vigilant. If you detect any non-Iranian submarine, monitor its movements from a safe distance, avoid contact, and promptly notify command. Record the acoustic signatures of every vessel you encounter. We want a record of everything in the water—for future use." He let that last sink in. "Our exercises, sinking replicas of U.S. destroyers, frigates, and warships, trained you in combat tactics we will use against American ships. You are ready."

"Commodore," Naceri asked. "So, we are not permitted to attack?"

Yazdi scowled. "At this time, you are not authorized to initiate an attack on any American or other flagged ships. The Americans must not detect a weapon fired from your submarines. Understood?"

Karini replied, "Allah, be praised. I never believed I would be honored to attack the Satan's ships."

Yazdi smiled. "The arrogant Americans are delusional if they think our government will not respond to an attack by them or their Israeli puppets. In the past, we have only mined the northern Straits of Hormuz and the Persian Gulf. They will not expect us to plant munitions in the southern entrance to the Straits."

"We will destroy them," Karini answered.

Yazdi placed a hand on the officer's shoulder. "Any more questions?"

"No, Sir," Karini replied.

"Good. Return to your submarine, and once the mines are aboard, execute your orders without delay." Commodore Yazdi stood. "With Allah's blessing."

"Praise be to Allah," Karini echoed. "By your leave?" He smiled, heading for the door. *After years of training and simulated attacks against the American navy, I will be the first to destroy one of their carriers. Allah be praised. The lion in me will roar when I sink my teeth into the rotting flesh of the infidels.*

Chapter 24

USS Buffalo; Gulf of Oman –

"Alpha Bravo, this is Whiskey Lima, over," The pilot's throaty voice and the background noise of the MH-60 Seahawk helicopter filled Control.

Scott pulled the red phone from its cradle.

"Whiskey Lima, this is Alpha Bravo. Hear you loud and clear. Over," Scott said, releasing the transmit key.

"No close contacts Captain," the XO reported.

"Diving Officer, surface," Scott ordered.

The lookout climbed up the ladder from control and opened the lower and upper hatches leading topside. The OOD, Lieutenant Steve Wilkinson, followed him.

"Whiskey Lima, this is Alpha Bravo," Scott said into his mic, "We are on the surface, navigational lights activated, Over."

"Roger," the chopper pilot replied. "Hold you 200 yards from my position."

Scott replaced the phone and climbed the three stories to the bridge. The wind turbulence, rotor noise, and salt spray from the twin turboshaft engines drowned out communications between control and the bridge. He noted the Seahawk's door-mounted Browning GAU/A .50 caliber machine gun and the serious-looking gunner manning the mount. He saw the forward outer hatch open, and a crewman emerged on deck. He felt the boat lift and fall back in the calm sea as he maintained eye contact on the Seahawk. If squadron's calculations were correct, the sky should be free of Russian and Chinese satellites at this moment. "Bridge, Control," Scott shouted into the mic over the noise, "do you hold any surface search radars?"

"No, Sir."

The ship was under emission control, restricting Buffalo's electronic signals during her surface period, limiting counter detection.

"Let's hope this is over fast. Having this Seahawk sitting off our starboard side is like waving a flashlight in a coal bin," Scott said.

"Whiskey Lima, this is Alpha Bravo, ready to receive cargo. Over,"

The Seahawk shifted to port and started her approach from the stern. The side doors opened, and four Commandos moved past the door gunner and slid down the Static Line to Buffalo's deck. Two more men soon followed them. Seconds later, a large package was lowered and stowed below. The men moved to the hatch and disappeared.

"Clear the bridge! Clear the bridge! OOD, submerge. Make depth six-zero feet," Scott ordered, waving to the pilot. He watched the Seahawk bank to the left and disappear into the black sky. Mission accomplished.

The port lookout stepped down from the platform and hurried down the hatch. Scott came after, followed by the starboard lookout, who secured both the pressure hull and the lower hatches.

"Last man down," the starboard lookout announced.

Repeating the order, the Chief-of-the-Watch pulled the

149

diving alarm twice, setting off the traditional klaxon sound, an unmistakable grating noise, somewhere between a honking truck horn and an angry bull. "Dive! Dive," he announced.

Scott hoped the operation had gone undetected.

Entering the wardroom, Scott saw six men dressed in dark camouflage uniforms standing around the table. "Welcome aboard," he said.

"Thank you, Captain. I'm Commander, Mike Walsh. May I introduce you to Team 6. Machinist Mate First Class, Willie Hamerman; Boatswain Mate First Class, Bob Rose; Boatswain Mate Second Class, Mark Stanley; Information System Technician Second Class, Bruce Freeman, and Hospital Corpsman, Third Class, Chad Barnes."

"Welcome men," Scott said.

The men nodded.

"You're traveling light, Commander," Scott said.

"Yes, Sir. Except for a 'special' package, I asked your Weapons officer to store in the munitions locker. Our equipment was packed in the ASDV before its installation aboard Buffalo." Walsh glanced at Master Chief Norris, who was taking notes.

"I'm sure everything was taken care of," Scott said.

Commander Walsh's tall frame and broad shoulders filled the space leading into the pantry. At 6' 4, he looked directly into Scott's eyes when he spoke. "Thank you, Sir. I expected as much."

Scott accepted the sealed envelope Walsh pulled from a black bag, noting the Commander's hands were the size of small shovels.

"My orders and clearances," Walsh said.

Scott turned to Varney. "Commander, this is my very capable XO, Lieutenant Commander, Tom Varney."

"Welcome aboard," Varney said, smiling at the SEALs.

"Please be seated, men," Scott said.

Brady, a Second Class Culinary Specialist, hustled into the room, and placed cups and carafes of coffee on the table. He then hurried out and returned with a tray full of assorted sandwiches.

"Thanks, Brady," Scott said. "Eat up, men. You must be hungry."

While Scott looked over their documents, the SEALs poured themselves coffee and dove into the pile of sandwiches.

Varney studied the SEAL Team. Intelligence Specialist (IS) 2 Freeman had a long scar on the left side of his cheek. The sandwich Freeman held was all but hidden by the enormity of his hand. The Corpsman, (HM) 3 Barns, on the other hand, was not a massive, muscular individual but had a determined look in his eyes.

"When will we be entering the Gulf, Captain?" Walsh asked.

"Tomorrow. Around 1100. XO, we will have a briefing after breakfast. Get Drs. Thomas, Stone, and Lace. Include Lieutenant Morton."

Varney noted the order.

Scott glanced at the orders Walsh had given him. He noted Buffalo was to deploy the ASDV near the naval base at Bandar-e-Abbas. "Your orders don't indicate when we're to place your team on the beach, Commander."

Walsh stopped eating. "Specific orders will be issued later.

For now, we're just along for the ride."

Scott had a feeling Walsh was holding something back. "You're aware we're carrying an Unmanned Underwater Vehicle, called Hunter on board?" He asked, curious as to how much Walsh knew.

"It was mentioned in my brief before we departed Bahrain," Walsh replied.

"The engineers, from NUWC, will deploy Hunter to survey the sea bottom before we launch the ASDV. That should eliminate any concerns as water conditions at your debarkation point," Scott said.

"That will be helpful," Walsh replied.

Scott nodded. "Dr. Lace, our science officer, discovered a mini-submersible capable of carrying two frogmen searching inside the harbor entrance which the Iranians have blocked with a net."

"It looks like our foray just became a little more complicated, boys," Commander Walsh grinned. "We'd love to go head to head with our Iranian counterparts."

Scott wasn't sure Walsh was taking this mission as seriously as he wanted. "Commander, I don't run from a fight, but let me remind you that once you are deployed, Buffalo is not here. We are to be invisible to the Iranians, as per the President's orders."

"I understand, Captain," Walsh said.

Scott hoped Walsh did. "The COB will show you to your berthing area after you've finished eating. Anything else I can do?"

"No. Thank you, Captain."

Scott and the XO left for Scott's stateroom.

Once the door was closed, Varney said, "I think the Guards

will find it more than a little challenging to fight them."

Scott shook his head. "Tom, remember, the SEALs must do all they can to avoid initiating a confrontation. Our orders of engagement are clear." He looked hard at Varney. "We have to make sure Walsh understands that."

"Yes, Sir."

After Varney left, Scott sat down at his desk. He closed his eyes. *Putting SEALs ashore is always risky. On Iranian territory....*

Chapter 25

USS Buffalo; Gulf of Oman –

After the morning meal, Scott asked the XO, Commander Walsh, Dr. Lace, the two NUWC Engineers, and Master Chief Jack Norris to remain.

"Dr. Stone, did you receive a reply regarding downloading Hunter's data into our Fire Control System?" Scott asked.

"Yes, Sir. The upgrade will be completed and tested by noon eastern standard time tomorrow," Stone replied.

Scott smiled. "So, once the upgrade is tested, we should be able to view what Hunter sees on our monitor?" Scott asked.

"Correct, Captain," Stone said. "It will be like looking out a window."

"It will be like Captain Nemo enjoying a picture window of our underwater world," Dr. Thomas added with a broad smile.

Scott didn't smile. This was too serious. Lives rested on Hunter and these two scientists.

"Captain," Dr. Stone asked. "Can you authorize me access to the submersible's sonar and tactical systems?"

"Why do you need that?" Scott asked.

Stone replied, "I believe I can attach my computer with footage of Hunter's video to the ASDV's monitors. If that connection can be made, the ASDV operator will see in real-time what Hunter sees. Instead of just looking at acoustic returns, you will have a visual.".

Thomas added, "You will also be able to compare your sonar returns with the visual images."

Scott nodded. "That would be a valuable capability. Doctor, please contact Master Chief Norris, our ASDV expert, and pilot. He'll be delighted to show off his baby."

"Thank you, Sir," Drs. Thomas and Stone said at the same time.

Scott noted a puzzled expression on Janice's face. "Dr. Lace, do you have a question?"

"No, Sir. I just wanted to update you about the currents between Qeshm and Jazireh-ye Hormuz. Tidal currents between the two islands run between four to six knots, becoming stronger during the full lunar and spring tides."

Morton added, "The bottom is mostly sand and mud. Satellite pictures collected over the last two years indicate water clarity averages between 10 and 15 feet, depending on traffic and sandstorms."

Janice nodded in agreement.

Walsh aimed his eyes at Janice. "Do you know the distance from the breakwater to the piers?" he asked.

"Yes, Sir. It's about one mile to the first pier," Janice replied, "but the water is too shallow for the ASDV."

Walsh nodded.

Janice continued, "You'll have to disembark from the ASDV at least another mile from the breakwater."

Thomas interrupted, "Commander, once Hunter surveys the area, we'll know for certain the distance and depth of the water."

Janice glanced at Dr. Thomas. "That is correct."

"Thank you, Dr. Lace. That is very helpful," Walsh said.

Janice smiled. "That's my job. And please call me, Janice?"

Walsh smiled back. "I assume you're an experienced SCUBA diver?"

"Yes, Sir. I am." Janice shot a glance at Scott.

Scott wondered if she was thinking back to the times they dove together in the Caribbean.

Walsh was still smiling. "I thought so. How would you like to accompany us on a practice dive? You'll stay in the ASDV and monitor the electronics."

Janice glanced at Scott's face.

Walsh's invitation caught Scott off guard. He wanted to say, "Commander Walsh, leave the woman I love alone." He wanted to say that but instead said, "Commander Walsh, Dr. Lace, and Lieutenant Morton have a tremendous amount of data they must analyze. I doubt either has time to leave their task—"

Janice wanted to protest that she was no longer his concern but replied, "Lieutenant Morton is fully capable of analyzing the required data." She saw the dark look on Scott's face and continued, "I welcome the opportunity to join your team, Commander. Thank you."

Scott was annoyed but couldn't show it. "XO set ultra-quiet conditions once we enter the Straits."

A knock at the door was followed by IT1 Weathers entering the room. "Captain, we received an urgent message." He handed the clipboard to Scott.

Janice focused on Scott's face. He looked worried.

Scott picked up the phone from under the table and called Control. Without waiting for a response, he asked, "how long before we enter the Straits of Hormuz, Jeff?"

"We'll make the turn for the first leg in 20 minutes," the navigator responded. "Is everything okay?"

"Slow to five knots and move us away from the entrance toward the eastern coastline. I'll be up in a minute." Scott looked at the others. "We just received an alert that the Iranian navy has a new class of destroyer actively conducting acoustic searches in the Gulf and the Straits."

Master Chief Norris said. "There've never been any Intel reports of active sonar aboard their surface ships. This is going to get interesting."

Scott replied, "It will be a game of cat and mouse. They're also deploying helicopters from ships, equipped with hydrophones to detect subsurface contacts."

"Is that dangerous?" Stone asked.

"Buffalo was not designed for shallow water. We are a deep-water submarine playing in their swimming pool. Our primary mission is to conduct surveillance and identify all mining operations in the Gulf, as you know. Buffalo is required to land the SEALs in hostile territory without being detected." He eyed them sternly. "We must tread lightly and not be seen or heard by the Iranian navy. We're not here to provoke a confrontation, but to accomplish our mission as expeditiously as possible."

"This boat and crew are ready for whatever Iran wants to toss our way," Varney said.

Scott placed both his hands flat on the table and said in his most authoritative voice, "We're not here to start anything, but, make no mistake, if it's a fight they want, we won't disappoint them!"

Chapter 26

USS Buffalo; Straits of Hormuz –

After reading his message traffic, Scott looked over at the XO and said. "The threat to Buffalo grows tenfold when we're in shallow waters, Tom."

"Their destroyers won't be a problem as long as they don't spot us. We can alter our course to avoid them based on knowledge of their current locations," Varney replied.

"Dr. Lace, do you have something to add?" Scott asked. He locked eyes with her.

"Yes. Your Senior Chief knows extracting passive narrow-band and broadband lines from the background environment is difficult along a coastline. We don't know to any degree of certainty just what Iranian passive sonar limitations are. Because of this uncertainty, I recommend Buffalo stick close to the coastline. That will make it difficult for their destroyers to detect us in the clutter."

Tom Varney nodded, "I agree, we should hug the coastline. They won't think of us doing that. But we don't have a clear knowledge of the shallows at this point. Do we?"

"True, but once Hunter is in the water, Buffalo will be able to map those areas," Lieutenant Morton said.

Thomas added, "That is the value of Hunter on this kind of

mission."

Scott realized they would require more time than he might have to conduct this kind of survey. "Okay, for now, we'll continue on present heading until we reach the upper portion of the northern channel, and then continue north along the coast until we are off the city of Kuhestak. From there, we will move toward Jazireh-ye Larak Island south of the Bandar-e-Abbas Naval Base and there deploy Hunter. According to our charts, the depth in the area is between 164 to 246 feet, adequate for us to traverse. We can stand off and monitor Iran's surface traffic from the Bandar-e-Abbas Naval Base." He looked at Varney. "XO, contact Fifth Fleet. Request additional satellite pictures of the Straits of Hormuz, Persian Gulf, and the Bandar-e-Abbas Naval Base. I want Intel to provide the latest locations and numbers of all Iranian boats along the coastline."

"Yes, Sir," Varney said.

"Thanks, people. XO, please join me in Control," Scott said.

Leaving the wardroom Scott and the XO headed for Control.

"Come right 10 degrees," Scott ordered after taking his position. "Sounding?"

"Two-Hundred Ninety-three fathoms below the keel," the Navigator responded.

"Captain, Sonar reports gaining contact on a tanker heading into the Persian Gulf," Lt. Obermeier said. "Classified Sierra 44."

"Very well, Lieutenant," Scott said. ..."Sonar, speed of Sierra 44?"

"Conn." the intercom speaker crackled, "Sierra 44 is making twelve knots."

"Very well; Navigator, distance to the turn?" Scott asked.

"Four thousand yards," Obermeier responded.

"Scott, addressing the men in Control, "we will disguise our movement by shadowing Sierra 44, a massive and noisy tanker, entering the Persian Gulf. Once she turns into the northern shipping lane, Buffalo will break off and hug the eastern Iranian coastline, proceeding north. We'll take station 15,000 yards off Kuhestak City in 350 feet of water. We'll remain in this area, monitoring shipping traffic. That should give sonar an excellent opportunity to collect acoustic data on their surface craft."

"Captain, I hold the middle of the channel to be 14,200 yards," the Navigator reported.

"Very well."

"Captain, how long do you intend to remain in this area?" the XO asked.

"Five hours, XO. Once we retrieve Hunter and obtain a good NAVSAT fix, we'll move. Based on my experience in these waters, I believe this location is the best position to monitor marine traffic around the Bandar-e-Abbas Naval Base. Should we be ordered to drop the SEALs for an incursion, we'll also be in an excellent position. We can move into deeper water quickly. I don't believe their destroyers will search in this area due to shipping. Should they do so, we can reenter the Straits."

Varney thought Scott had taken everything into account but knew staying in shallow water by the Iranian coastline was a considerable risk.

After giving his commands, Scott returned to the wardroom.

Drs. Lace, Stone, Thomas, and Lieutenant Morton were involved in a discussion. "Good afternoon," he said. "May I join you?"

Janice looked up. "We were about to leave."

Scott said. "I would like to discuss with you our current status." He saw Commander Walsh enter. "Commander Walsh, please join us?" Scott pointed toward an empty chair.

Janice thought she saw Commander Walsh's eyes land on Morton, as he took a seat across from her. *Was there a spark of interest in Morton's eyes?*

"XO." Scott began, "Drs. Stone and Thomas, within several hours, we'll be repositioning Buffalo on the eastern edge of the outer channel where we have the best chance of not being detected. After careful review, I'm approving your search pattern for Hunter."

"Lieutenant Morton, may I borrow your chart, please?" Varney asked.

Morton slid the chart to the XO. She saw Walsh studying her but ignored it.

Varney pointed to the chart. "Buffalo will be stationary here while Hunter initiates her first search in the shipping lanes." He looked up. "I have questions about the ability of Hunter to search the bottom while attached to the tether."

Thomas and Stone looked surprised. "I thought we addressed those earlier, "Thomas said.

Varney replied, "You indicated during your initial briefing that .... Am I correct in understanding Hunter can be deployed to a maximum range of 10,000 yards?"

"That is correct, XO," Dr. Stone replied.

"I think there'd be a considerable drag on the tether while she opens that distance from Buffalo," Varney said.

Scott looked at Varney with interest.

Dr. Thomas replied, "XO, there is a surprisingly minimal amount of drag. The tether wire is extremely light but strong, which reduces friction through the water when the UUV is moving."

Scott saw Janice's hand raised. "Dr. Lace, do you have a comment?"

"Yes, Sir. I'm sure Dr. Stone is aware there are other factors that may reduce Hunter's speed. One is the current."

"True. Another is whether Hunter's on ship or battery power," Scott said.

Stone replied, "Drawing power from Buffalo, Hunter will maintain the desired speed—"

"But what if the tether gets cut?" Varney asked.

Thomas replied, "If the tether is cut, then the speed will depend on the drain of the batteries."

Stone jumped in, "But I assure you—"

Scott held up his hand and interrupted. "Okay, I think we understand what to expect. Thanks," he said. "XO, anything else?"

"How are your studies progressing?" Varney asked, turning to Janice.

"Thank you. We've just about completed the algorithms that will project the currents expected along the coastline, harbor, and Straits of Hormuz to your Navigator. We need to enter more data. But we're getting there."

"Very good. Anything else?" Scott asked.

There wasn't any response from the others sitting at the table.

Scott turned to the two engineers, "It's showtime. Prepare Hunter for the water on my order."

Dr. Thomas and Dr. Stone jumped up and left the wardroom, relieved to get the Captain's approval finally. "This is what we worked for, Fred," Thomas said as they rushed down to the torpedo room.

"We've got to show that skeptical captain just what our baby can do," Dr. Stone replied.

Still in the wardroom, Scott looked at Tom and said, "This UUV better work as advertised. If not, it's going to be secured in the torpedo room no matter what those brothers say." He became aware Janice was watching him. "That will be all, Dr. Lace."

Janice rose from her chair. "Yes, Sir," she said, once again thinking that getting roped into this mission had been a gigantic mistake.

Chapter 27

IRIN Noor, Kilo-903, Bandar-e-Abbas Naval Depot-

Captain Giv Alizadeh watched from the bridge. His crew was replenishing Noor's arsenal. He wished he had a cigarette, but smoking was prohibited around weapons. He knew submarine K-903 was far superior. The removal of sound shorts in the machinery spaces, rubberizing the hull, and advanced electronic equipment made his boat a deadly predator. Should the Israeli enemy attack Iran's nuclear facilities, the Noor would be ordered to defend the Gulf. He relished the dream of attacking an American carrier. Laying mines was the first step in destroying their fleet and blocking America's flow of oil. But it was only the first step.

Returning to Bandar-e- Abbas provided little time to reflect on the success of his operation. To fulfill his second set of orders, he was working his crew to near exhaustion. His mantra had become 'baad amadh bashem' (*I must be ready*). He believed his men were taking the two days of blistering heat and hard work in stride. They seemed to have a strong sense of commitment to the significant challenges ahead. They were willing to make sacrifices of themselves for the glory they sensed lay ahead of them.

Alizadeh was aware Noor's sister ships, INIS Taregh K-901

and INIS Yunes K-902, were also executing their orders, laying mines in their sectors of the Straits of Hormuz. All was going to plan.

Stepping out on the main deck, Alizadeh walked aft, inspecting the black rubber noise-reducing tiles covering the sides of the boat. His XO, Lieutenant Commander Gilani, and his Engineering Officer were reviewing maintenance and Operational records for machinery. They were also checking for any deflection on the sound isolation mounts for Noor's two 1,500 KW diesel engines. Muting all unnecessary sound was essential. An American submarine might be lurking, waiting to detect them.

XO Gilani signaled the completion of the weapons loadout.

Alizadeh asked, "Good. How is the engineering review?"

Gilani responded with a smile, "Noor is ready to go to sea, Sir."

"Very well. Pass the word to get underway at 2200." Alizadeh lit a long-awaited cigarette.

"Have we received our new orders?" Gilani asked.

"No, but I expect a message to arrive within the hour now that we completed our loadout."

As if on cue, "Captain, we just received a second message from Commodore Yazdi." Accepting the board, the CO flipped the lid, and after reading the radio traffic, smiled. "Let's go to sea, XO."

Forty minutes later, K-903 was off the eastern tip of Qeshm Island. Alizadeh's orders were to remain on the surface and proceed to the southwestern tip between the two commercial channels. Once in position and radar contact established with Damavand, he was to submerge and close in on the destroyer and begin the wargames. If they detected his boat, Damavand

165

or Jamaran were to simulate an attack by dropping one-pound exercise bombs which could cause no damage to his sub. The exercises were to continue for 24 hours.

Alizadeh was excited, believing these tests were a precursor to what the Iranians would unleash on enemy vessels. He turned to his XO, "Gilani, my friend, we are about to make history."

A smile crept across the XO's face. Commodore Yazdi's orders offered the promise of exciting days to come.

Chapter 28

USS Buffalo; Persian Gulf –

"OOD set ultra-quiet conditions," Scott ordered. "Pass the word."

Sonar Technician Sorenson refocused on the patterns on his display. The hypnotic effect of staring at lines on a greenish background was always a problem. On occasion, operators would miss transients that later were revealed to submarines, potentially hostile. The background noise from the pumping stations, surface craft, and high-speed patrol boats added to the problem. "There it is again," he pointed to the upper right corner of the display.

Varney came closer.

"I can't identify this new contact," Sorenson mumbled, rotating the pointer below the dark shape. "Any ideas, Senior Chief?"

"Check the spherical hull array. There's something there all right. If I had to guess, it's an Iranian diesel submarine. There are only a few new diesel electrics' capable of sustained operation in the shallows. Qaeem is one of them. She's being masked by background noise. You better report it."

"Conn, intermittent contact off the port beam, bearing 090 degrees, designated Sierra 50." Richardson watched the young operator adjust his controls.

"Sonar, Conn, classification?" Scott asked.

"Sierra 50 probable diesel submarine, registered Master 1."

"Ask Control how far we are from Jazireh-ye Larak Island?" the Senior Chief ordered Sorenson, comparing the broadband display with the contact.

"Five thousand yards," Scott answered, entering the sonar room, wanting to see for himself. "What do you have, Sorenson?" He nodded to Richardson, then directed his attention to the display. "It could be hostile." He turned to the Senior Chief, "It's still a long shot, but I believe there might be a diesel boat lurking in the shadows. Good job grabbing it. Either we stumbled on him, or he's been trailing us for a while."

"Sounds about right," Sorenson said, "but, Sir, I don't think they know we're here."

Scott looked at Richardson.

Sorenson placed his hands against his headphones.

Senior Chief Richardson pressed the left headset against his ear. He nodded to Scott.

"What do you think?" Scott asked, still focused on the moving object on the screen.

"Noise coming from Master 1," Sorenson said. "It sounds like an LP blower. She may be surfacing."

Scott nodded. It was too soon to feel relief.

"If it wasn't for the fact she was up against the island, I don't think our sensors would have detected her," the Senior Chief said, still looking at the two displays.

Scott nodded, all too well aware that an enemy submarine could have been dangerously close, and they might not have known.

IRIN Damavand, M-77; Persian Gulf –

"Captain, radar reports a possible surfaced submarine sight-ing—between Damavand and Larak Island," the operator called on the phone in Captain Javadi's stateroom.

'Seyyed,' bastard, Captain Javadi muttered under his breath, "Captain Alizadeh of the K-903 was supposed to signal us. He is not in the correct sector. Officer of the deck, come left, head down the reported bearing of the radar contact. XO, inform Jamarand we have contact on our playmate. Contrary to orders, my old friend, Captain Alizadeh, decided to begin the games unannounced." *We'll see my over-eager friend. We'll see. He smiled.*

USS Buffalo -

Sorenson let out a soft, "Oh, Shit."

"What's going on?" Scott asked.

"Sonar just acquired two new high-speed broadband con-tacts, bearing 090 degrees relative and closing. Designate Sierra 51 and 52, possible warships."

Scott walked quickly to Control. "OOD, reduce speed to ahead one-third." He stepped up on the elevated platform and grabbed the periscope. "XO, let's take a look." He rotated the control ring into the UP position. The stainless-steel pole rose out of its well. Lifting the eyepatch, he pressed his eye against the rubber buffer. "She's broached with her search scopes extended."

"Conn, Sonar, Master 1 is now venting and increasing speed, she appears to be submerging. Sierra 51 and 52 are altering course toward her." He looked up. "I believe Sierra 51 and 52 are the new Iranian destroyers." He looked again. "Reclassifying 51 and 52 as Master 2 and 3 respectively."

Scott stood next to Tom Varney, watching the bearing dots starting to stack up on the tactical display. "I believe, XO, we stumbled into a training exercise between the destroyers and one of their submarines. We may get a rare chance to assess their ASW capabilities sooner than we thought."

"That's good," Varney replied, aware how carefully the Iranians guarded their weapons.

Scott said, "OOD, come right to new course 090 degrees. We should open the area, XO, and let them play their game."

Varney was a little concerned that the new course was set in the same general direction as the destroyers. He wondered if Scott was taking undue risks.

Scott felt the boat turning. He waited for Buffalo to steady on her new course. "Let's see if we can minimize our profile and remain in her baffles, XO."

Varney's doubts were put to rest as he recognized the Captain's plan to remain concealed while gathering data on the Iranian exercise and the capabilities of the enemy vessels.

As the two destroyers bore down on Buffalo, Scott sensed the tension increase in the control crew.

"Ten thousand yards and closing," Varney announced, watching the Signal-to-Noise level increasing.

A transmission from high-power active sonar lashed out from one of the Iranian vessels. The single ping was audible throughout the boat.

"Range to Master 2 and 3?" Scott asked.

"Nine thousand yards and closing," Varney reported. "It's a hell of a gamble getting this close."

"I agree, but with the shallows off our portside, we had only two choices: continue paralleling the coastline and provide a beam aspect for them to detect or follow the Kilo and stay in its baffle. That seemed the safest. When she changes course, we'll maintain a bow aspect and close the surface ships." Scott felt his heart rate accelerate. *Washington's orders to remain undetected echoed in his brain.*

IRIN Noor, K-903

"Captain," the sonar operator said, listening to his headset. "I'm detecting a dipping sonar off our port beam. It could be coming from one of our Moudge class destroyers." He looked up. "I believe it is."

Giv Alizadeh was surprised. He was supposed to initiate the exercise, and his boat hadn't even reached the designated coordinates. *What the hell is Damavand's Captain doing?* "XO," he said loud enough for the entire control room party to hear, "If he wants to break the rules and win an easy victory in this game, we'll make it impossible for him to detect us. Set ultra-quiet. Use only the economic engine to maintain sufficient headway for ship control. Let's see just how good his dipper is!"

Gilani nodded and said, "OOD, continue to close the coast, drop speed to 10 knots."

Alizadeh laughed, let the games begin, you ambitious bastard.

IRIN Damavand

"Captain, OOD, our helicopter electronics warfare officer reports multiple contacts on his sonar. He requests guidance on which contact he is to pursue."

Multiple contacts? There was only supposed to be one Kilo involved in this training exercise. Could an American have slipped into the mix? "Radio, inform Jamaran, our dipper holds two contacts. Ask for him to verify." He turned to his XO, "XO, come right 10 degrees, make turns for 30 knots. Let's see just what we can find out about these contacts." One can hope, he thought, wishing this wasn't a game.

USS Buffalo

Richardson was staring at the display. "Conn, both destroyers are racing to the coastline. Wait! Master 3 just slowed. It's turning starboard. Crap! I'm picking up rotor noise off our starboard side. Master 1 just increased speed."

"She altered course," Scott said, peering at the blips on the screen. "He's heading for shallow water. Nav, how far are we from the first channel?"

"Ten thousand yards," Obermeier responded.

"Master 2 has gone silent and changed course," Sonar said. The bearing dots from the destroyer raced across the screen.

"Detecting rotor noise," Richardson shouted. "It's a helicopter."

Scott shouted, "OOD, come left 5 degrees and increase speed to 15 knots. Sorenson, find me a tanker to hide under."

"Conn, I lost Master 1. Master 2 increased speed," Sorenson replied, sounding alarmed.

"The helicopter? Where is it? We don't want to get locked between the destroyer and the dipping sonar."

"Captain, the rotor noise from the helicopter is gone," Richardson said.

Varney peered at the display boards. "Captain, recommend we continue to the channel. I don't believe the Iranian knows what he's tracking."

"I agree," Scott said. "OOD, make turns for 15 knots. Maneuvering, increase turns slowly. Bearing and range to the nearest tanker?"

"Captain, we have an active dipper between us and the tanker," Sorensen said.

Varney reported, "We're below the noise detection threshold of the dipper."

"Remain on course. Range to the channel?" Scott asked again.

"Five thousand yards," Obermeier replied.

"Master 2 just increased speed to 30 knots," Sorenson announced.

"XO, I think the Iranians are testing their systems," Scott said. He fell silent, waiting for the next Iranian move.

Varney stared at the dots on the display as the surface ships raced closer to Buffalo. The active transmissions from the surface ships and helicopter bounced against Buffalo's hull.

All eyes glanced up when the sound of thrashing screws

passed overhead.

Scott felt the shock when two explosions struck near Buf-falo's hull.

Chapter 29

USS Buffalo; Persian Gulf–

"Damage report maneuvering," the Officer of the Deck asked over the sound powered phones.

"Conn, no damage in the engineering spaces. What the hell just happened?" asked Dennis Fender, the engineering officer.

"Small underwater bombs, maybe hand grenades," Varney replied. "They're using them to simulate an attack or to harass us."

"They'd do a lot more if they knew we were under them," Scott said. "XO, come right 10 degrees."

Buffalo changed course.

Two more small explosions.

Scott was grateful the bombs didn't impact Buffalo's movement.

"Master 2 slowed and is coming right, matching our course change, Captain," Sorensen said.

"A game of cat and mouse," Scott said. "OOD, resume original course, and continue to close the tanker." He looked at Varney. "XO, generate a firing solution for Master 2."

"Master 2 appears to be trying to cut us off from reaching the tanker," Richardson said, staring at the bearing dots on the weapon console.

"That's not gonna happen," Scott said, adrenaline now coursing through his veins. "Sonar, range to the tanker?"

"Five hundred yards and closing," Sorenson responded. "I no longer hold the active dipper."

"Where the hell did he go?" Scott asked, annoyed at the cat and mouse game, with Iran playing the cat for the time being. "Thoughts, XO?"

"Proceed under the tanker. Don't slow until we emerge from her portside, make a hard turn to starboard, and enter her baffles." Varney drew the suggested pattern on the DRT. "Match her speed and remain in her baffle area, heading toward the Straits of Hormuz. If I were the pilot of the dipper, I'd be waiting for you on the other side of the tanker."

"Control lost contact on the Kilo submarine due to increased noise from the tanker," Sorenson said.

Scott was deep in thought. "Okay. Nothing we can do about the helicopter. Even if the pilot gets a sniff of us, he knows we're going to use the tanker to hide under, and he can't fire at us with the tanker so close." He smiled at Varney. "We can't let the second destroyer lock us between her and her sister ship."

"We can't fire at her," Varney said.

"No. Not unless she fires on us."

"So, what do we do?" Varney wondered if Scott was up to this kind of challenge.

"We can't fire on them, and the tanker is too close for them to fire on us. Okay. We stay under the tanker until dark or until we have enough noise to hide our escape. Then we hightail it out of here."

Varney wished he could think of an alternative, but knew Scott was right. The next hours would test Scott's strategy.

The sound of munitions exploding a short distance away was all Scott needed. "XO, get us out of here."

Varney ordered the course he and Scott laid out.

Scott ordered ultra-silent and quarters for all unneeded personnel. He waited in suspense as Buffalo began the risky escape from the Iranian tanker and the war games, a short distance away.

After forty tense minutes, Scott ordered Buffalo to turn east, toward Jazireh-ye Larak island. He was relieved they had shaken off the two destroyers but watched for enemy subs. He turned to Varney, "I can't wait to see what other surprises are in store for us, Tom. Are you having fun yet?"

Tom smiled, "The most I've had in years."

"Well, one thing we've learned is that If it comes to trading blows, Buffalo is ready."

Varney still wondered if Scott was.

IRIN Noor, K-903, Persian Gulf-

Aizadeh had a decision to make. "XO, have radio send this to Damavand, and Jamarand, copy to Bandar-e-Abbas, attention Commodore Yazdi. "Noor, trailing possible American submarine. Request surface units break off war game attacks and remain clear of the area. Urgent."

"Do you think there is an enemy submarine nearby?" Jalil, the Noor's XO, asked.

"It's hard to say, Jalil, since our friends on the surface made so much noise and alerted the entire Gulf to our presence. But we shall see." He remained focused on the displays, itching to see an enemy submarine to attack.

Ten minutes later, the radioman handed the Captain a reply.

Alizadeh smiled. "XO, we're to remain and attempt to reacquire the contact, if it was an American submarine. Our noisy friends are ordered to stay clear. We may have some help from our new Qaaem submarine, laying mines not far from here."

"That is good news, Sir," the XO said.

"I have the Conn," Alizadeh announced. "Let's go hunting these infidels."

USS Buffalo

"Conn. Hold narrowband contact off our port beam. Believe we've reacquired the Master 1," Sorenson said. "I thought we shook him."

"Sonar, is Senior Chief Richardson still with you?" Scott asked, knowing he was the best person for identifying transients.

"Yes, Sir, and Dr. Lace," Sorenson responded.

Great, Scott thought, wishing he hadn't put her in danger like this. "OOD, slow to six knots and remain on this heading. Verify ultra-quiet conditions, and all additional personnel are in their racks." He glanced at Varney. "Tom, let's develop a firing solution on this guy."

"Conn, transients from Master 1, indicate flooding noise. Wait, the tube door just opened."

Scott understood there were few unspoken threats worse than letting another boat hear your ship's outer torpedo tube doors open. "Sonar, is she still off our port beam?" He allowed his voice to show no hint of his stress.

"Yes, Sir. She's hugging the island," Sorenson responded.

"OOD, Steady as you go," Scott ordered. "Range to target, XO?"

"Twenty-five hundred yards and holding steady."

"Torpedo or mine, XO?"

"Gotta be a mine, Captain. They're too close to launch a torpedo. I believe they don't know we're here," Varney said, looking on as the Navigator marked an annotation on the Dead Reckoning Table.

"I agree, XO." Scott quickly weighed his options. "Chief, make ready to launch acoustic countermeasures, but only on my order." He picked up the mic again. "Sonar, I believe he intends to launch a mine."

The tension in the Control Room was palpable. Everyone knew if the CO was wrong and a torpedo was launched Buffalo would have minutes to evade. Perhaps no time at all.

"OOD, make turns for 5 knots," Scott ordered. "Continue to slide back into her baffles just in case we were detected."

"Loud underwater metallic noise from the target," Sorenson said.

Scott clenched his fists, waiting for confirmation there wasn't a torpedo in the water. He counted the seconds. A torpedo would end it all.

"Conn sounds like Master 1 launched... a mine."

Scott heard the sighs of relief. "We're not out of the woods yet. Let's continue to move astern of the target, XO, Sonar, do we have a tape on this target? Classification?"

"Qaeem," Janice replied.

The XO looked at Scott.

Scott was surprised but didn't want to show it. "Dr. Lace is experienced at identifying vessels," he said. "Damn good at it too."

Varney nodded.

"Conn, new contact, Sierra 55, off our starboard bow. Possible submarine."

"What?" Scott said, an uneasy feeling creeping up his back. He headed for sonar. "What's going on?" He leaned over Sorensen.

"The contact just popped up on display," Sorensen pointed to the dark line.

"Any idea what flag?"

"Kilo, according to the acoustic signature, designation, Master 4."

The Senior Chief said, "I concur, Captain."

"Keep sending updates on both Master 1 and Master 4 to Control," Scott said, leaving sonar.

"XO, range to the new target?" Scott asked, stepping closer to Varney, who was evaluating the dots on the Fire Control Tactical Display.

"Three Thousand yards at six knots." Varney looked up. "If we don't change course, we could collide. Your orders?" Varney felt tension building in his shoulders.

Scott looked at the tactical display on the FC Console. He had only seconds to decide before his submarine plowed head-on into the enemy sub. "OOD come left three degrees," he ordered, making up his mind.

"You're threading the needle?" Varney asked, unsure if he would have made the risky decision to maneuver between two hostile contacts.

"If we make a slow turn and pass between the two Iranian

submarines, we might just mask our presence, XO," Scott said. "It's a long shot, but the only other option is to turn starboard and race toward the Straits of Hormuz and possibly into a worse trap."

"It's still very risky," Varney said.

Scott nodded. "Let's look at what we know. If the Qaaem just launched a mine, it's unlikely she has any idea about what happened earlier with the destroyers and the Helicopter. If she does suspect our presence, we'd have a lot more company, and not just having mines being tossed at us. I think neither submarine realizes our boat is between them."

"You are guessing though," Varney said, glad he wasn't making this decision.

Scott smiled. "Sometimes, you have to go with your gut. I tend to be a risk-taker, Tom if you hadn't realized by now."

Varney had figured that out about his new CO. "I just hope you guessed right," he said softly.

"Me too," Scott said.

Both men held their breath, watching the range close between the Kilo and Buffalo.

"OOD, come back to the base course," Scott ordered.

Varney didn't like it, but there was nothing he could do but pray that his CO was right.

IRIN Noor, K903

"Captain, Sonar, holds a transient. Classification unknown," the XO announced.

"Officer of the Deck, let's close and see what we hold,"

Captain Giv Alizadeh said.

"Aye, Sir. Helm, come left 10 degrees."

Watching the distance to the contact diminish, Alizadeh made a command decision to drop stealth mode and go active. If an enemy submarine was near, he wanted to catch that big fish before it had a chance to escape. "Sonar, transmit active search, full power," he ordered.

"Aye, Sir," Gilani answered.

Moments later, a 200-dB double ping shot into the water. The unexpected speed of the return shook the control party.

"It's one of ours," Sonar shouted.

"Left full rudder. Ahead full. Cavitate!" Alizadeh screamed, praying to avoid a collision with another Iranian submarine. "Collision quarters," he shouted to the XO, whose face showed terror.

USS Buffalo-

The men in control detected it first: the slow throbbing swish of the Kilo's screws. The thrashing sound washed over, around, and through the hull. A loud double ping from the Kilo's active sonar bounced off Buffalo's hull. Seconds later, Scott heard it again.

"Conn, Master 4 is cavitating," Senior Chief Richardson reported. "She's changing course."

"They're evading, believing they're closing too fast on the other submarine," Varney said. "You did it."

"Not so fast. OOD, turn three degrees to starboard," Scott ordered. "Let's place him out of our baffles, Tom. If he comes around, we can assume our deception didn't work."

Varney saw there was a cautious side to his new CO that was reassuring.

Scott watched the clock advancing. It felt as if each second matched his heartbeat.

The men knew the enemy submarine was near. Scott may have fooled it into thinking it was about to collide into its sister sub, but what if the Iranian realized it was a deception?

After ten minutes without any apparent course change by the Kilo, Scott was almost ready to make his next move.

"Control lost Master 4," Sorenson reported. "I think she's returning to base."

"Navigator, give me a course to the mile marker off Kuhestak City," Scott ordered.

"Control, lost all contacts," Sorenson announced. "Looking good, Sir."

Varney released a smile.

Scott wasn't ready to relax yet. "XO, once we clear the area, we'll deploy Hunter east of Jazireh-ye Larak island. We'll sanitize the bottom for mines."

"Aye, Sir." Varney returned to his usual position.

Seeing he was alone, Scott wiped the sweat from his temples. He felt his anxiety subsiding. He hoped the Iranian still believed his sub had almost rammed another friendly ship. If he did, he wouldn't risk the embarrassment and repercussions of reporting it to his superiors. For the time being, Buffalo was still invisible. Or so he hoped.

Chapter 30

USS Buffalo; Persian Gulf –

Dr. Fred Stone glanced at the digital readouts on the right of the 17-inch tactical display. Hunter's current position was indicated by a blue V. A white dotted line extending from the center of the V denoted the direction of the vehicle. The dots trailing behind the symbol displayed a 30-minute track history. Traveling at 5 knots, paralleling Buffalo's track at a range of 6,000 yards, the UUV was exiting the southernmost outer shipping lane. According to the waypoint, Hunter would reverse course in two minutes, cutting back across the pair of shipping lanes.

Dr. Thomas, sitting to his brother's left side, was monitoring data collected from Hunter's computer. He compared the two digital readouts. "Looks okay from here," he said. "My readings correlate with your numbers, Fred. Depth from the bottom is fluctuating between 10 to 15 feet, depending on the ripples of sand along the floor. All those months of testing and preparations are paying off."

"Let's not become too excited," Stone said. "We still have months of testing. Once Commander Scott becomes confident of Hunter's capabilities, I hesitate to guess what our tasks might be. Wait a second. We're picking up a hard return,"

Thomas interrupted, switching to video. "It's a mine!" He stared at a semi-submerged cylinder.

Dr. Thomas pulled back on the throttle, and Hunter hovered over the torpedo-like object off its bow. The orange bull-nosed weapon lay covered by a layer of sediment. "Jesus, Fred, I wonder how long this sucker's been down here?"

"I don't know." Stone grabbed the intercom. "Captain, Hunter, detected what appears to be a mine or a torpedo," he said. "I'm transferring the video image to Control."

Scott turned to Varney. "Having the video inputted to fire control was an excellent idea," he said, examining the picture. He then called back. "Dr. Stone, hold Hunter at that location. The contact looks like a raising rocket mine that can be activated by a surface ship or submarine. Good catch, gentlemen."

"I wasn't aware Iran had these kinds of mines," Varney said, studying the images.

"Neither was I, Tom." Scott said, moving closer to the screen. "Dr. Stone, move Hunter to the left side of the mine. I want to see the aft end of the weapon."

An audible alert surprised them.

"Captain, we're picking up a return of another object," Dr. Thomas said.

"Okay, let's see what else Hunter found," Scott said, watching the mini-sub maneuver past the mine.

Dr. Stone moved Hunter's video eye to the left. The pulsing sounds cycled more rapidly.

"Stop," Scott said.

The image of a long thin cylinder filled the screen. The nose was buried in the sand.

"It looks like it's been in the water for some time," Scott

said, studying the object's shape. "Although with the shifting sandy sea bottom, it could have been placed there only a few weeks ago."

"What the hell is that?" Varney asked.

"It looks like another torpedo-mine, but much longer and thinner," Scott replied. "Dr. Stone, move Hunter higher, I want to see the back end of that thing. Be careful. You don't want to set that thing off."

Hunter lifted off the sandy bottom and propelled up toward the tail end of the weapon.

"Dr. Stone, can Hunter remain hovering right there?" Scott asked.

"Yes, Sir."

"Tom, look at the six tubes extending from the back of the weapon. It's a rocket torpedo," Scott said. "Dr. Stone, take pictures of this torpedo from every possible angle." He felt uneasy at finding another lethal weapon, only 5,000 yards from his ship.

"Should we alert Fifth Fleet?" Varney asked.

"Not yet Tom. We're too close to hostiles. We'll wait until dark when we can come to periscope depth and transmit the message much faster. We don't want enemy vessels spotting the wire antenna."

Varney nodded. Scott thinks of everything, he thought.

Scott was still staring at the image of the torpedo. "Hell, Tom, floating mines and bottom mines we can work around, but remote-controlled torpedo-mines or rocket-mines increased the threat level a hell of a lot. I wonder how many more of these predators are on the bottom waiting to be launched."

"I gotta admit, Skipper; like you, I was a bit unhappy, when DARPA ordered the engineering geeks aboard and stuck us with the testing of this UUV. Now, I'm damned glad they did! Hunter's technological capabilities may keep us from getting killed in this process."

Scott was still skeptical but had to agree. "XO, draft a communique reporting what we've learned and attach the pictures. Send it to Fifth Fleet. I'll be in my stateroom. Navigator, please chart the location of these mines." He spoke into the intercom, "Dr. Stone, after you finish taking the photographs continue to search along our route. I don't want Buffalo to find more surprises."

"Dr. Thomas, any alerts when you circled the weapon," Varney asked.

"Nothing. Hunter was less than five feet from the torpedo." He looked at Scott. "I'd say this proves she won't trigger any torpedoes."

Scott frowned. "Let's not become over-confident." He left Control and entered his stateroom, still wondering how Intel missed these torpedoes. He sat down at his desk, turned his laptop on, and tapped in his password. Opening the onboard classified library, he typed 'Torpedo-Mines' and hit 'enter' on the search bar. A list of the world's mines, by country, filled the monitor. Iran was not included. They *must be either Russian or Chinese, he thought, highlighting the list of Russian undersea sentries.* He scrolled down until he found what he was looking for. "That's it," he said. "The Iranian navy is deploying Russian rocket torpedo-mines from their submarines," Logging out, he returned to Control. "Tom, add to your communique that the mine is a Russian launched rocket torpedo," he said.

"A torpedo?" Varney said.

"Yeah. It may carry a 700kg warhead and can do 170 knots.

From what I read, these mines can be activated acoustically or magnetically."

"Good thin Hunter spotted it," Varney said.

Scott replied, "Yep. A mine like that has a blast radius of 2,500 yards."

"That's enough to put a big hole in any ship," Varney said.

"I think Iran must want it to be only activated by an operator. If it were set to be triggered magnetically or acoustically, the mine would be triggered by a commercial ship," Scott said.

Varney sighed. "I agree. But it's still lethal."

Scott replied, "We'll need Hunter's help to avoid the mines. Let's send two SEALs from the ASDV to see if they can deactivate the mine. They're trained in demolitions."

"Great idea, Skipper. We can talk to Commander Walsh after Hunter completes the search cycle. Later tonight, we can return to the area and deploy the ASDV."

"Tom, add to your communique for fleet to alert our surface ships passing in the area to search for floating antennae. Warn that they could be attached to these mines," Scott said.

"Captain," Navigator Obermeier cut in. "Hold our position 3,000 yards from our next leg. Recommend making turns for three knots."

"Very well, Nav."

Chief Richardson reported, "Conn broadband noise bearing 090 degrees, designate Sierra 65. Hold two additional broadband contacts bearing 120 degrees designate Sierra 66 and 67. Sierra 65 classified a large tanker. Losing Sierra 65 in our baffles. Sierra 66 just went active. Running a tape on her now."

Scott glanced at the SNR reading. Well below the counter detection threshold, he thought.

Sierra 67 just went active, reclassified 66 and 67 as Iranian destroyers," Senior Chief Richardson announced.

"OOD, get us out of here," Scott ordered. "There are too many hostile fish in this water." He wondered what the hell the Iranians were up to.

Chapter 31

USS Buffalo; Persian Gulf –

"Conn, underwater explosion detected," Senior Chief Richardson reported, "Captain, intermittent broadband contact off our portside, designated Sierra 68. Wait, I'm reclassifying this contact as a submarine."

"Chief, any idea what flag?" Scott asked.

"No, Sir. But the absence of a reactor coolant pump and reduction gear frequencies, I would bet Sierra 68 is a diesel, but we have insufficient information to determine the type."

"What the hell is going on here?" Scott asked.

"Not only are we dodging two Iranian diesels, but now have to contend with a third submarine?" Varney said.

"Designate Sierra 68, Master 7. Range to Master 7?" Scott asked.

"Two thousand yards and opening. Sierra 66 and 67 designated Master 8 and 9 changed course and increased speed," Varney reported, looking over the operator's shoulder.

"Senior Chief, I need the classification of the third submarine," Scott said, hoping it wasn't another hostile.

"Conn, reanalyzed the acoustic signature of Master 7. Best guess, it's a Dolphin II-class submarine. Either German or Israeli."

Scott was aware that a Dolphin II had been sold to Israel by Germany. The Dolphin was rumored to have a 1,500-mile range and carried nuclear-tipped cruise missiles. This recent purchase increased Iran's paranoia for the security of their non-existent, atomic facilities. He glanced toward the overhead screen showing the active transmissions from the Iranian destroyers passing 7,000 yards off Buffalo's portside.

"Control, Master 8, and Master 9 changed course and are closing, Master 7."

Scott eyed the acoustic receiver. "XO let's remain outside detection range. Helm, come left 10 degrees. We'll sit in the destroyer's baffles. Can you think of a better way to collect data, XO?" He asked.

"Sir, what about, Hunter?" Varney asked.

"Thanks, Tom. Dr. Thomas, increase Hunter's speed and let me know how long you can keep her ahead of my position," Scott said.

"Maximum speed of Hunter on the tether is 8 knots," Thomas responded. "According to our sensors, Buffalo is now at 10 knots. We can't keep up. You need to slow down, or we'll have to cut the tether. We've got 20 minutes."

"Keep me informed when I must change course," Scott said.

Israel Naval Submarine Tannin Persian Gulf -

"Well, Yoshi, is this enough action for you?" Lev Zak asked. After a quiet week, Tannin had stumbled into the middle of what he assumed were Iranian naval exercises just north of the Musandam peninsula at the narrowest point of the Straits of

Hormuz. In the wrong place at the wrong time, she now found herself between at least two Iranian surface craft. He thought they had caught her scent and were aggressively searching the area. "Sonar," he asked, "Do you hold good bearings on the contacts?"

Petty Officer Kahan responded, "Yes, Sir. We are between them, but they're making so much noise they must be interfering with each of their active returns. I also had a momentary line on the same 60 Hz coolant pump of the American 688."

Colonel Zak looked thoughtfully at the screen. "Very well. XO, let's get the hell out of here. Diving Officer, record soundings every 30 seconds and maintain depth between 15 and 20 meters off the bottom. Officer of the Deck, maintain ultra-quiet conditions. We're going to creep out of here at 5 knots."

Moments after the CO gave his orders, the sound of distant explosions rattled Tannin's crew.

Zak hurried to the display. "At least it isn't us, but I believe the Americans are getting a pounding," he said, smiling. "Let's go home."

Iran's Quoy Sheyere; Persian Gulf –

Lieutenant Commander Saman Lajani, an ever-present cigarette dangling between his lips, stood in the pilothouse of his converted tank landing ship. He wondered who he'd angered to be assigned to this scow. His boat, purchased in the mid-1980s from the Netherlands, was badly rusting, and he thought grimly almost unseaworthy. He smiled bitterly when he considered its' name, Quoy Sheyere, Farsi, which meant 'Angry Lion.' "Her name should be something more appropriate, such as, 'Garbage Truck," he grumbled.

Lajani hadn't done poorly for a Kurdish Shi'ite boy when neither Iran nor Iraq cared a fig for their minorities. Achieving naval command, even if it was unglamorous, was something few Kurds had ever done. He surveyed the rust-spotted deck below, happy to let his XO, Lt. Basir Mohsen, supervise the laying of contact mines, a task he considered barely worthy of his attention.

The XO directed the crane operator to lower the sling assembly into the wide-open deck hatch.

Lajani shook his head. Such a monotonous task, he thought.

The XO signaled the crane operator to raise the mine.

A nylon strap holding the mine loosened.

"Look out!" Mohsen screamed.

Lajani recoiled helplessly as the sling gave way, and the mine crashed in the hold.

The first explosion tore off the deck hatch, hurling it through the pilothouse. Lajani stared in shock, where his arm had been. Blood gushed from the stump. He sagged to the deck.

A split second later, the rest of the mines detonated, blowing a massive hole in the portside, hurling shrapnel everywhere.

All aboard were killed.

Some died immediately from massive wounds. Others died slowly. Twelve drowned. The only evidence of the disaster was an oil slick dotted with debris and body parts on the once calm sea.

USS Buffalo; Persian Gulf –

"Captain, explosion west of our position," Sonar reported, marking the site.

"Say again, Sonar?"

"Second explosion, Sir! The same bearing. Picking up high-speed screws."

"Any idea what caused the explosions?" Scott asked, entering Sonar and leaning over Sorenson's right shoulder.

Senior Chief Richardson and Sorenson pointed at the two dense black dots on the spectrum analyzer's display.

"If I had my guess, I'd bet on mines."

"Okay, keep scanning along those bearings," Scott said, studying the dark line along the top of the spectrum analyzer. "Report any further activity in the area."

Sorenson pointed to the screen. "Two contacts increasing speed. They're heading to the site of the explosions."

A short time later, Scott, in Control, called for an update. "Sonar, how's it looking?" Scott asked. "Any more on the destroyers?"

"They're both pounding away using the same search frequency." Richardson looked up. "They have no idea how to conduct an active search. Their destroyers made so much noise it's difficult for even our sensors to pick-up other vessels."

Dr. Thomas's voice interrupted. "Captain, Hunter is 8,000 yards from our position."

Scott, in all the excitement, had almost forgotten about Hunter. "Okay, we can go back and get her now. OOD, reverse course, and close Hunter's position. Torpedo room; we're reversing course."

"Torpedo room, have Hunter go active," Scott ordered. I need to verify if Hunter is detectable, he thought.

194

"Hunter is active!" Dr. Stone said, depressing a toggle switch on the control panel. "Speed 5 knots and 6 feet above the sandy bottom."

"Are you detecting Hunter?" Scott asked.

Sorenson looked at his monitor and replied, "No, Sir."

"That answers that question," XO, Scott said. "If Sorenson can't detect Hunter, no one will."

"Conn, lost Master 7 due to background noise," Richardson announced over the overhead speaker.

"Captain, Master 7, before we lost her, appeared to be heading toward the Straits," the Navigator added.

"Anything else on the destroyers, Senior Chief?" Scott asked. "Negative, on the surface ships."

Dr. Thomas chimed in, "Captain, Hunter's sonar is like the secure fathometer. Its 'pings' are like fish farts, indistinguishable from biologics—"

Varney said, "Fish, farts?" He shook his head. "At least we don't need to worry about Hunter being detected."

Scott wasn't so sure. "Okay. But keep checking. I don't want Hunter's fish farts—I can't believe he said that—leading a destroyer to us."

Janice looked up from a chart she was studying with Morton.

Scott walked forward, not wanting to disrupt the conversation. He thought Janice shot him a glance but wasn't sure.

"Evening, Sir," Obermeier said, interrupting Scott's thoughts.

"Lieutenant," Scott said. He liked the young supply officer, two years fresh out of the academy.

"What are the three of you cooking up?" Scott asked, feeling more relaxed now that the Iranians had pulled away.

"We were discussing our evaluations of the coastal condi-

195

tions, Sir," Janice said, fidgeting with a pencil in her hand.

"Well, 'Chop,'" using Terry Washington's nickname for Supply Officers, " Sonar's assessment is that the explosions were possibly the result of mines near Queshm Island."

"Any idea what set them off?" Janice asked, looking concerned.

Scott faced her. "We don't know. I suspect as tension grows between Iran and Israel, and us, the Revolutionary Guards will place more mines at key locations to disrupt shipping. We're moving to the location of the explosion, to investigate."

Janice frowned. "Dr. Thomas reported Hunter is now 4,000 yards ahead of our current position, near Qushm Island. Based on Patricia and my analyses, that would be an ideal location for the Iranians to place mines."

"We're picking up Hunter before we transit north to investigate the explosions," Scott replied. "Time will tell what other surprises the Iranians have in store for us."

"Yes, Sir," Janice replied. And time will tell what fate has in store for me, she thought, wishing Scott wasn't so cold to her.

Scott turned to Washington, "I'll be in my stateroom, please, inform the XO."

"Aye, Sir," Terry Washington said.

Janice watched Scott leave the area. I can't focus on my work when he's near, she thought. What the hell is wrong with me?

"Dr. Lace? Janice?"

Janice realized it was Morton. "Excuse me, Pat, I was thinking of the speed of the current leading into the harbor."

Morton, grinned and whispered, "Is that what you were thinking about?"

Janice drove her eyes back to the chart on the table.

Scott closed his stateroom door and sat down on the couch.

196

He breathed a sigh of relief to be a few minutes free from the scrutiny of his crew. It was a massive responsibility. He leaned back, closing his eyes. It was impossible to shut out the sounds of the ship. He could still hear the explosions, pings, and other noises rattling in his brain. Then, he saw Janice's face. What am I going to do about her?

Five hours went by without a hitch. The destroyers were no longer in the area. Sonar reported Master 8 and 9 were heading toward the Straits of Hormuz. Hunter was mapping the seabed near Buffalo.

Scott wondered if Hunter would be able to discover what caused the earlier explosions. The ship that had gone down after those blasts had been close. Was it targeted? Were the Iranians hunting for bigger game and accidentally blew up another vessel? Blowing up an American submarine-like Buffalo would be a significant coup. Were they ready to do that? "Not if I can help it," he said, ending all hope of sleep.

Chapter 32

USS Buffalo; Persian Gulf –

Hunter commenced her sixth hour, searching along the sandy floor for hidden munitions.

Dr. Thomas, recording the digital readout of Hunter's depth, noticed the submersible was slowing. "Fred, did you reduce Hunter's speed?"

"No, why?" Fred replied, looking at the portable monitor in the torpedo room. A flashing red light above the amperage meter flashed on.

Thomas cut the power to the motor. "The warning light on the amperage meter just came on. Stopping thruster." He noted Hunter's depth had also decreased. The video image displayed on his monitor revealed the water was clear, allowing him to see the bottom was littered with bottles, metal, and assorted cans. Fred shot Glen a worried look. "Either we have a motor failure, or the tether is snagged." He leaned closer to his brother. "A motor problem this early in the testing won't look good."

Glen Thomas fired back, "Well, let's hope it's just snagged."

Dr. Stone reported, "Captain, a warning light from Hunter, indicates excessive current being drawn from the batteries is causing the battery compartment's temperature to increase.

We're going to secure the UUV until we can determine what's causing the problem."

Just what I need, Scott thought. "Keep me informed." He switched to Control. "OOD, All Stop," Scott ordered.

"All stop, Captain. Is everything okay?"

"Just dandy," Scott replied. He sat on the seat, extending from the railing surrounding the twin periscope wells, reading the message traffic. "Sonar?"

Senior Chief Richardson replied, "Sir."

"Chief," Scott said, "your information was on the money. Intel reports the submarine we encountered yesterday was a Dolphin II Class diesel-electric. She was spotted via satellite when she surfaced to recharge her batteries. It had to be the same boat."

"Roger, but it doesn't answer the question. Is she a German or an Israeli submarine?" Richardson asked.

"I'd be willing to bet she's Israeli. If the Germans were operating here, it would be a radical departure from NATO protocol. Keep your eyes and ears open. She may return. If so, it's going to become a little crowded."

Varney said, "Let's hope she continues toward the Arabian Sea. I would prefer not to go head-to-head with a friendly by accident. We're going to have enough problems with the Iranian diesel electrics without mixing it up with the Israelis."

"Captain, reversing Hunter's course 180 degrees to determine if the tether is snagged on an obstruction," Dr. Thomas reported.

"Keep the OOD informed. We will hover while you investigate." Scott looked at Tom. "The loss of what could be an excellent underwater resource would be unfortunate this early in our operation."

"I agree. Hunter's systems will be beneficial."

Twenty minutes later, Dr. Stone contacted Scott. "Captain, you need to look at what Hunter found."

Scott and Varney studied the image of a bow as it became visible through the murky water. They saw a cavernous hole amidships.

The Captain and XO watched with interest as Hunter traversed along her tether toward the wreck's stern. A long gash ran from the deck down to below the waterline.

Stone nosed Hunter toward the wreck's pilothouse.

"Oh, my God," murmured a sailor standing behind Scott.

Scott recoiled when a human face filled the screen. "I believe we now know what sonar detected," he said, a somber expression on his face as the olive-colored face of a man with a dark beard swayed with the current. The sailor's eyes were wide open, staring, even in death, into the camera. One arm swung into view, a hand severed at the wrist.

Shifting Hunter's field of view showed another man, in a life vest, was entangled, face down, in several lines, preventing him from drifting to the surface.

"Jesus, what a shitty way to die," Juststone mumbled.

Varney had to agree.

"Conn, detecting high-speed screws closing our location," Sorensen announced over the open mic.

"Dr. Stone, pull Hunter back from the wreck," Scott ordered. "The owners may want to investigate and retrieve the bodies."

"We're almost there, should be just another five or 10 minutes," came the response.

"Sonar, how close is the new contact?" Scott asked.

"Two Thousand yards and closing fast," Richardson replied.

"Dr. Stone, you have 5 minutes to retrieve Hunter. If you

can't untangle the tether, cut the wire, and get the UUV out of there." He heard grumbling on the other end of the line and prepared to kick someone's ass if they ignored his orders.

Chapter 33

USS Buffalo; Persian Gulf –

Dr. Stone reluctantly increased Hunters' forward motion to comply with the Captain's order. He tensed as the noise of approaching surface ships became audible.

The Iranian vessel's sunken pilothouse loomed out of the haze.

"There's the problem, Captain. Hunter's tether is caught between the pilothouse and the radar mount." He pushed the Speed Down button. Using the joystick and thruster, he maneuvered the UUV toward the radar mount, hoping the tether would lift upward when there was slack between the two vehicles.

"Can you get it free?" Thomas asked.

To Stone's great relief, the tether started to rise. He reversed Hunter's motor.

The UUV backed away from the wreck, exposing the stern.

"Mines!" Varney shouted.

The images of several gray horned mines on the seabed that had been hidden by the sunken minelayer came into view.

Scott stared hard at the scene. One mine was floating among the carnage, swaying back and forth with the current. As he looked closer, he saw it was anchored to a lead weight by a thick chain.

Varney pointed to the mine on the screen. "Captain, that mine could be active. We could lose Hunter."

"OOD start opening the area," Scott ordered. "Dr. Stone, send Hunter to deeper water now! Get away from those mines."

"I counted three mines on the bottom plus the floater," Varney said, peering hard. "They appear to be the horned contact type. They could be alive."

"I figure each mine contains enough TNT to put a sizeable hole in a ship," Scott said.

"Do you think a mine like that caused the explosions?" Varney asked.

"I don't know. But that explosion, if it was an accident, should slow down their mine planting, in this area, at least. What a damn waste of life, though."

"Conn, the high-speed surface contact is slowing over the wreck," Senior Chief Richardson said.

"We'll wait here until they leave," Scott said. "Hopefully, taking care of their dead will be their priority now."

Three hours later, Scott granted permission for Hunter to resume sweeping the seabed north of the sunken minelayer. No more mines were detected.

"You were right. I guess that accident put a dent in their plans," Varney said.

"I wonder how many men they lost," Scott replied, grateful his ship had been spared at least one danger.

Buffalo moved into deeper water, waiting for commercial shipping to resume sailing the Persian Gulf. Several times, Scott suspended Hunter's search for mines when supertankers closed to within 2,000 yards. With a comfortable depth of 200 feet, and with Hunter still exploring, he had no intention of placing Buffalo needlessly in harm's way.

"There's a lot of traffic," Richardson said as the noise created by passing ships made it difficult to identify potential hostiles.

Scott considered moving farther away from the traffic but wanted to wait until Hunter completed her third and final leg.

Sonar reported another explosion. The site of the blast correlated with the position of the destroyed minelayer.

"It's good we got out of there," Scott said to his XO. "Whatever happened is keeping them busy."

"Control," Sorensen said, "New contact, Sierra 70, classified possible Kilo."

"Looks like I spoke too soon," Scott said. "Range to target?"

"Ten thousand yards off our starboard beam and opening."

"Keep an eye on her," Scott said.

"Conn lost Sierra 70 due to background noise," Richardson replied.

"Chief, where is Hunter right now?" Scott asked, thinking it was a pain to have to keep track of the UUV and all these contacts.

"Four-thousand yards off our starboard beam," Richardson responded. "Pretty close, Sir."

Scott grabbed the phone. "Dr. Thomas, Stone, bring Hunter home now!" He slammed the phone down. "Nav, plot a course to move us north toward the island of Larka. Torpedo Room, prepare to retrieve Hunter."

"Captain," the Navigator said. "Recommend we change course left to 030 degrees, speed 10 knots to reach our rendezvous point."

Stone entered the new course and speed and engaged the

autopilot.

"Autopilot is engaged," Varney said.

Sorensen shouted, "The contact is changed course. She's moving to intercept us."

"Navigator, when is the next satellite pass?" Scott asked.

"2300, Sir!"

Scott leaned over the chart table with Varney. "Tom, we've found one of their Kilos. There could be more of their subs patrolling the coast."

"I agree," the XO responded.

"Their mines are just the start. I think they're ready to attack any ships they view as hostile. When I was at the Pentagon, there was a report, Iran was building a replica of the USS Nimitz in the Bandar-e-Abbas Shipyard, for war games, to simulate attacks against our carriers."

"You're kidding?" Varney said.

"Given the mining of the Straits and the war games we've witnessed, there's a real possibility Washington might force us into the fray, as a preemptive measure."

"Without provocation?"

"Hopefully, not, but we were ordered to monitor the Naval activity around their base. That could be considered by the Iranians sufficient provocation for an attack."

"I'll draft a message to Fleet and find out what developed in the past six hours," Varney suggested.

"Include your report of the Iranian minelayer exploding, presumably while laying mines. Add pictures when we take our next Sat fix at 2300," Scott ordered. "And add, we detected an Israeli Dolphin II Class submarine operating in the Gulf."

"Do you think she might return?" Varney asked.

"I wouldn't be surprised."

Varney looked up from his board. "Sir, we still haven't seen any messages directing our SEALs to infiltrate the Bandar-e-Abbas Naval Base," he said. "Maybe, they realize it's too hot out here?"

"Tom, when you least expect it, the SEALs will receive their marching orders, and then, none of us will be able to sleep."

Chapter 34

Bandar 'Abbas Naval Base Iran –

Admiral Al Jujair fumed at the report he received from Damavand's Captain.

"Damavand states during the training exercise, his sonar operators and our helicopter detected not one but two submerged hostile submarines. Why was I not told of this before now, Admiral, Mokri?" Jujair demand.

"Admiral, verification of the second submarine did not occur until after the exercise. Damavand's CO was the officer in charge. He directed Jamaran's Captain to break off his attack on the second contact believing it was one of ours. Jamaran was then directed to join Damavand and search for the contacts."

"Was the second submarine an American?" Jujair asked.

"No, Sir," Mokri answered. "Our ship and helicopter could not verify the type of contact. Our command did receive a report earlier this month that an Israeli Dolphin Class submarine was spotted transmitting the Suez channel. She might have been the submarine we detected during the war games."

"Where are our destroyers now?" Admiral Jujair asked.

"Both are searching the northern section of the Persian

Gulf off the Musandam Peninsula. If an American or Israeli submarine is in the area, I felt stationing the units there might result in a detection."

"How many Boghammars and Bladerunners are helping in the search," Jujair asked.

"Fifty from the Bandar 'Abbas Naval Base," Admiral Mokri replied.

"Your orders are to establish a search area starting south of Qushm Island extending east toward Musandam across the two commercial shipping channels. Once the barrier is in place, direct the squadrons to move north. There is no need to search the shallows. American 688 boats need over 200 feet of water. If there is an American or Israeli submarine operating in the area, we will push him into the arms of our waiting destroyers," Jujair said.

"I will relay your orders," Admiral Mokri replied. He hurried out of the conference room, his Chief of Staff in hot pursuit.

Assembling his officers, Admiral Mokri relayed his new orders.

"So, the reports are true?" Captain Alvand asked. "An American submarine was detected during the training exercise."

"There is no physical evidence, but I am not taking a chance," Mokri responded. "If they are there, we will be ready for them."

Chapter 35

USS Buffalo; Persian Gulf –

"Captain, your presence is requested in radio," the XO called. He was paging through grainy black and white pictures when Scott entered. He handed Scott one of three satellite photos along with an attached intelligence report.

"Thank you, Tom," Scott said.

"Captain, this is a recent photo of Iran's Fordow nuclear complex. The Iranian government has increased the number of Surface to Air Missile sites near their facilities," Varney said.

Scott checked out the photo. "If Iran develops nuclear weapons, and Israel launches an attack against Iran's Fordow Fuel Enrichment Plant, we'll be dragged into World War III. I hope Washington and our NATO allies are prepared to fight Iran and every Arab country in the Middle East that supports Iran. You can bet we'll see a replay of the burning oil fields in Kuwait in 1991. Remember the long lines at the gas pumps we experienced in 1974? This really could be a shit storm if Russia gets involved."

"Here, look at our OP Area," Tom said, handing the second picture to Scott.

Scott's eyes narrowed. "I see the reason for the increased

activity. With a possible attack at the nuclear enrichment facility and the increase in Iranian naval ships in the Persian Gulf, commercial ships and tankers are trying to leave."

"There's more," Tom said, sliding the last picture and messages to Scott.

Scott studied the image of Jet Skis and Bladerunners dotting the surface. After reading all the text accompanying the pictures, his face furrowed.

Along the eastern side of the naval base, tied against a long cement pier, were three Ghadir class diesel submarines. "It looks like the submarine preparing to leave, based on the location of the tugboat, tied outboard. The remaining two submarines are still loading torpedoes. Several flatbed trailers loaded with weapon containers are stacked next to the crane." He pointed to the top of the dock.

"This could be for show, as Dr. Lace noted earlier," Varney said. "The Iranians know we maintain satellite coverage of the entire Gulf."

"I agree. You can see two patrol boats are moving toward the harbor entrance. My question is, how long before someone pulls the trigger?"

"Are you referring to the Israelis?" Varney asked.

"With the President not backing their 'Red Line,' I believe they might go ahead with a preemptive attack. Buffalo will be right in the middle. We're the only asset on the scene and could become the go-to guys to eliminate threats against our fleet," Scott said.

Varney handed the Intel report to Scott. "This is the entire package from today's message traffic. Should we stream the floating wire, Sir?"

"With the increase in traffic and the swarms of Iranian boats,

I think we should hold off, Tom."

Varney nodded.

Scott read aloud, ''Iran has stepped up production on the Boghammar II, difficult to detect on radar. The boats are capable of speeds of 50 knots and carry twin 50 caliber machine guns. Fifty are already positioned at key points with another 25 anticipated within the next week."

"More trouble," Varney said.

Scott continued the report, 'Several Kaman Class Fast Attack missile/torpedo boats and four Patrol Torpedo boats are harassing ships entering and leaving the Straits. Preparations are underway for the Iranians to send six of the Kaman Class fast attack, missile/torpedo units into the Persian Gulf in days'.

"It's getting crowded," Varney said.

"Tom, inform the OODs all periscope observations, including Coms and Transit passes, will be conducted at night. Each duty section must be vigilant when coming to periscope depth. Order sonar to conduct sweeps of the area before proceeding to PD. I don't want to be seen, Also ask Senior Chief Richardson if they recorded sound tapes on Iran's small craft yet."

"Captain, did you see the flatbeds? They appear to be dropping a new fleet of Jet Skis into the water," Varney said, pointing to a photograph taken of the Iranian coastline near their primary weapons facility.

Scott studied the photo. "They're like a nest of hornets waiting to attack. Any more good news?"

"Here are two satellite pictures," Weathers said, handing them to Scott.

Scott read an attached message and exploded, "Splash! What the hell is Splash?" He slammed the table. "Christ, what next? Fifth Fleet is ordering Team 6 to initiate Splash." He turned to the radioman, "Petty officer Weathers, has Team 6 received any messages since their boarding?"

"No, Sir."

"Tom, find Commander Walsh and bring him to the wardroom. The SEALs always have their agenda. I don't like being kept in the dark."

Commander Mike Walsh sat across from the XO in the wardroom.

Scott was, reading the message aloud, "Splash! Please, indulge me, Commander, what's 'Splash?'"

Walsh pulled a sealed envelope from his black leather case and handed it to Scott. "I was to hand this to you if the word 'Splash' was included in a message. You will be issued a separate set of orders within the next 24 hours."

Scott pulled the paper from the envelope. "Upon the issuance of these orders, Commander Walsh is to proceed to Point Shadow and extract Dr. Aslan Mehman, whose codename is Alias." He looked up. "Who is Dr. Aslan Mehman?"

"I was only told he's a nuclear physicist," Walsh said.

"He must be important to send your team to pick him up," Varney commented.

"There's more, XO," Scott said. "Team 6, after the extraction, is to infiltrate the Bandar-e-Abbas Naval Base, and based on Dr. Mehman's information, plant explosives at the weapon facility." He looked at Varney. "It says the facility houses nuclear and conventional torpedoes."

"We are ordered to do what?" Varney asked.

Walsh looked Scott squarely in the eyes. "Yes, Commander, based on intelligence, Iran may be building naval-based nuclear weapons that could endanger our fleet. It falls upon us to destroy this facility. Dr. Mehman is the key to this info, which is why we need to get him out before we do anything else."

"When and where are you to extract this professor?" Scott asked.

"Point Shadow is on the south end of Larak Island. Extraction is at 1800Z on the evening of the 2nd. Dr. Mehman will be vacationing with his grandparents. Our instructions are to send three men to get him. My men will bring him back to Buffalo, so we can get the information we need."

"So, Washington wants you to destroy this facility with this scientist's information, but without Iran suspecting we did it?" Scott asked.

"Sounds about right." A sardonic smile appeared on Walsh's face. "The professor will brief us on the location and contents of the weapons facility. Our instructions are to make the destruction of the facility appear to be an accident."

Scott shook his head. "Iran's reaction will be to intensify the search for us. They'll be determined to find out who was responsible. Washington isn't placing us in a good position. Destroying their weapons facility will create hell if we're discovered." He turned to Varney, "XO, have Navigator lay out a course to Larak Island. Check with Dr. Thomas and see if Hunter is ready to go back into the water. I want to map the incursion point ahead of time."

"Captain," Weathers interrupted, "Received a message

from Admiral Westfield."

"Thanks, Weathers." Scott accepted the message board. He read the communique, signed it, and handed it to the XO. "This reaffirms 'Splash,' but with one additional spin."

Varney looked curious.

Scott shook his head. "Dr. Mehman is to remain aboard Buffalo until we're directed to transfer him to another naval unit." Another complication, he thought, resealing the envelope.

Walsh stood. "Sir, may I leave to inform my men?"

"Yes," Scott said.

Walsh left.

Varney scrutinized the photos on the table. "Enemy fast attack boats will hamper the SEALs' retrieval of Dr. Mehman. They're everywhere."

"You're right. The trick will be not to get caught," Scott said.

"That will be some trick," Varney replied.

Chapter 36

USS Buffalo; Persian Gulf –

The hydraulic rammer pushed Hunter into Tube 1. Chief Machinists Mate Juststone attached the wire dispenser on the breech door and connected the data transmission link cable. "Ready to verify connections," he said.

Dr. Thomas lifted the cover on the control unit and applied power to Hunter.

The dark green screen came to life, displaying the course, speed, and depth parameters he entered before launch. The V, symbolizing the UUV, sat in the center.

Thomas selected the 100-yard range scale and verified ten amber rings were visible on the Geo Plot to the left of the Tactical Screen.

"System checks complete," Dr. Stone reported to Control. "I'll head to Control and view the operations from there," he said to his brother.

Dr. Thomas nodded, eyes glued to the screen.

"Shutting the breach door," Chief Machinist Mate Juststone announced. "Hunter is ready to launch."

Hunter rested on the sandy floor five thousand yards from Buffalo.

Buffalo crept toward Larak Island. Her speed was a mere two knots above the six-knot current. Running in 180 feet of water, with only 50 feet under the keel and a scant 65 feet of water above the top of her sail, she was rigged for ultra-quiet.

Commanded to shut down, Dr. Stone and Thomas waited for Buffalo to launch the Advanced SEAL Delivery Vehicle sitting astern of Buffalo's sail.

"Captain, we're 15,000 yards from Larak Island," the Navigator announced.

"Conn," we're picking up a low cycling diesel engine off our portside.

"Range?" Scott asked.

"Seven thousand yards," Senior Chief Richardson responded.

"All Stop," Scott ordered. "Dr. Thomas, move Hunter 7,000 yards off our port bow."

"What the hell?" Senior Chief Fire Control Technician Jack Russell said. "Captain, Hunter detected what appears to be a sunken craft sitting on the bottom."

Scott stepped over to the monitor. "Dr. Stone, hold Hunter right where she is." He reached up over the console and retrieved the blue volume of Jane's Fighting Ships. Opening the section on Iranian naval vessels, he found what he was looking for. "North Korean, Taedong-B semi-submersible attack. The craft is fitted with a snorkel allowing it to hover to 82 feet. She holds a crew of 3 and carries two 324mm torpedoes and small arms." He handed the book to Varney. "Take a look at the profile, XO. They can place this submersible in the channel or the shallows and wait for an unsuspecting ship to pass before launching torpedoes. Sonar, do you still hold the noise source off our beam?"

"Yes, Sir. The SNR is less than 10 dB. It sounds like a diesel kicker on a fishing boat. Wait, one, I'm picking up an increased noise level."

"Cut a sound tape on the contact and label it Taedong Fast Attack Craft," Scott ordered. "Send the bearings to fire control. Let's track this." He turned to Dr. Stone. "Dr. Stone, keep Hunter tracking the submersible," he ordered. "OOD, close Hunter, and prepare to retrieve the UUV if required. XO, let's forward the data to Fifth Fleet on our next Nav fix."

Buffalo continued to shadow Hunter and the submersible until depth, and time constraints forced Buffalo and Hunter to break off and head for Larak Island.

"Captain, 3,000 yards from Larak Island. Recommend we launch the submersible here and remain at this location until they return," the Navigator said.

"Master Chief, get those SEALs on board and notify me when you are ready to depart," Scott ordered.

Sorenson's tone was urgent. "Sonar, detecting several explosions astern," he said. "Source unknown."

Scott hurried to Sorenson's station.

Master Chief Norris climbed up through the aft escape hatch and entered the ASDV. Stepping through the forward water-tight door, he proceeded to the pilot's seat and sat down.

"Master Chief, an internal pressure gauge in the submersible is holding at one atmosphere," Janice Lace reported, having boarded earlier. "Laser viewer and side-scan sonar are in standby in preparation for us to disengage from Buffalo."

"Master Chief, all equipment and personnel are aboard," Walsh reported, standing in the Lockout Chamber.

Norris acknowledged the report and said, "Air banks, battery banks, and the forward and aft venting valves, all green. Access hatch connecting Buffalo indicates open."

Dr. Lace checked off the pre-launch list as Norris verified each item. "Activating the side-scan sonar." She waited for the computer to sequence through its system checks.

Powered up, the lower monitor displayed the ASDV heading, sector scan selections, power levels, course, and speed readouts. All were zero at present.

Lace powered up the secure fathometer and placed it in standby. She looked at the tactical console and Hunter's video feed. She adjusted the gain on the side of the monitor to brighten up the display from Hunter's camera.

The bottom current swirled sand around Hunter's lens.

"Master Chief, Hunter's video indicates there are no obstructions between us and the island. Looks like smooth sailing," Lace reported.

"Commander Walsh, let's button her up and head for the island," Norris said.

Norris glanced at two remaining red lights.

A dull thud sounded from behind him as the lower hatch was shut and secured.

Looking up, Norris saw one of the red lights turn green. "Ready to disengage," the Master Chief informed the OOD. "Permission to deploy?"

"Granted. Good hunting," Scott replied.

Pressing the locking switch, Norris saw the light on the panel above his head turn green, indicating that the docking collar had disengaged. He felt the submersible sway as he pulled back on the reverse thrusters.

Janice Lace adjusted the gain again on the screen and sat back. "Ten-thousand yards from the drop point," she announced, looking at the readings on the tactical video.

Norris pushed the power handle forward and added a hard-right rudder causing the ASDV to bank away from Buffalo's sail. The whine from the electric motors increased. "Estimate time of arrival 50 minutes," he announced over the communication mic.

Clear of Buffalo's sail, Lace entered an initial 60-degree search sector between 300 degrees to 030 degrees, a 10-meter range scale at 200 kHz. She adjusted the gain and the pulse width. "Transmitting now," she said, pressing the activate button.

The sound wave from the transducer was faint in Lace's headset. She had calculated earlier the amount of power required by Hunter to conduct an active search without alerting enemy acoustic sensors on the seabed. Adjusting her earphones, she listened to the crackling sound of the pulse traveling through the water. Eyes glued to the display, she waited for any reflection caused by sounds bouncing off an underwater object. To her relief, none appeared.

Hunter's video confirmed the area was devoid of contacts. The fathometer showed 60 feet below the submersible's hull.

"Master Chief, sonar indicates a shelf 500 yards dead ahead, depth 100 feet and rising," Lace reported.

Norris pulled back on the thrusters and brought the submersible to a stop. "Releasing forward and aft anchors," he said.

The crew felt sudden weightlessness when the two 300-pound lead weights dropped from the submersible.

"Anchors holding," Norris announced.

"Commander Walsh," Janice said into her mouthpiece. "We are stationary and holding at 72 feet. It's time."

"We're entering the Lockout Chamber now," Walsh replied.

Norris adjusted the ballast to compensate for the added weight in the Lockout Chamber. "Roger. Strobe will be activated in 30 minutes. Good Luck!" He knew the strobe light would help the SEALs find Hunter when they returned. If they returned.

Chapter 37

Advanced SEAL Delivery Vehicle; Persian Gulf –

Walsh and Rose stood, backs pressed against the Monel clad chamber wall waiting for Hamerman to finish loading the three Diver Propulsion Vehicles. The black underwater scooters could maintain continuous cruise at 6 knots for eight hours.

Hamerman pulled the hatch shut and locked it into place.

Lace noted the light change from red to green. The inner-chamber hatch was locked.

"Flooding chamber," Walsh reported through his mike pulling down the red handle that opened the valve to the sea.

Norris started the electric trim pump, removing water from the internal ballast tanks to compensate for the extra weight of the water filling the Lockout Chamber.

Rose bent down, rotated the wheel that unlocked the outer hatch, and lifted the heavy cover.

The Outer Chamber Hatch light switched from green to red, indicating it was open.

Janice watched the lights intently. A green light showed the hatch was again shut. The SEALs had deployed.

Commander Walsh, Rose, and Hamerman adjusted their buoyancy vests and dropped through the escape hatch.

Checking the navigation board strapped to his scooter, Walsh gave the thumbs-up signal and pressed the switch on the handlebar of his mini-scooter. Leading the way, he turned in the direction of the extraction coordinates.

The water was murky.

The less transparent, the better, Walsh thought. There are too many possibilities of us being seen from shore. Raising his clenched fist, he dropped the scooter. He eased his body toward the surface, lifted his head, exposing only his eyes. "There he is," he hissed into his mouthpiece.

A gray-haired man was walking toward the water's edge. A blue mask and snorkel were hanging around the man's neck.

He meets the description, Walsh thought. "Got him in sight," he said into his throat mike and ducked back underwater to retrieve his scooter.

Moving two hundred yards closer, Walsh raised his fist again and let his scooter drop. "Rose, follow me," he said, moving to the surface.

Walsh had his knife ready. He saw the man walking along the shore. It has to be him. But what if it isn't? His hand tightened on the knife. "No one move. Wait for the splash," Walsh ordered and ducked underwater.

A short swim and Walsh watched silently as the man he believed was Alias, now in mask and fins, entered the water.

The man kicked his fins, water splashing as he swam gradually farther away from the shore. He kicked his fins hard three times.

Was that the signal? Walsh had no choice. He had to take the chance. His black-gloved hand reached up. "Now," he shouted.

The target jumped when Walsh's hand locked around his wrist and pulled him under. He tried to tear away from the glove, but another hand pulled the snorkel from his mouth and replaced it with a rubber mouthpiece.

Held underwater by powerful hands, the man sucked in the compressed air from the SEAL's buddy hose.

Walsh pulled him deeper into the dark water as he dragged the target away from the shore. The knife was still ready if needed.

Hamerman, catching up to the small party, placed the man's hand through a loop in a cord and tightened a slipknot around his wrist.

Walsh motioned for Mehman to follow him.

The man, no longer struggling to break free, nodded his head.

The SEALS picked up their scooters from the sandy bottom.

Hamerman, the largest, held onto their prize as the scooters pulled them away from the shore.

"Beacon in site. Mother, package is in tow," Walsh called to Norris.

"Roger!" Norris replied. "Back to work, Doc, coffee break's over."

"Did I miss it, Master Chief?" Janice laughed, then turned

to face the display monitors. She was the first to detect the sounds through her headphones: "High-speed screws. They're bearing down on us."

Norris retracted both anchors.

The noise was louder.

"Silent operations," Norris ordered. "Walsh, stay put."

A loud thud was followed by a scraping noise moving up and over ASDV's hull.

"Damn it," Norris said, "Grappling hook." He looked at Janice. "Thank God, there is nothing the hook can grab."

The hook scraped slowly across the hull again.

Walsh's voice came over the com, "Master Chief, get the hell out of here. We'll follow," he said.

Lace looked alarmed. "That's risky, isn't it?"

"No choice," Norris replied, retracting the anchors all the way and lifting ASDV off the bottom. He then opened the area as the surface ship bore down on them.

Lace heard Walsh shout into his mic, "Let's go, boys." She knew the SEALS were trying to chase after the submersible.

Norris smiled. "The Iranian is still at our previous site. I hear her searching for us with her grappling hook. We lost him." He reduced speed. "Walsh, you there?"

"Right behind you," Walsh said.

Norris slowed the ASDV to a dead stop.

Reaching the ASDV, Walsh dropped his scooter, reached up, and grabbed the hatch ring. He unlocked the hatch and entered the chamber, pulling Dr. Mehman with him. He then shut and locked the escape hatch and pressurized the compartment, draining the water from the Lockout Chamber. Opening the door leading into the SEAL's bay, he motioned Dr. Mehman to sit against the diving suits on the wall. He heard the remaining

SEALs enter the chamber. We made it, he thought, wondering if this man was worth all the risk.

"Commander Walsh," Lace called over the intercom. "Is everyone okay?"

"Yes, Dr. Lace. All safely aboard."

Once convinced all was secure, Norris let the electric motors whine and headed back to Buffalo.

"Welcome aboard, Dr. Mehman. Did you enjoy your ride?" Walsh asked.

Mehman looked shaken but smiled. "It was a bit frightening." He looked around the red-lit compartment filled with diving equipment. "This is quite a large submersible. Does your government have a lot of these?"

Commander Walsh didn't want to give out any information. Not until he verified that this man was the genuine article. He smiled and replied, "We'll be transferring you to the USS Buffalo soon, so sit back and enjoy the ride."

Rose handed Dr. Mehman a towel to dry off and a blanket to keep warm.

The physicist dried his face and hands, then wrapped the blanket around himself. Leaning back against the diving suits, he closed his eyes.

Walsh never took his eyes off their guest.

"Activating autopilot," Norris announced, sitting back. He flipped all electrical switches to off except the one marked 'Auxiliary Power.' We made it, he thought, as he heard the sound of Hunter's collar locking onto the docking station on

Buffalo.

Lace was the first to climb down the ladder into Buffalo's passageway. Turning, she almost bumped into Scott. She looked up into his eyes, fantasizing what it would be like if he put his arms around her.

Scott's arms remained locked to his sides. He was tempted to pull her close when she nearly crashed into him but held back. Not a good idea, he thought. "Welcome back," he said, fighting to keep his voice steady. "Debriefing in the wardroom in 20 minutes." He turned sharply and proceeded down the passageway to Control.

"Yes, Sir!" Janice said, watching Scott walk away. Once he was gone, she fell against the bulkhead. I can't believe I almost fell on him. She quickly regained her composure when Norris, Dr. Mehman, and the SEALs came down the ladder. "Captain wants to debrief in the wardroom in 20 minutes," she said.

Walsh nodded.

"Any problems to report Master Chief?" the Engineering Officer asked, walking toward them with two crew members.

Norris replied, "Nope, Engineer. Recharge the batteries and check the oil. She did a great job."

"You heard the man," Lieutenant Commander Fender laughed, sending the two ASDV trained sailors up through the escape hatch to check the seals and confirm the air and batteries were being recharged.

Back in Control, Scott thought of his close call with Janice. He wondered what she would have done if he had grabbed her. He glanced at the radar monitor. "Officer of the Deck, return to the East channel." Phase one of the mission was complete, but he knew the most challenging part was yet to come. Blowing up a highly-guarded weapons facility without being detected would be very tricky. I'm damn sure Buffalo is going to be right in the middle of whatever happens, he thought surveying the men standing at their duty stations and knowing he was responsible for their lives.

Chapter 38

USS Buffalo; Persian Gulf –

Scott entered the wardroom to find the CO, XO, Dr. Mehman, and Commander Walsh sitting at the table.

The Steward poured coffee into Dr. Mehman's mug from a sterling silver carafe.

"I have been told navy coffee is strong," Mehman, said. "Yes, very refreshing, and with a lovely aroma, but not strong. Paani Kam Chai, my usual hot tea beverage is much, much stronger," he said, savoring the aroma.

"Wait until it sits for several hours under the warmer. You can stand a spoon up in the cup," Varney replied.

Scott sat down. He looked over at the small man, in his mid-60s, with sloping shoulders, and graying hair, wearing oversized blue submarine coveralls. The too-long sleeves of his 'poopie suit' were rolled up, exposing his long thin fingers. He had a warm smile and eyes the size of quarters. His bushy eyebrows reminded him of Andy Rooney, a news commentator. "Dr. Mehman, I hope you're comfortable?"

"Yes, Captain. Thank you."

Scott checked his dossier. "I understand you received your doctorate from the Massachusetts Institute of Technology?" He decided to start with basic information to set the scientist at ease.

Mehman put down his coffee. "That is correct. When the Shah was placed in power, he was encouraged to allow university students to study in the United States. I chose nuclear physics at MIT. After receiving my doctorate, I remained in the states for another ten years. I argued it was necessary to study nuclear power plants in the U.S. So, they let me remain. Once satisfied, I had a complete understanding of all facets of construction and operation, I returned to my homeland. My desire was to help build nuclear power facilities, such as I found in your nation."

Scott nodded. "Then why did you defect?"

Mehman frowned. "You are most direct. I disagree with the current regime. After Ahmadinejad was elected president, he demanded Iran become a nuclear power."

"Wasn't that why you studied in America?" Scott asked.

"At first, I praised his decision to move into the 21st Century. But I began to realize that this was not his true intent. His continued defiance of the European Union and the U.S., regarding the development of Weapons of Mass Destruction, was I felt dangerous. I believed he was placing us on a collision course with Israel and your powerful nation, as well as Germany, France, and Britain. Sanctions against my country served to increase our hardships and reinforced the bitterness and intransigence many of my countrymen feel toward the West—"

"You mean the intransigence of your leaders?" Scott interrupted.

Mehman nodded." Yes. I suppose. At any rate, I do not share the ideological beliefs of the people now in power. I must do what I believe is right to protect the country I love."

229

"We all feel that way," Scott said.

Mehman sipped his coffee and said, "It surely must be realized by the West that a preemptive attack by Israel against our nuclear facilities would result in a unified response by every Islamic state? I also fear there are extremists in the Islamic Republic of Iran who don't intend to wait for Israel to launch such an attack. The weapons facility I worked in for the past three years was ordered to step up torpedo production. I interpret this to mean the Iranian navy intends to attack U.S. ships."

"That would be a tragic miscalculation," Scott said.

Mehman nodded. "That is why I decided I can no longer sit back and help the radicals destroy my country."

"But why now?" Scott asked.

"It came to my attention that our submarines are placing mines at various strategic locations in the Persian Gulf. That is a dangerous provocation. Is it not?"

Scott nodded. "We found several mines that support your assumption."

Mehman sipped thoughtfully at his coffee. "Mining the straits is a suicidal act."

Scott looked down at the detailed report he'd received from Intel concerning his new guest. "I have a few more questions I'm required to ask you." He knew it was to authenticate Mehman's identity. "What was the code name you used when contacting your handler?"

Mehman smiled. "Dottyback! It's a fish, native to tropical reefs."

"What was the first grade you received from Dr. Howard's physics class?"

"Ah, you are trying to ascertain my identity. Very good."

Mehman smiled, "It is a bit embarrassing. I received a C minus. It took me a while to adjust to the Western method of teaching. And early on, I had a language barrier to overcome."

Scott laughed. "I believe all the officers in this room can attest to the difficulty in understanding the foreign instructors we had." He replaced the sheet of paper in the scientist's dossier. "Dr. Mehman, with your extensive background in nuclear physics, why were you working in a torpedo factory?"

"The hardliners moved us away from developing domestic nuclear power for civilian use toward the development of nuclear weapons. I felt compelled to speak out. I won no battles in my attempts at persuading members of the Islamic Republic party to reverse this direction. I only managed to erode whatever support I had within the Government." He paused. "I was given a choice: either accept a position in this factory or be labeled a traitor and be placed in prison. Truly, not much of a choice."

Scott made a note in the folder. "According to your reports, there are nuclear weapons stored in several buildings at the Bandar-e-Abbas Naval Base. Is that correct?"

"Correct. I've brought documents and facility plans with me," Mehman said.

"But I saw no package," Scott said, turning with a quizzical look at Commander Walsh, who had been listening silently.

"Would someone find my fins and get me a computer?" Mehman asked.

Scott signaled Wilkinson.

Wilkinson got up and left the wardroom.

"Weps?" Scott called after him. "Please ask Dr. Lace and Lieutenant Morton to join us."

Mehman held out his mug, "More coffee, please?" He held

his cup for a refill. "I can assure you what you are about to undertake will not be easy. The facility is well protected. In the past, several attempts by Mossad failed."

"How do you know that?" Walsh asked.

"Rumors, at first. Then the results of an interrogation of a detainee suspected of being one of Mossad's infiltrators." He sighed. "Later, interrogators from the Quds Force of the Islamic Revolutionary Guard Corps made sure everyone understood what would happen to traitors." He shrugged his shoulders. "The alleged informant died a painful death."

The Weapons Officer returned and handed Dr. Mehman's fins to the Captain, who examined them and then passed them to the doctor.

Dr. Lace and Lieutenant Morton entered the room.

Scott's eyes fixed on Janice as Varney made the introductions, "Dr. Lace, Lieutenant Morton, I would like you to meet Dr. Aslan Mehman."

"A pleasure to meet you, Sir," Lace said, shaking Dr. Mehman's hand. She then sat down at the opposite end of the wardroom table, keeping her eyes averted from Scott.

Morton sat beside Janice, glancing at Walsh.

"A sharp knife, if you please," Dr. Mehman asked, removing the heel strap from one of the fins. "This is the only way I could think of to smuggle out the information your government might require." He held up the strap. "I mapped out the facilities, recorded the locations of cameras, trip lights, and guard rotations. Would you like to look at the heel strap, Commander?" He handed the strap to Walsh.

Walsh, a puzzled look on his face, took the strap, turned it over several times. "It looks ordinary." He then placed it in the palm of his hand, trying to determine if it was heavier than it should be. "I don't see anything here." He handed the strap back to Dr. Mehman.

Dr. Mehman looked pleased. Then, taking the knife, he sliced along the top edge of the strap and removed a long thin piece of black plastic. Picking up the knife again, he poked at the side of the plastic and then peeled back the covering. He held up a small memory card. "The information you require is stored on this card. There is a second card located in the other strap, in case I lost a fin in the water."

"Ingenious," Scott said. "But how did you obtain the camera to take the pictures?"

"My handler provided me the camera and cards."

Dr. Mehman was about to insert the memory card into the computer, but Scott stopped his hand. "XO, do we have a computer off-line?"

"This one is, Sir," Varney replied.

Scott should have known Varney would be a step ahead of him. There was no way he was going to allow this Iranian to implant a computer chip into one of the ship's computers. He still didn't trust him. "XO, have Wilkinson take over. He's our computer guru."

The computer whiz examined the chip and then inserted it into the laptop. He then connected the computer to a projector, switched on the power, and adjusted the focus.

A picture of a harbor appeared on the screen.

"What are we looking at?" Scott asked.

"It is two thousand meters from the entrance of the harbor to the floating dry-dock. The warehouse housing nuclear weapons is adjacent to the dry-dock." Dr. Mehman stood and placed his finger on the screen.

"Dr. Lace, how deep is the water in the harbor?" Scott asked.

"About 45 feet," Janice replied.,

"That's a problem," Scott said.

Janice nodded. "Commander Walsh, I recommend your team stays close to this side of the dock. There is a large concentration of silt on the bottom. If your men stir it up, it may be seen by prying eyes from the dock."

"That's good to know," Walsh said, smiling at Janice.

Scott noted the smile.

Mehman spoke again, "You can see it is only about 200 meters to the building from the water."

The phone beneath the table buzzed.

"Captain here," Scott said, glancing apologetically at the scientist.

He listened silently and said, "I'll be right up," He replaced the phone. "We must delay the briefing. Lieutenant Morton, would you remain here with Dr. Mehman? Dr. Lace, would you please report to sonar? The Senior Chief might be able to use your expertise."

"Yes, Sir," both responded.

"Captain, I would like to remain behind and ask Dr. Mehman several more questions if you don't mind?" Commander Walsh asked, glancing at Morton.

"Fine. XO, join me in Control. Sonar just detected a Qaaem submarine," Scott said.

"Let's hope Mehman's information is correct," Varney said to Scott.

Scott was thinking the same thing.

Chapter 39

Qaaem Q-104, IRINSGhaaem; Bandar 'Abbas Naval Base, Iran

-

Captain Kashani, leaned forward and said good-bye to his wife, Jasmin. Both now, in their mid-fifties, they had been married for over 30 years. This was not the first time she stood pier-side while her husband went to sea. She smiled and released his hand. "Go with Allah's blessing," she said softly.

Kashani turned and walked proudly toward the gangway.

"Ghaaem, arriving."

Jasmin smiled again, hearing his title announced when he crossed over onto the deck of the Islamic Republic's newest submarine. She felt proud watching him ascend to the deck.

"Welcome aboard, Sir," XO, Lieutenant Commander Nouri Azizi, at attention, saluted. "Ship's company assembled for your inspection."

Kashani returned the salute and walked down along the sail toward the men, all standing at attention, dressed in pressed white uniforms and berets. He recognized several faces from the Yunes, a submarine he served on as XO. "Welcome!" Kashani's voice boomed from the speakers. "The Islamic Republic of Iran is providing us this superior submarine to destroy our enemy. Each of you was handpicked because of your training and experience. During our voyage, we will be conducting intensive drills to hone our skills. You will be pushed to your physical limits. When you reach that exhausted state, I will ask the XO to push you harder. This is how we will defeat the American Satan and all its allies. Allah be with you all."

The men repeated the final chant, "Allah be with us."

Kashani smiled proudly. "XO, dismiss the men and prepare for sea."

"Dismissed," the XO shouted.

Kashani watched approvingly as his men hurried toward the aft escape hatch. He remained behind, surveying the sleek black hull of his new ship. It was time to go. Excited, Kashani waved a final good-bye to his wife, still standing on the jetty, and entered the submarine. Descending the ladder, he walked forward, through the spotless halls, and entered his quarters. Closing the door, he sat down at his desk and ripped open the envelope containing his orders. He had not revealed to his wife the true nature of his mission. He did not want her to worry.

USS Buffalo; Persian Gulf –

"I have the Conn," Scott announced, entering Control. After the extraction of Dr. Mehman, Buffalo remained off Larak Island, tracking traffic and recording sonic tapes for future classification.

"Sierra 72 reclassified Master 10, is tracking off our port quarter," Lieutenant Steve Wilkinson reported.

"Are you sure the contact is a Qaaem submarine?" Scott asked.

"Senior Chief Richardson is convinced it's one of the new Iranian diesels," Wilkinson replied.

"XO, let's close and develop a track on this contact," Scott ordered, heading for sonar. "What do you hear, Senior Chief?" he asked, spotting Janice standing nearby.

Sorenson pointed to the bearing line on the passive display. "There, Captain."

"Okay, Senior Chief, what makes you think this spike came from the Qaaem?" Scott asked.

"I spent several hours going through Squadron 15's acoustic library to determine if any other boats had this specific broadband and narrowband signal." Sorenson said.

Lace said, "We had this on file already?"

"Yes, Dr. Lace," Sorenson replied. "The acoustic records from three of our other boats all recorded the same tonal characteristics. This leaves no doubt in my mind it's a Qaaem."

Scott looked at Chief Norris, who nodded and said, "The lad's done his homework. So has Dr. Lace."

"Well done, son," Scott said. "Thank you, Dr. Lace."

Sorenson smiled.

Lace nodded.

Scott wished he could break the ice with her. He left Sonar deep in thought and headed back to Control. Once there, he ordered, "OOD set the Fire Control Tracking Party. We have a visitor." He then ordered Varney to alter the course. He did not want Buffalo counter-detected as she tracked the enemy submarine.

After initiating two-course changes, the XO announced Master 10 was tracking 100 degrees, speed 5 knots with a range of three thousand yards off Buffalo's port bow.

"OOD, place us in her port baffle region," Scott ordered.

"Sonar, Control, Master 10 is altering course," Sorenson reported.

"Recommend reducing speed, we're starting to close," the XO said, keeping his eyes on the fire control readouts.

"Drop ten turns," Scott ordered. "We will hold our position until we figure out what the contact is doing. Their skipper doesn't seem concerned with counter detection." He wondered why an Iranian skipper was being this relaxed about being shadowed by an American sub. What were the Iranians up to?

Chapter 40

Iranian Qaaem, Q-104; Persian Gulf – –

"Open the outer door, tube one," Captain Kashani ordered. "Come to course 020 degrees, speed five knots."

The OOD relayed the orders to the helmsman.

Kashani smiled. Once these new torpedo-mines are in the water, he thought, we will have control over all who pass. "XO, standby Tube One."

A hush fell over Control. The officers and crew prepared to shoot their first torpedo-mine into the commercial shipping lanes.

🔹

USS Buffalo; Persian Gulf –

"Did you hear that, Sorenson?" The Senior Chief asked. "It sounded like a torpedo door opening on their boat."

Sorenson pressed his headset closer to his ears. "Conn, Master 10 opened her outer torpedo tube doors," he reported, a worried edge in his voice.

"Messenger, pass the word to remain rigged for ultra-quiet," the OOD ordered.

"Captain," Varney relayed, "Master 10 continues to track 100 degrees, speed 5 knots, range three thousand yards off our port bow."

"Remain in her baffles," Scott ordered. "If she launches a torpedo, I want to have the time to evade."

Iranian Qaaem, Q-104; Persian Gulf – –

"Shoot Tube One," Kashani ordered.

Q-104 quivered from the recoil of high-pressure air pushing against the piston forcing the torpedo-mine from the tube. The sound resonated throughout the boat.

Standing behind the fire control operators, the XO observed the presets being downloaded from the Weapons Control Console to the torpedo. "Weapon continuity confirmed," the XO said. "Weapon running hot."

USS Buffalo; Persian Gulf –

"Holy Shit!" Sorenson pressed his hands on his earphones. "Conn, torpedo in the water! Torpedo in the water!"

A black line emerged on the bearing time recorder.

"Diving Officer, sound General Quarters," Scott ordered.

The OOD flipped down the lever to the 1MC, "Man Battle Stations, Torpedo," Lt. Obermeier broadcast to the crew.

The alarm sounded through the boat as men ran to their battle stations.

"Left full rudder. Ahead Flank," Scott ordered.

"Control," Sorenson shouted, "Torpedo is opening."

Tell me something I don't know, Scott thought, knowing he had just given away his position. "Say again," he said, his heart pounding, adrenalin surging through his body.

"Torpedo is heading toward the commercial lanes," Sorenson said.

"Belay my last," Scott ordered, again wondering what the Iranians were up to, sending weapons into the commercial lanes. "Resume previous course and speed," he ordered. "Sonar, are you still tracking the torpedo?"

"Control, torpedo is opening, bearing 090 degrees off our starboard bow," Sorenson said, sounding calmer.

Looking over the XO's shoulder, Scott watched the bearing dots stacking on the tactical console. "Tom, send a message off to Fifth Fleet, Intelligence Branch after dark, and find out if the submarines we saw in the satellite photos are still in port. I want to find out what the hell is going on."

Chapter 41

Qaaem Q-104; Persian Gulf –

"Command, shut down," Captain Kashani ordered.

"Shut down confirmed," his XO replied, looking at the readouts on the Weapons Control Console.

"Sonar reports possible cavitation just outside our starboard baffles," Sonarman 2nd Class Namazi shouted.

"Is that definite, Namazi?" The Captain asked, leaving Control and stepping into sonar.

"I can't be sure! The spike popped on my display, then disappeared. The high pitched noise from our running torpedo did not help," Namazi complained, pressing the headphones on his ears.

"Is it possible the spike was a reflection of our torpedo's cavitation against another submerged hull?" Kashani asked, excited there might be an American lurking nearby.

"I can't be sure. I am still becoming familiar with this new sonar system," Namazi replied.

"Okay. Stay with it. I'm sure you will be able to identify the source," Kashani said, wondering if he should have sought a more experienced sonar operator. "OOD, execute a baffle clear to starboard and increase speed to 10 knots," he ordered. "I want to clear the area and work our way into the commercial shipping channel, just in case we are being tailed by an American submarine. Remain on the new course for 30 minutes, then reverse course and head back to the second designated torpedo launch point. We will shoot our second torpedo-mine and see if sonar detects any response."

The XO asked, "Captain. Do you believe there is an American submarine operating in this area?"

"It seems likely. XO, send out a report that we detected a possible American submarine in our area. Give them our location. I'll be in my stateroom." As he headed for his quarters, he had a thought. *Did we detect an American sub, or could it have been that Israeli submarine reported leaving the Suez Canal last month? That could change everything.*

Kashani entered his stateroom and sat at his desk. He opened his logbook and entered the time and location of the first torpedo-mine he had planted. He then unsealed his latest report from Intelligence. He read again to expect an American battle group with an accompanying SSN 688 to enter the Persian Gulf over the next several weeks. Could he have already encountered one of their ships? Were the Israelis and American boats already operating in the Straits of Hormuz? He examined the stats of the American sub and what was known about the Israeli vessel. Both were a formidable enemy, he knew, but he was confident no American or Israeli submarines were as stealthy, as quiet, as his Ghaaem. He sat back and closed his eyes. He decided. Yes, he would relish the honor to be the first Iranian captain to sink an American nuclear submarine. With Allah's blessing," he said.

USS Buffalo; Persian Gulf –

"Control, Sonar. No longer hold the torpedo," Sorenson reported.

"Going to Sonar, XO," Scott said.

"Captain," Sorenson said, seeing Scott enter, "the torpedo slowed, then just died somewhere out in the channel."

"How long did she run?" Scott asked, leaning over the monitor.

"Five minutes. I guess the weapons top speed was 50 knots, which would place it 9,000 yards from our current position."

"Keep up the good work," Scott said and left for Control.

Back in Control, Scott walked over to the Dead Reckoning Table and looked at the recorded bearings of the torpedo marked on the paper. "If the initial bearings of the torpedo are correct, the Qaaem was 2,000 yards off our port quarter, XO," he surmised. "Sonar, do you still hold Master 10?"

"No, Sir. I believe she changed course. Detection appears to occur only when her starboard side is exposed to our acoustic sensors," Sorenson replied.

"That confirms what we are looking at on the Dead Reckoning Trace, Tom. Let's assume she detected our cavitation and initiated a baffle clear. Her last position had her heading out into the channels. OOD come right thirty degrees, speed five knots. Let's open, then reverse course and see if we can detect the target when she clears baffles. Great job, Sorenson."

Thirty minutes later, unable to reacquire the target, Scott announced, "Secure from Battle Stations, Torpedo. Maintain ultra-quiet conditions." He looked at Varney. "We avoided trouble this time, but she's still somewhere out there."

The CO and the XO satisfied there was nothing more to be done, returned to the wardroom where they had left Dr. Mehman with two guards by the door.

Scott sat down and signaled Varney to join him. He had more questions for Mehman after this latest contact. He noted the scientist seemed more relaxed. He wondered if having Janice remain with him helped. He asked the two guards to stay outside the room and close the door. He smiled at the doctor, who was nursing a mug of coffee. "You know my XO, Tom Varney, and of course, Dr. Lace."

Mehman nodded. "Dr. Lace has been most charming."

"Good," Scott said, shooting a glance at Janice and then turning his attention to Dr. Mehman. "Dr. Mehman, I have a few more questions for you."

"Yes, I expected that," Mehman said.

Scott aimed his eyes at the scientist's face. "Are the Iranians developing wire-guided torpedo-mines?" he asked.

"This facility," Mehman said, pointing to a building on the map, "is where they fabricate their new torpedo-mines. So, yes, is my answer."

Scott nodded. "Are these torpedoes being loaded aboard their new Qaaem Class Submarines?"

Mehman shifted in his seat. "Again, yes. I know a total of 20 torpedo-mines were fabricated over the past year. They were designated to be loaded on the newer class submarines."

Scott sighed. He wondered if their informant would answer the big question. "Are these torpedoes capable of carrying nuclear warheads," he asked, hoping the answer would be no.

Mehman hesitated.

"Dr. Mehman, I ask again. Can these new torpedoes carry nuclear warheads?"

Mehman bit his lip and replied slowly, "Yes. I believe they are nuclear-capable."

Scott turned to his XO. "Tom, I believe Iran is mining the channel with those torpedo-mines. If I am correct, all hell may break loose." He grabbed the phone from under the table. "OOD send the NUWC engineers to the wardroom asap." He turned to Varney, "Contact sonar and see if you can establish a Datum where the torpedo stopped running."

"Yes, Sir." Varney hurried from the room.

Scott studied Mehman. The scientist looked nervous. Was he hiding something? "Dr. Mehman, you've been a big help. I need to ask you a few more questions."

Mehman nodded.

"Do you think it's possible to remove the warhead from a torpedo and disarm the detonator after it's deployed?" Scott asked.

Mehman looked at his hands. "Yes. If you could place it on board...Yes, I could disarm the weapon. Yes."

Scott didn't relish the idea of putting an armed torpedo on board his ship. "Can you disconnect the warhead from the torpedo body while in the water, without detonating the warhead?"

Mehman closed his eyes. "Yes. I believe there is a way to remove the warhead from the body that will not detonate the weapon. The depth of the water would be a factor."

"Dr. Lace?" Scott said, looking into her blue eyes. "How deep is the channel at this point?"

Janice examined the chart. "Over 190 feet in some places."

"What are you thinking?" Commander Walsh, who had just joined them, asked, puzzled by the question.

Scott looked up. "I'm thinking that we can retrieve the warhead before blowing the weapons facility to prevent it from being detonated by the furious Iranians."

Walsh looked surprised. "You want my SEALs to retrieve hot warheads?"

Scott nodded.

Drs. Stone and Thomas entered the room. "You sent for us?"

Scott shifted over. "Sit down, please, gentlemen. Is Hunter ready to launch again?" he asked.

Thomas replied, "Yes, Sir. Batteries are up, and system checks indicate no abnormalities."

Scott looked hard at Dr. Stone. "Can the UUV get close enough to read the writing on a torpedo or mine?"

The two scientists looked at each other. Dr. Stone answered, "Yes. But what specifically are you asking, Sir?"

"Can Hunter approach a magnetic mine without detonating it?"

Thomas replied, "Hunter's body, as you know, is a non-metallic composite material." He looked thoughtful. "The only thing capable of influencing a mine would be the DC motor."

Stone jumped in, "And we shielded the motor and tested it against all types of detonators. You've read the reports."

Scott nodded. "Then we go," he said, getting up from the table. "Thank you all. Thank you, Dr. Mehman."

Mehman nodded.

Scott turned to Janice. "I appreciate you remaining here with the Doctor. He seems more relaxed with your company."

He wished he could tell her that he had felt that way with her too, but this wasn't the time.

"Yes, Sir," Janice said and sat down at the table again.

Scott smiled and then left the room, followed by the XO.

"What's happening?" Dr. Thomas asked as he and Stone headed for Hunter.

"Looks like we're going after a torpedo-mine," Commander Walsh said. "You'd better recheck your equipment. It's going to be a long night, and my men's lives depend on you two." He hurried to get his crew up to date.

Scott headed to Control. "Tom," he said, "I don't want the rest of the crew to know about what we're attempting. If those mines are nuclear, or if Mehman is playing us, we're in big trouble."

Chapter 42

USS Buffalo; Persian Gulf –

"XO, give me a bearing and range to the position of the torpedo?" Scott asked. What I'm about to do goes against Washington's orders, Scott thought. If I just ignore the weapon, it could come back and destroy Buffalo later. It could also jeopardize the safety of the battle group.

Varney and the OOD stood over the DRT plotting table. "Come right to course 100 degrees," Varney said. "I estimate datum 15,000 yards from our current position, Captain."

"Right standard rudder, make turns for seven knots. Sonar, any sniff on the Qaaem?" Scott asked.

"Negative. We're still sifting through the broadband and narrowband traces to extrapolate her lines from the background noise. There's a lot of surface traffic in the area."

"What about Iranian Destroyers?" Scott asked, concerned about the sub-killers.

"Lost contact near the Naval Port of Bandar-e-Abbas," Senior Chief Richardson replied. "They most likely returned to port or are conducting a passive search along the coastline."

"Stay with it, Senior Chief. I don't want to be boxed in between the Destroyers and that submarine." Scott rubbed his temples. He'd been up for 36 hours, except for short naps, and was feeling the energy drain from his body. "XO, ask Drs. Thomas, Stone, Lace, Commander Walsh, Lieutenant Morton, and Master Chief Norris, to meet me back in the wardroom. I want you and Dr. Mehman there also." He looked at Tom. "Things are getting hot."

Varney nodded, concerned that Scott appeared to be driving on fumes.

♦

"Okay!" Scott declared. "Everyone's here. But where is Lieutenant Morton?"

"She just left to get Dr. Mehman," Dr. Lace said, surprised he'd noticed.

Scott began, "Okay. We can't wait. I want you to know that I intend to go after the underwater torpedo-mine we detected earlier."

There was a low murmur as those seated around the table weighed the danger of this new threat. A hot mine they knew little about could endanger all of them.

Scott understood what they were thinking but saw little choice. "Dr. Thomas, I need you to put Hunter back into the water. I want Hunter to transmit all videos to our computers live asap. Any questions?"

"When do you anticipate we launch?" Stone asked.

"Within the next five minutes. You can leave and get ready."

Dr. Stone jumped to his feet and hurried out of the wardroom just as Lieutenant Morton and Dr. Mehman entered.

"Please sit down," Varney directed.

Scott waited until they were seated. "Dr. Mehman, you

stated you could help in the removal of the warhead from the torpedo body. Is that correct?"

"Yes, but I need to look at the weapon to determine if removal of the warhead could detonate it. The weapons I helped assemble would not detonate, but others?"

"Will you know that by sight?" Walsh asked.

Mehman nodded. "I believe so. I am familiar with most of the new torpedoes."

"But not all?" Walsh asked.

"Dr. Mehman, assuming you recognize the type of torpedo, can the warhead be defused in the water?" Scott asked.

Mehman's brow furrowed. "In the tests, I was involved in, saltwater penetration inside the weapon's core rendered it useless. The engineers were working on this problem. How far they have gotten, I don't know."

Scott felt frustrated. "But you believe it can be done without detonating it?"

Walsh leaned forward.

Mehman nodded.

Scott looked at Walsh. "Once you defuse it, I want it brought back to us."

Morton looked at Walsh and asked, "How can they bring it back?"

Scott noted concern in Morton's voice and saw Walsh looking at her. A new wrinkle, he thought. "Master Chief, the submersible carries enough compressed air to lift a complement of SEALs and their gear. Correct?"

"Correct, Captain," Norris replied.

"Dr. Mehman, how much does the warhead weigh?" Scott asked.

"Sixty kilograms," Mehman responded.

SHALLOW WATER

"About 132 pounds, give or take," Janice interjected.

"So, if we limit what we carry in the ASDV," Scott continued, "We should be able to load the warhead and bring it back to the boat."

"Yes," Norris responded. "I'll ensure the air banks are full."

"Good," Scott said.

"Sir, are you sure you want to bring a nuclear device aboard Buffalo? Isn't there a risk of radiation?" Varney asked, wondering if this was one of Scott's risky decisions.

Scott looked surprised but realized Varney was voicing what most of those around the table were probably thinking. "Dr. Mehman, once the weapon is neutralized and the cover replaced, should we be concerned about radiation?"

"No. The weapon will be harmless, but I would still put it in a lead container and secure it," Mehman replied.

"We have such a container on board," Varney said.

"I'll make it ready," Norris replied.

"Dr. Mehman. Do you know how many nuclear warheads were manufactured in your facility?" Scott asked.

"Two. At least that is what I am aware of. I understand Iran was negotiating with the North Koreans for ten. The Koreans need oil, and Iran reached a deal."

"Do you know where the other nuclear warhead is?" Scott asked.

"Yes! They were both loaded aboard the Ghaaem, hull number Q-104. She left port two days ago," Dr. Mehman answered.

"So, XO, if it was Q-104 who launched the torpedo-mine, there is only one remaining aboard," Scott said.

"That is correct," Mehman said.

Scott made a note on his pad. "Good. Unless there are other

252

questions, I suggest we prepare to retrieve a warhead," he said and stood.

The others stood as Scott left the room. Then they returned to their stations, each nursing silent thoughts about what they were about to do.

Morton caught up to Walsh. "Mike," she said, "This is very risky, isn't it?"

Walsh smiled. "It's what we do."

"I know. I just didn't think about it much before."

"Neither did I." He looked at her and smiled again. "You think about things, and I will too. Okay?"

Morton walked away.

Walsh had a feeling she'd already thought about them. He had to bury his thoughts for now. He had to get his men ready.

Scott headed for his stateroom. He felt drained but knew soon he would have to be at his most alert. His crew depended on that. He stretched out on his couch and closed his eyes. He had to be ready for whatever hostilities Buffalo might encounter. One wrong decision could have devastating consequences.

Buffalo crept at five knots along the floor following the torpedo track.

The crew members who knew what Buffalo was hunting, felt as if it was taking hours.

"Captain, estimate we are 2,000 yards from Datum," Lieutenant Steve Wilkinson, the OOD reported, interrupting Scott's restless nap.

"Thanks, Weps, I'll be right there," Scott said, forcing himself up from the couch. He entered the head, filled the stainless-steel sink with cold water, and splashed some on his face. He looked in the mirror at the thirty-eight-year-old sailor he had become, crows feet next to both eyes, water trickling down his hard-jawed face. Am I ready for this, he asked his reflection. "Damn, I wish you could answer," he said aloud and left the room.

Back in his desk, he studied his half-written report. He held his pen, trying to come up with the words he needed to explain why he decided to delay the destruction of the weapons facility until after going after the torpedo-mine, That mine, possibly armed with a nuclear warhead, posed an immediate danger. Only Buffalo has the SEAL Team and Dr. Mehman, who may be able to disarm it. "I'm risking my command," he said, "but I've no choice." He sealed his report and left his stateroom.

Chapter 43

USS Buffalo; Persian Gulf –

"Make sure there is a chain fall hoist in the submersible," Master Chief Norris ordered. "Are your men ready, Commander Walsh?"

"Yes, Master Chief. Hamerman and Rose are checking their gear in the submersible."

"Okay, I'm ready if you are. Let's climb aboard and wait for the order to launch. Dr. Mehman, if you would please follow me?"

Mehman hesitated and then climbed up through the aft escape hatch. Patricia Morton stood beside Mike Walsh, nervously awaiting her turn to enter. Their shoulders pressed against each other in the crowded passageway. "Thanks for allowing me on this mission, Commander," Morton said.

"After you," Walsh replied, climbing up the ladder after her. Once we are back in Guam, I intend to ask her out, he thought, wondering if she'd let that happen.

Janice Lace was seated in the forward compartment when Norris entered. "Systems checked out, Dr. Lace?" he asked.

"Yes, Master Chief."

"Then let's saddle up and get the show on the road."

"Patricia, sit here behind the sensor consoles," Lace indicated the operator's chair. "You've seen most of this technology before, just not in this package."

Morton stepped over the first seat and sat down pressed against the bulkhead. "This is tight quarters," she said, squeezing in to let Norris enter.

Dr. Mehman, still standing, studied the monitors and controls.

Morton reached above her head and retrieved the headset, positioning the mic over her mouth, establishing communications with Buffalo.

Dr. Mehman glanced over at Norris, who was pressing buttons and flipping switches on the power box above his head. Within seconds, small red and green lights blinked on. The two monitors lit up, and the instruments, dials and digital panels came to life. "Master Chief, what are these controls for?" Dr. Mehman asked. I am eager to better understand the operation of your vehicle.

Norris wasn't sure how much he should reveal to their visitor. "I'm the Navigator and Pilot of this small sub. I operate the forward and reverse thrusters, ballast control system, and anchors. Lieutenant Morton will monitor the active and passive displays. Please sit down behind us, Dr. Mehman, and strap in. We're about to head out."

Dr. Mehman sat behind Norris while Lace buckled herself in the seat behind Morton.

Assured they were all strapped in, Norris flipped the switch unlocking the docking collar and pulled back the joystick for the reverse thrusters.

The mini-sub backed slowly from its port.

"Dark Shadow, we are airborne," Norris announced into his mic.

"Roger!" the OOD aboard Buffalo responded. "Smooth sailing."

Patricia Morton locked in the heading and entered the sonar sector search parameters on her console. She watched the first active pulse fan outward on her screen.

"Dark Shadow, this is Mother, Hunter is 2,000 yards off our port bow," the OOD reported.

"Two-thousand yards off your port bow," Norris responded. "Sharp eyes, Lieutenant."

Patricia kept her eyes glued to the monitor and concentrated on the sound in the headset.

The minisub was moving smoothly through the water. The crew was beginning to relax.

"Contact!" Morton announced, interrupting the silence. "Hold Hunter 120 degrees, range 100 yards ahead of our position."

Norris pulled back on the forward thrusters. Hunter's stern came into sight.

"Mother, Hunter has visual on the torpedo-mine," Morton reported, adjusting the video gain on her scope.

The standard 'click, click', meaning "message received and understood." was heard over the Com system, aka Gertrude.

Norris reversed the thrusters, stopping the ASDVs forward movement. He dropped the forward and aft anchors and trimmed the submersible. "Touch down!" he radioed to the after compartment.

"Package is 100 yards off our bow," Morton announced to Commander Walsh over the intercom.

Behind her, Janice Lace heard the water filling the Lockout Chamber and the opening and closing of the hatch. The lights from the chamber switched from red to green.

Scott, listening aboard Buffalo, knew there was no turning back now.

"Now we wait," Patricia said, switching from active to passive on the Sonar Console.

"Coffee, anyone?" Janice offered, unscrewing the cap from the top of the thermos and pouring the steaming coffee into their cups.

"Will we be able to see Commander Walsh and his men remove the warhead from the torpedo body?" Dr. Mehman asked, peering out at sea.

"Yes, once they hook up the external cable," Norris replied, sensing the tension in the informant's voice.

Walsh, Hamerman, and Rose stood beneath the submersible and set their stopwatches for 30 minutes. Each had an underwater light strapped to their wrist. Hamerman held a spool of wire, one end connected to the submersible's communication system. He signaled he was ready.

"Follow me," Walsh ordered, moving along Hunter's tether, trying not to stir up the sediment on the seafloor. "We can catch the current."

The six-knot current helped propel the three SEALs toward Hunter.

"Hold Hunter's light," Walsh announced into his mic.

The UUV sat on the light-colored sand. Behind it was the Iranian torpedo-mine.

"Package insight," Walsh said, swimming toward the torpedo. "Rose, cut the tether."

Rose pulled a set of bolt cutters from the black canvas tool bag. Made of composite material, Mehman had assured them the tool would not set off the mine. He hoped the Iranian was telling the truth.

Hamerman, well-rehearsed, swam to his predetermined position and dropped the spool of wire down on the floor. He carefully unraveled 50 feet of cable and attached a connector to one of the leads on his face mask. He then handed the other two leads to Walsh and Rose.

"Comms and video check," Walsh called into his throat mic.

"Hold you on video and hear you loud and clear," Patricia Morton responded.

Dr. Mehman, leaning in between Norris and Patricia, peered at the video being transmitted from Walsh's head-mounted camera. The men's movements around the torpedo-mine caused the water to become murky. "It is difficult to see," he said.

"Slow down, you're kicking up sand and silt," Norris cautioned. "Okay, better. But try not to shuffle your fins if you can?"

Watching the video feed from inside the ASDV, the small crew waited anxiously as the SEALs prepared to remove the warhead.

"Alright, let's start," Commander Walsh ordered, glancing at the illuminated dials on his watch. "Dr. Mehman, are you there?"

"Just speak into the mic, Dr. Mehman," Lace said.

Mehman pulled the mic closer. "Proceed to the green faceplate on the top of the warhead. Yes, that one," he said after Walsh pointed it out.

Walsh swam closer.

"Pan the camera toward the top screw on the left. Stop! Okay, I recognize the weapon. Proceed with the removal of the screws holding the plate," Mehman said.

Walsh pulled a set of non-metallic metric wrenches from his bag. He moved his gloved hand to the screw.

Morton held her breath as Walsh started to withdraw the first of 10 Allen screws holding the plate. "So far, so good," he said. "Rose, start removing the screws from the opposite end."

Rose moved toward the plate and carefully undid a screw. He dropped it into a black bag hanging from his belt.

Mehman said, "Pull the faceplate up carefully."

Using a flat head composite screwdriver, Walsh then pried under one end of the plate, lifting it from the casing. Air bubbles seeped from the edge of the broken gasket. "It's leaking air," he said.

"That's normal," Dr. Mehman replied. "Don't lose the plate."

Removing the plate and dropping it into his bag, Walsh bent his head over the opening. He was about to reach for a wire.

"Don't touch anything until I look at the insides," Dr. Mehman warned. He moved closer to the monitor studying the pattern of wires in the warhead. "Commander, turn your head left."

Walsh turned the camera.

"Stop!" Mehman ordered. "Stop there."

Walsh glanced at the time. *Twenty minutes left.* "Hurry, up

Doc; we're running out of time. Hamerman help Rose remove the screws from the body of the warhead." Walsh seemed almost calm. He'd faced death many times and was prepared to die if the weapon detonated. He just didn't want his men to die with him. What was taking the doctor so long?

Mehman said, "Okay. Remove the gray timer cover in front of the small white plate."

Walsh removed the cover and aimed his camera at the opening.

Mehman said, "Now lift the white plate to expose the detonator wires."

Walsh hoped Mehman knew what he was doing.

Mehman said, "See the magnetic switch in the upper left-hand corner?" Walsh pointed to a switch with the composite screwdriver.

"Yes. That is the one. You must cut the blue and white wire leading into the switch," Mehman said, removing his glasses and wiping his face with a paper towel.

As Walsh examined the wires, he realized he was unable to distinguish the colors well enough to determine which to cut. "The wires both look the same," he grunted. "I can't tell which to cut." He moved his hand from one wire to the other. "Select one, Doc. Hurry. We're running out of time." He waved to Rose and Hamerman. "Get back. Get back."

Mehman put his glasses back on and paused.

Scott wondered if he'd been tragically wrong to trust him. He was an Iranian. Could this be a trap?

Janice Lace also wondered if Mehman was on the level. She had sat with him, talked to him. I trust him, she decided. "Doctor, please?" she said, giving him an encouraging smile.

Morton was staring at Mike Walsh. He had waved the

other divers away from the mine. Her hand tightened on the armrests of her chair.

Janice stared into Mehman's face. "You have to help him now," she urged.

Mehman nodded. "Commander, cut the top wire!"

Walsh closed his eyes and cut the wire.

Patricia Morton felt Janice Lace squeeze her shoulder. She closed her eyes and said a silent prayer.

Scott was riveted on the screen. It was difficult to see. He prayed the silence of the sea wouldn't be shattered by a massive explosion.

Seconds passed.

"Still here," Walsh said as if nothing dangerous had happened.

Dr. Lace released her grip on Morton. "Walsh did it," she said.

Morton released her grip on the armrest. "Is it over?"

A voice on the com interrupted. It was the OOD on Buffalo. "Dark Shadow, detect underwater explosions astern. High-speed surface craft are closing."

Morton shot her eyes to Janice. "What does that mean?"

Janice looked anxiously at Norris.

Norris radioed Walsh. "Commander, Mother reports explosions astern of her position. Get the hell out of the water!"

Walsh heard the explosions. "Hurry, roll it over and remove the other screws from the warhead," he commanded. "Master Chief, bring over the ASDV. We'll direct you."

"On my way," Norris responded, retracting the anchors and increasing the speed on the thrusters.

An explosion off the portside rocked the submersible, jarring the crew in their seats.

Walsh saw the explosive flash seconds before the shock wave picked him up and slammed him against the torpedo.

Patricia gasped. "Mike is down. Mike is down."

"He's lost his mouthpiece," Hamerman shouted.

"Rose, get that mouthpiece back into Mike's mouth," Patricia yelled, watching the bubbles pouring upward.

Rose, stunned still from the explosion, pushed off the sea bottom and raced to Walsh's side. He replaced the mouthpiece and held it against his friend's lips. "Commander," Rose shouted, shaking him, trying to revive him. "Master Chief, get the ASDV over here now," he shouted.

Hamerman was now holding the mouthpiece.

Norris steered the submersible closer.

"Hamerman, help me pull the Commander," Rose shouted, grabbing one arm and lifting Walsh.

Norris carefully maneuvered the 50-ton vehicle toward Rose.

"Come left! Higher! About five feet," Rose ordered, straining to hold Walsh while Hamerman held the mouthpiece.

"Slow! Slow! Stop!" Rose shouted.

As the submersible moved above them, Rose reached up and released the hatch. Pulling himself up into the chamber, he turned and grabbed Walsh. Slamming the heavy cover down, he locked the hatch and drained the water from the compartment.

Patricia and Janice waited until they heard the water had been drained from the chamber. Then they unlocked the portal and helped Rose pull Walsh into the aft compartment. "You've got to get that torpedo," Patricia shouted. "We'll take care of him."

Rose re-entered the escape chamber, sealed the doors,

flooded the compartment. He then lowered the hook on the chain fall.

Hamerman, still in the water, swam back to the mine. He attached the hook to the warhead. "Okay, lift," he ordered.

Norris started the hoist motor, and the chain began to pull the torpedo toward the sub.

"We've got her," Hamerman shouted but waited for the warhead to disappear into the belly of the submersible before he disconnected the communication and video cable from the hull. He then scrambled up through the hydraulic hatch and turned the air pressure valve on and waited for the water to drain out. Looking at his stopwatch, Hamerman saw zero's flashing on the digital readout. "That was close," he said, breathing a sigh of relief and then remembering Walsh.

Rose hurried into the SEAL's compartment and saw the blonde lieutenant pressing down on Walsh's chest.

The torpedo on board, Norris gunned the submersible back to Buffalo.

"Stand back," Hospital Corpsman Chad Barns ordered Morton as he peeled the film from the Automatic External Defibrillator pads. Checking around him, he pressed the pads to Walsh's chest. "Clear," he shouted and pressed the AED button.

Walsh spasmed and jerked from the 200 joules coursing through his body.

Morton pressed her index and middle fingers against his carotid artery. "Again," she demanded.

Pressing harder, to ensure good contact on the big man's chest, Barns pressed the button.

Morton felt for a pulse.

Barns shook his head.

"I feel it. I've got a pulse," Morton said.

The AED indicated an increasingly steady rhythm.

Barns leaned forward.

Walsh coughed and spat up seawater. Looking up, through foggy eyes, he saw Patricia's face smiling down at him. "I must be in heaven," he said softly.

"Welcome back, sailor," Morton said, cradling his head in her lap. "Barns, do you want to look at the lump on the back of his head?"

"You seem to have everything under control," Barns replied, a smile on his face.

Morton smiled as she pulled the blanket up toward Walsh's chin. "Rest. I'll be back soon." She started to leave when she felt Walsh grab her arm.

"Thanks, Patricia," he said, looking into her eyes and smiling.

Patricia shivered at his touch. "I'm glad you're okay."

Chapter 44

USS Buffalo; Persian Gulf –

Scott, satisfied Walsh was okay, returned to Control. "XO, Draft a message informing SUBPAC, COMSUBRON-15, and Command Task Force-54 we detected a Qaaem Class submarine launching a nuclear torpedo-mine in the channels. Inform them I delayed our current orders to retrieve the warhead. The weapon's been defused and onboard with the help of Alias. I want this sent during our next satellite fix."

Varney nodded. "They did a great job, Sir." He smiled. "You made the right decision."

Scott frowned. "They did a great job."

Sorenson's voice interrupted, "Control, detect another noise spike. Bearing 270 degrees. Classified as submarine torpedo tube outer door."

Not again, Scott thought. "On my way. Man Battle Stations, XO." Scott hurried into the sonar shack.

"Torpedo in the water, Sir!" Sorenson shouted.

Scott stuck his head back out into the passageway and yelled, "XO, steady as you go. Talk to me, Sorenson," he said, eyes glued to the dark line on the waterfall display.

"Torpedo down doppler," Sorenson replied, sounding calmer. "She's heading toward the eastern channel, away from us."

"I concur," spoke up Sonarman Price, watching the torpedoes 50 Hz line on his monitor. Price, a Tennessean, with a broad southern drawl was not rattled by the detection of a high-speed torpedo.

"That's good news for a change," Scott said.

Sorenson pressed his hands against his headsets. "Conn, torpedo shut down."

"Run time?" Scott asked, relieved the weapon was not directed at Buffalo.

Sorenson looked at the time stamp at detection and loss of the torpedo. "Five minutes, Sir."

"Petty officer Price, were you able to record a tonal from the enemy submarine?" Scott asked.

"I picked out a weak 55 Hz line from the firing platform," Price replied, pointing to the display. "Wait! The target must be in a turn. The signal's getting weaker."

Scott smiled. "Excellent job, both of you. Record everything you have on that submarine. I'm sure we'll run across her again."

"Are we going after this torpedo?" Varney asked when things appeared calmer.

"Tom, I'd love nothing better than to defuse every one of their mines, but we must complete our assignment."

Varney nodded.

Scott asked, "Nav, how far are we from Bandar-e-Abbas Naval Base?"

"One hundred seventy miles." Lt. Obermeier replied.

"Tom, ask Commander Walsh and Dr. Lace to please join me in Control," Scott said.

Commander Walsh and Dr. Lace entered Control a few

minutes later.

Scott studied Janice. There was a small smile on her lips. Did he imagine it? "Good to see looking so fit, Commander Walsh."

Walsh smiled. "Ready for duty, Sir."

Varney spoke. "Commander Walsh, we are 170 miles from your designated drop area," he pointed to the chart. "From there, it is another 17 miles to the harbor entrance. Dr. Lace estimates it will take you three and a half hours at five knots to reach the entrance."

"When is high tide"? Walsh asked.

"Nav?" Scott asked.

"Twenty-four hundred tomorrow," Nav replied.

"Dr. Lace, your recommendation?" Scott smiled at her, something he had avoided previously.

"I recommend you deploy the ASDV around 1800. That gives you three and a half hours on the incoming tide to reach the net. Estimate another two hours to swim to the pier," Janice said, pointing to the egress spot on the chart.

"That places us there just before midnight," Walsh said. "Dr. Mehman recommended we enter the complex after midnight, just after the mid-watch relieves the evening watch." He shook his head. "I estimate we'll need 45 minutes to place the charges. Let's say by 0130; we are heading back to the ASDV with the outgoing tide."

Lace nodded. "You should make rendezvous with the submersible in three hours."

"That works for me," Walsh replied. "Thank you, Dr. Lace."

"Sounds like we have a plan," Scott said. "Nav, when is the next satellite pass over this area?"

"In thirty minutes, Captain. We are preparing to clear

baffles now."

Janice looked at Scott. "Sir, this might be an excellent time for you to rest before we arrive at our destination." She had noticed how tired Scott appeared.

Scott smiled, but said, "XO, add the following message with the coordinates of the second mine torpedo. Report that Buffalo was unable to retrieve the second deployed warhead, due to our previous commitment."

"Yes, Sir," Varney said.

Scott looked up at his navigator and smiled. "I'll be in my stateroom as Dr. Lace ordered."

Lace caught his smile, but in front of the others, he didn't return it.

The office of the President; Washington, DC –

The President's Secretary, Mrs. Beverly Yancy, knocked on the Oval Office door and entered.

"Let me ring you back, Sam," President Washburn said, hanging up the phone.

"Mr. President, Dr. Ure would like five minutes, Sir," Yancy said.

"He always wants five minutes. Please show him in."

Dr. Ure hurried into the Oval Office. "Mr. President, I just received a message from Commander, Submarine Pacific Fleet, readdressed from Commander Scott's mission report."

"What is it?" Washburn stood, hoping it wasn't bad news.

"Sir, Scott delayed deploying Team 6—"

"He did what?" Washburn shouted.

"He was ordered to destroy the weapon facility, but delayed it—"

"What the hell for? Weren't his orders clear? Was he not ordered to destroy that building?"

"Yes Mr. President, but–"

"There is no, but." Washburn sat on the couch. "Please, explain to me why he disobeyed written orders?" Was I wrong to approve Scott for such a delicate mission? God, I hope not.

Ure remained standing, knowing his job was on the line. "Sir. Mr. President, Scott had clear orders, but...but made a command decision—"

"Tell me what he did," Washburn demanded.

"Sir, he decided to extract a nuclear warhead from a torpedo-mine the Iranians fired into commercial shipping channels."

The President looked shocked. "A nuclear warhead? A torpedo-mine in commercial channels? What the hell is going on?"

"It appears before Scott transited north to fulfill his mission, Buffalo detected two torpedo-mines were fired into these channels. Scott relayed that believes one of Iran's new Qaaem diesel submarines was responsible for launching these torpe-does."

"Let me get this straight; the Iranians mined a shipping channel?"

"According to Scott, yes. He further states the Naval Undersea Warfare Center, engineers, using Hunter, found the first mine and Team 6, with Alias's assistance, successfully disarmed the weapon in the water—"

"They disarmed an Iranian torpedo?"

"Yes, Sir, and transported it back to the boat."

Washburn sat back down on the couch. "That was taking

quite a risk."

Ure nodded.

"Where's Buffalo now?"

"At present, they are proceeding north toward Bandar-e-Abbas, Naval Base...to complete the primary mission."

"President Washburn, though annoyed, realized the significance of the report. If the Iranians mined a commercial shipping channel, with a nuclear warhead, this represented a serious escalation in their actions. "I want all of this verified," he said. "If that man risked his crew and ship recklessly, I'll have his head on a pole in the East garden."

"If you remember, Mr. President," Ure added, "this was one of the reasons you agreed to give Scott another command. He is one of those rare officers willing to take the initiative, think on his own, and he gets results. Scott always reads between the lines. You asked him to do a job, and you can see he is well on his way."

"But he took a dangerous side trip," Washburn said, still considering removing Scott from command for disobeying orders.

"Sir, Scott took a necessary risk. He knew that once the Iranians learned that their nuclear manufacturing facility was destroyed, they would most likely detonate this ship-killer with unknown casualties and the disruption of traffic in the Straits. A nuclear warhead—"

Washburn nodded. "I see. But it was still risky."

Ure nodded. "Of course, Sir, there is also the bonus that he removed a nuclear device from a rogue nation's inventory and is bringing us the evidence."

President Washburn smiled. "Your Commander's got balls." He laughed. Okay, I see your point. A mine sinking one of our surface ships or our carriers would've resulted in open hostilities between the U.S. and Iran. Not to mention the loss of lives and Naval ships. The radiation would have caused untold damage. Reckless behavior by our Iranian friends."

"If we can prove it," Ure said. "Mr. President, after Scott completes his orders and eliminates the weapons facility, I recommend you order Scott to transfer the warhead as soon as possible to one of our carriers. If Iran intends to deploy nuclear torpedo-mines, we need to learn everything we can about them as fast as possible."

Washburn thought for a moment before responding. "Where and when can we achieve this transfer?"

Ure thought for a second. "I suggest we arrange for the weapon and Dr. Mehman to be picked up in the Gulf of Oman."

"Good. Make it happen, Jack. But then send Buffalo back to the Straits. We've forgotten another complication. We still don't know if the Israelis might bomb the nuclear facility since Scott hasn't done it yet. If the Israelis learn about the mining of international shipping lanes with nuclear torpedoes, they could strike preemptively, which could destabilize the entire region."

"That's why I think Scott made the correct decision, Sir."

"He was also lucky. Why didn't he call for backup to help with the mine?"

"None of our other subs have his submersibles and Dr. Mehman, who was instrumental in defusing the weapon. Scott knew that and made an on-site decision that had the best chance for a successful outcome."

Washburn brushed back his hair. "Okay, let him run for now, but keep an eye on him. I want no more chances. See also what your Intel people have on the weapon he captured, and schedule a meeting with the National Security Council to discuss our response to Iran's ruthless behavior."

"I will, Sir," Ure responded, turning and backtracking to the door.

Washburn sat down behind his desk. *Christ, all I need are nuclear torpedoes in commercial lanes just waiting for some unsuspecting ship to get too close. Scott is a loose cannon. He's been lucky so far, but what if his luck runs out?*

Chapter 45

USS Buffalo; Persian Gulf –

Commander Scott was seated facing Mike Walsh, SEAL Team 6, and Dr. Mehman. He was eager to place the SEALs onshore and get them back safely. He listened quietly as Dr. Lace briefed the team on current conditions, as recorded by Hunter, the Unmanned Underwater Vehicle. Having Patricia aboard helped Janice in providing technical assistance. Walsh appreciates her too, he thought.

Dr. Mehman was listening intently to the discussion.

"I've input the times of mean low water over the next several days onto the laptop I installed in the submersible." Morton said.

Dr. Lace continued, "Dr. Thomas provided video and bottom measurements obtained during Hunter's survey of the harbor yesterday. He confirms there is a net across the harbor entrance. Your debarkation point should be 500 yards from the net," Janice said, shining a laser pointer at the projected map.

"Thank you, Dr. Lace," Scott said.

"Captain, have we received updated satellite pictures of the harbor?" Walsh asked.

Scott nodded. "Yes. My Information Technicians are

274

processing the images now. I'm waiting for the —"

A knock at the door was followed by Weathers entering. He handed a folder to Scott. "Sir, here are the photos we received from Fifth Fleet."

"Thanks, Weathers," Scott said, opening the folder. He examined the first picture, then the second. "Two of the Qaaem's are no longer at their berth." He handed the copies to Commander Walsh. "Dr. Mehman, can you add any information about the Qaaems?"

Mehman shrugged. "You are aware this class was retrofitted with an Air-Independent Propulsion System. With the additional massive air cylinder, she does not have to recharge her batteries and can remain submerged for weeks."

Scott studied his photo of the Qaaem. "I can see her hull has been extended to support the additional air tanks. That could be the reason our satellites did not detect them. Do you know what weapons the Qaaems carry?"

Mehman nodded. "I believe each is fitted with two torpedo-mines and 15 war shots. To my knowledge, there weren't any nuclear weapons aboard."

"That's good to know. Thanks. Anything else?" Scott looked around the table.

"Captain, see the channel left of the basin? There is only one pier along the west side of the warehouses. That's where we should exit the water." Walsh pointed. "It looks like there's excellent cover from here to the facility."

"Okay," Scott said. "Dr. Mehman, where's the factory on this chart?"

"It's the rectangular white-roofed building," Dr. Mehman said.

Lace walked over to the map. "Wouldn't it be better to exit

275

the water between the docks, near the south of the building?"

Walsh looked at the map. "Yes, if the two Corvettes weren't sitting at the dock. Though we intend to hit the facility at midnight, there will be patrols and security around those ships. While that may be the optimal spot, the risk of being seen is too great."

"Interested in taking out the two Kilos?" Scott asked spotting the two submarines nested along the pier.

"That's not in our orders," Walsh replied. "Maybe you'll tag one or two before this is over, though." He added, "I believe Dr. Mehman's information and the facility layouts should be sufficient to complete this mission."

"What about getting out after the operation?" Morton asked.

Walsh smiled. "I'll leave one man tending the equipment and covering our escape route. The rest will go with me. We will infiltrate the building and plant the explosives. Then off we go, fading away into the sunset."

"How long will it take to set the charges?" Scott asked.

"Dr. Mehman, you mentioned the guards conduct a sweep of each building once per hour?" Walsh asked.

Mehman shook his head. "Not accurate, Sir. Two guards sweep the grounds for 30 minutes and then enter the facility. When not out walking around the factory, they sit in the guard room, presumably monitoring the panel of security cameras."

"Do you know where the video recorders are?" Walsh asked. "We don't want to leave any evidence."

"I don't know," Mehman answered.

"Those tapes must be removed. We can't take chances they'll survive the explosion." Scott glanced at Walsh. "Dr. Mehman, you may leave now."

Mehman looked at Scott and nodded.

Scott waited until Mehman left and said in a low voice to Walsh, "You may have to eliminate the guards. Remember, we're not here."

"That will cut into our time," Rose remarked.

Walsh replied, "The Captain is right. We can't leave any trace that we were here." He glanced at Scott. "If those bastards are already planting their nuclear-armed torpedoes in the Gulf, we can't give them more time."

Scott extended his hand. "I'm confident you'll succeed."

Walsh turned to his men. "Yes, Sir, we will. Each of you check your gear. When you're done, check it again. I don't want any screw ups. Now, get it done, then eat and get some rest." He remained seated as his men left the wardroom. He leaned toward Scott, "I just hope the info we're getting from this defector is accurate."

Scott hoped so too. "Anyone else?"

"Commander Walsh," Janice said, "Lieutenant Morton and I anticipate your team will not reach the pickup point until 0430."

"A bit later than I'd like."

Janice nodded, "It might be sooner because of the tide. But don't count on it."

"Understood," Walsh said.

Scott looked at his board. "After the ASDV deploys, Buffalo will move into deeper water, between 190 and 225 feet in depth, approximately 6,000 yards from the debarkation point."

Walsh studied the chart.

Scott continued, "Master Chief, while you wait for the SEALs, monitor any submarine activity near the Naval Base. Collect information on the noise radiated from their vessels. You never know what might happen when the weapons depot is destroyed." He looked at Janice. "I'm assigning Dr. Lace to go with you."

Janice was surprised. She had thought she was going to remain with Scott on board Buffalo. What was he doing?

"Good choice," Norris said, "Dr. Lace knows the ASDV inside and out almost as good as I do." He laughed.

Janice wasn't laughing.

"Good. Master Chief, I'm glad you agree," Scott replied. "Also get with the navigator and work out alternative rendezvous coordinates." He paused. "Select at least three possible locations."

"Yes, Sir. Dr.Lace can enter the locations into the Nav," Norris said.

Janice nodded.

Scott glanced at his checklist. "Lt. Washington will provide food, clothing, blankets, and water for six days... in case you're delayed." He glanced at Janice. "That's not very likely, but we should be prepared."

"Should that happen, here is the nightly communication schedule," Varney said, handing a copy to Norris.

A knock on the wardroom door, followed by the Messenger of the Watch interupted. "Excuse me Captain, the Engineer asked me to hand this report to the Master Chief."

Norris accepted the papers. "Captain, engineering has completed system checks on the ASDV. Batteries are topped, air banks full, and equipment stowed for sea. There is enough air to last seven days if all goes well."

"Seven days?" Janice looked uneasy.

"We'll find you," Scott said and smiled at her. I won't leave you. Not ever again, he thought.

Chapter 46

USS Buffalo; Persian Gulf –

"Captain in Control," Lieutenant Steve Wilkinson announced.

"Report," Scott said.

Nav replied, "Twenty Thousand yards from the drop point. Expect to reach Datum in seven hours."

Scott glanced at the clock. "I'll be in my stateroom." He headed down the passageway and entered his quarters. "What are you doing here?"

Janice was sitting in the chair against the wall. She sprang from the chair and wrapped her arms around Scott, her head against his shoulder. "Why did you order me to go on this dangerous mission? I want to remain with you."

Scott placed his arms around Janice and held her for a brief second. He then gently pushed her away. "Sit down, please," he said, pulling the chair over.

Janice remained standing.

Scott smiled. "Janice, you know you're the only person other than Norris who can operate the ASDV. I had no choice."

"What about Patricia?" Janice asked.

"She doesn't have your experience." Scott sighed. "The last few years, I lost two things I care about. You and my command." He set his jaw. "I won't repeat either of my mistakes."

Janice sat down. "You could lose me—"

Scott leaned toward Janice. "You're as safe on the ASDV as you would be aboard Buffalo. Janice, I've thought long and hard about our relationship—"

"So did I."

Scott bit his lip. "I was the one who walked away."

"Why did you do that?"

"I don't know. I do know I didn't want to hurt you."

Janice said in a low voice. "You did hurt me, so tell me why?"

"I guess it was my fear of commitment...and not wanting to leave the Navy—"

"I never said you had to leave. I was happy—"

"I get that now." Scott knew he was in deep water. "At that time, the thought of marriage, a family, scared the hell out of me." He saw Janice's jaw tighten. "I was wrong. I was very wrong. It took a while to understand what I threw away—"

"Do you really know now?"

Scott nodded. "I believe it's not too late. I love you, Janice. I always have." He took her hands in his. "I want to marry you and maybe, one day, raise a bunch of kids." He laughed but quickly got serious again. "After this mission, I plan to submit my retirement papers. We'll move to Hawaii, or wherever you want to live."

Janice looked at her hands and said, "After this mission?"

Scott nodded. "I made a promise to the men of this ship and the President. I have to keep that promise."

Janice pulled her hands away.

Scott looked into her eyes. "You wouldn't respect me if I broke my promise. Now, would you? Now dry your eyes and get ready," he muttered, trying to sound firm, but wishing she'd stay. "I really need you on that ASDV, but want you to believe I love you."

Janice stood up slowly. "You didn't ask if I love you."

"Do you?" Scott asked, unsure of her tone.

Janice stopped by the door. "Thank you for your honesty, Sir. I'll consider your proposal."

Scott stared at the door long after she left.

"Okay! Since you returned from our meeting with the Captain you've been moping and pacing and driving me crazy," Patricia growled from her bunk after being awakened by Janice. She pulled back the curtains that enclosed her bed. "Would you mind telling me what's going on so I can get some sleep?"

Janice stopped pacing. "Sure. Why not? He's doing this for spite. One minute, he says he's in love with me. The next, he places me in extreme danger—"

Morton sprang awaked. "Hold on! The Captain said he loves you?"

Janice didn't reply.

There was a soft rap at the door.

"What is it?" Janice asked, reaching for the knob, hoping it was Scott.

"Dr. Lace, one hour before launch," a voice announced from the other side of the door.

"Thanks, I'll be right there."

"Are you okay?" Morton asked.

"We'll talk later, Pat," Janice said, pulling on her clothes and rushing from the room.

Morton shook her head. She wondered what Janice would say if she shared that she thought she was falling in love with Mike Walsh. She dressed quickly. If Janice was leaving, so was Walsh. She hoped for a few minutes alone with him before he left.

The Duty Messenger rapped twice on Scott's stateroom door. "Captain, the OOD wants to inform you that we're one hour from the drop point."

"Ask the XO to join me in my stateroom," Scott said, rising from his chair and splashing cold water on his face.

The XO knocked and entered the room. "Captain, you sent for me?"

"Tom, after the SEALs blow up the weapons factory, set GQ...we can expect a hostile response."

"Yes, Sir." Varney had a nightmare vision of what a hostile response might mean.

Janice Lace watched for the 'ready' light to illuminate on the ASDV's upper console. She waited impatiently for the sonar system to step through its internal checklist.

Norris sat down next to her, reviewing the navigational coordinates on the lower window. Above his head, was a display of the sea bottom as recorded by Hunter.

Commander Walsh's voice boomed through the submersible. "Stow your gear and take seats, men. Rose, when we arrive at our drop point, you'll follow Freeman into the chamber and out into the water."

"Understood," Rose replied.

Janice heard Walsh's orders. Reality hit. *Am I helping take these men to their death?* She cut that thought off quickly. She had to remain focused if they were going to survive.

A muffled thud sounded behind Janice as the Lockout Chamber doors were shut and sealed.

"Dr. Lace? Janice," Norris said, unable to get her attention.

"I'm sorry, Master Chief. What is it?"

"Are you all right?" Norris asked.

"Yes." Janice realized all of her concentration had to be on her duties. Scott was right. She was the best choice and a professional. "System checks are complete and operational," she confirmed, fully focused on the present.

"Let's go then. Control, Shadow, ready to detach from Mother," Norris reported over Gertrude.

"Standby, Shadow." The OOD on Buffalo responded.

Janice observed the speed dial as Buffalo slowed.

"Shadow, Control, permission to launch," Varney said. "God speed."

"Here we go," Norris said, pressing the decoupling button.

Janice felt the submersible shift and heard the high-pitched whine from the electrical motors.

The ASDV tilted and veered away from Buffalo's hull.

Walsh sat locked in his seat, deep in thought. Taking a desk job and dating Morton is looking better and better by the minute. If I survive this mission? He looked around and saw his men leaning back in their seats. He knew he couldn't let anything distract him, not with their lives depending on his leadership.

The pitch from the electrical motors grew louder.

Walsh suspected his men were now deep within themselves, pushing all thoughts of death and failure on this mission into a black box in the back of their minds. "Failure is not an option." As SEALs, they were trained to keep anything from distracting them, anything from stopping the completion of their operation. I'm out of practice, he thought, his mind drifting back to Morton. He leaned his head against the headrest and closed his eyes. Would he survive to come back to her? Yes, I will, he promised.

"Commander Walsh," Norris said. "We're 2,000 yards from the net. Ready to deploy anchors on your command."

"Deploy anchors," Walsh said. "Okay, girls, showtime," standing in the aisle.

Rose was already at the Lockout Chamber, ready to assist the other divers.

Walsh exited first. The others followed.

Rose pulled out their scooters.

Once clear of the ASDV, they descended to the sandy floor, taking the scooters with them.

Walsh spoke into his mic, "Everyone hear?"

Thumbs went up.

"Good. Remember, guys, slow and easy. Conserve your oxygen." Walsh started his scooter and led the way.

Rose brought up the rear.

Cutting through the water behind his scooter, Walsh began

to relax. He could almost fool himself into believing this was a pleasurable underwater diversion. Almost.

"You seem tense, Doc," Master Chief Norris said to Janice, who was peering hard at the screen. "He'll be fine."

"Walsh," Janice said.

Norris smiled. "You know that's not who I mean."

"Oh." Janice looked at him. "Does it show?"

"Heck, yeah." Norris had a trace of a smile on his face. "It's pretty darned obvious."

Janice nodded. "I guess I didn't realize how strong my feelings were until he assigned me to this mission."

"The Captain wouldn't have done that unless he has confidence in you."

Janice faced him. "I've had a lot of time to think over our past, Master Chief. I kind of resented his love affair with the Navy."

"Captain Scott is a dedicated officer."

"I know." Janice hesitated. "You know, Jack, I blame myself for what happened. I now realize there's room for both of the things he loves most." She turned back to her panel. She'd said too much already.

Norris waited for Janice to continue. When she didn't, he focused his attention on monitoring the instruments, watchful for the unexpected.

Chapter 47

Bandar-e-Abbas; Naval Base, Iran −

Petty officer Bamdad pulled the rubber hood over his head and adjusted the facial opening. He signaled his partner Hijazi to follow.

Picking up their fins and masks, they preceded down the wooden ramp toward the tubular-shaped two-person mini-sub. Tonight, as on every night, the Special Forces frogmen were tasked with verifying the harbor net was secure and anchored on the seabed bottom.

Strapping on their air tanks, the divers stepped into the cockpit and latched themselves into their seats. The cockpit of the Iranian mini-sub was open to the sea allowing them easy access.

Petty Officer Hijazi tapped his partner's shoulder, the signal that he was ready to depart. He pushed forward on the lever starting the electric motor, turned on the bow searchlights, and maneuvered the mini-sub toward the net. "We're heading under." He pushed the yoke down and the vessel submerged. If all went well, they would return to their launch site and steaming cups of mint tea within the next two hours.

SEAL Team 6; Bandar-e-Abbas Naval Base, Iran –

The murky water of the harbor and moonless night made it difficult for the SEALs to see their men ahead. The only visible light came from their phosphorescent compasses, depth gauges, and the slight bioluminescence of tiny krill feeding on an algae bloom. Gliding with the inbound tide, the team closed the distance to the net.

Commander Walsh saw the light first. "Take bottom," he ordered, suspecting it might be an enemy vessel.

The SEALs ducked to the seafloor, holding their faces down to eliminate light reflecting off their masks.

Walsh waited anxiously as the mini-sub settled to the harbor floor.

Two Iranians pushed off out of the sub and swam to the net. The first diver veered left, while the second proceeded in the opposite direction.

"No one move," Walsh ordered. He saw the dim mini-sub's light through floating silt particles. He remained motionless. When the flashlight beams shot toward his location, his heart skipped a beat. Had the water been more transparent, there would have been no place to hide.

"Commander, they've got spearguns," Rose hissed.

Walsh clicked twice that he received the message. He was too close to the enemy divers to speak.

After checking the net, the frogmen swam toward the mini-sub.

Walsh breathed a sigh of relief but held his position.

The frogman on the left side of the net stopped moving.

"Don't move a muscle," Walsh whispered.

The frogman panned his light from left to right and back again.

Seconds felt like hours as Walsh fingered the knife at his side.

At last, the diver turned and finned back toward the mini-sub.

That was close, Walsh thought, moving his hand off the knife. He signaled the men to wait for the mini-sub to disappear into the blackness. "Let's go," he then ordered. Pressing the power switch on his scooter, he led the team toward the net. "Hamerman lift the chain-link fence," he said.

Hamerman examined the net for booby-traps. Finding none, he lifted it for the others to swim through.

Walsh, eyes alert for the mini-sub, followed the other team members as they entered the harbor.

Dropping the net, Hamerman rejoined the team.

The recurring whir of high-speed screws forced them to hug the bottom several times as they advanced toward their objective.

This is damn dangerous, Walsh thought. He rose to the surface to verify their location. "Ten minutes to showtime," he said. *This is it!* He felt the familiar tightness in his chest.

The other men were waiting for his signal.

"Shut down, scooters," Walsh commanded, hiding next to a steel ladder attached to the pier. Still checking the surface, he removed his fins and mask and placed them on his scooter. Taking a last look behind, he climbed up the ladder, hesitating at the top. After another look around, he crawled up onto the asphalt, looked around again, and then dashed in a crouched position to a stack of wooden crates and pallets. He concealed himself between them. Removing his rebreather and dry suit, he scanned the area for guards. So far, things were going smoothly. He signaled his men.

The men joined him behind the crates. They stripped off their suits and rebreathers.

"Let's get it done," Walsh whispered. "Rose, remain here. Bag the suits and change the oxygen bottles. The rest, follow me to those crates left of that truck." He scanned the area.

The night was moonless, but the wind was kicking up a lot of sand, making it difficult to see.

"Ready," Walsh asked.

The men gave the thumbs-up sign.

"Three-second intervals. Freeman with me," Walsh said, still scanning the open area in front of the weapon facility.

As the rest of the team remained concealed, Walsh and Freeman dashed toward the next stack of wooden boxes, behind a five-ton military cargo truck.

Walsh raised a fisted hand in the air.

Wondering why Walsh stopped their advance, the men took a knee and waited.

Walsh, now behind the truck, surveyed the surrounding buildings.

"Walsh, hold tight," Freeman whispered. "Driver in the truck... smoking a cigarette."

Walsh aimed his eyes at the truck. Damn, he thought. I was hoping to avoid this. "Freeman, eliminate the driver and take up a position under the truck," he ordered.

Freeman nodded and moved silently along the side of the truck. Removing the Beretta from his holster, suppressor mounted, he stepped in front of the driver's door, raised his gun in a two-hand stance and pulled the trigger.

Walsh heard the thud. "Okay! Move," he ordered and kept watch as each man hurried across the tarmac to the weapons depot. Each was holding a Koch MP7 machinegun with a suppressor attached ready to fire. "Freeman, report any activity, pronto," he ordered.

Freeman scurried under the truck.

Walsh raced toward the building. "Hamerman, there," he said, pointing to a shadowy area near the factory door.

Hamerman advanced to the building.

The others waited, pressed up against the wall, 140 yards from Freeman's position.

Freeman, a trained marksman, flipped down the legs on his MK-11 sniper rifle. He placed his eye against the rubber eyepiece and adjusted the optics. He focused the cross hairs on Hamerman's chest.

Hamerman reported, "Clear. Opening door now."

Two thuds in rapid succession barked in Walsh's ears. His heart pounded, ready to aid Hamerman.

"Room secured," Hamerman announced on his mic.

Walsh ordered, "Move in."

The others entered the building.

Freeman was alone. His hand tightened on the sniper rifle's trigger.

Freeman, concealed behind the truck's double tires, flipped down his night vision goggles and scanned the area. He felt safe now that the truck driver was neutralized, but he was sweating and nervous. He looked through his night vision goggles and spotted a sudden light.

A guard had opened the door. A second joined him.

Freeman prepared to fire. He held off when he saw the men were lighting cigarettes. He observed they were in fatigues and camouflage caps. A holster hung from each man's hip. No time to relax. His finger rested on the trigger.

One guard leaned against the building. An AK 47 hung from his shoulder. The other scanned the road while puffing at his cigarette.

Freeman remained ready to take action if either guard showed any sign of entering the building where Walsh and the others were.

After a long five minutes, the two guards stubbed out their cigarettes and reentered the building from which they had appeared.

Freeman breathed a sigh of relief but suddenly heard Walsh whisper, "Fan out. Rose, take the production line. I'll head for the far end of the building. The rest of you find the warheads. Set your timers 40 minutes."

Freeman checked his watch. *Thirty-five minutes to go. Damn!* He panned the perimeter.

A light went on.

Freeman aimed his rifle.

Two guards emerged from a warehouse south of Freeman's position.

Freeman held his breath.

The guards stopped in front of the building. They were talking.

Freeman was beginning to relax when one of the guards pointed toward the building in which Walsh was working.

Not again, Freeman thought, finger back on the trigger.

The other guard nodded, stubbed out his smoke, and started walking.

The first man threw down his cigarette and followed.

Freeman hissed into his mic, "Walsh, two guards heading your location."

'Click, Click,' came Walsh's response.

Freeman checked his sights.

The guards reached the corner of the building in which the team was operating.

Freeman braced himself.

After pausing for a few seconds, the men proceeded to the front door.

Suddenly, the second man grabbed the other's arm. They stopped walking.

Freeman couldn't believe it when the first man pulled out a cigarette and the second lit a match. Relieved, he called, "Walsh, they're having a smoke outside your door."

'Click, Click.'

Eyes blurred by sweat, the Iranians not an immediate threat, Freeman raised his night-vision goggles.

The taller of the two guards flipped his cigarette in the air.

Freeman thought the man was going to turn back.

The guard walked toward the factory building and pulled open the door.

Oh shit! Freeman flipped on his goggles. "Damn! Hamerman get ready, they're entering the building," Freeman hissed. He placed his eye against the rubber buffer of his rifle and released the safety.

Two thuds.

Hamerman's voice: "Shit, I missed one. Coming your way,

Freeman."

The door flew open. The guard bolted out. He ran toward the truck.

Freeman fired twice, hitting the man in the chest.

The guard stopped in his tracks, then fell to the ground.

Freeman scanned the perimeter, then dashed from under the truck toward the downed man. He placed a third shot in the man's head using his beretta handgun, grabbed him by the collar, and dragged the body back into the building.

Hamerman stepped up to Freeman. "Nice kill."

Freeman smiled. "I'm losing my touch. I aimed for the head."

Hamerman didn't laugh. "Keep us posted if any more shitheads show up." He headed back into the building.

Freeman looked up and down the tarmac and ran back to the truck. He looked at his stopwatch. Twenty-five minutes to go. *Come on, girls.*

Ten minutes passed slowly. What the hell is taking so long?

"All clear Freeman?" Walsh asked on the radio.

Freeman double-clicked.

Rose was removing the canisters and replacing the re-breathers. He didn't see a figure standing behind Freeman, knife drawn. Looking up at a soft noise, Rose shouted, "Freeman, behind you!"

Hearing Rose, Freeman flipped over in time to see the guard's knife raised above his head. He kicked the guard in the middle of his face with his right heel. He heard bone cracking.

Blood from his shattered nose gushed down the guard's face. He fell backward, dropping his knife.

Adrenaline racing, Freeman pulled his knife from the sheath strapped to his thigh. He jumped on top of the man who was

293

reaching for his knife. Cupping his hand against the guard's mouth, he shoved the razor-sharp blade into the guard's throat and pulled across, severing the carotid artery. Blood sprayed on Freeman's hands and face. "Clear," he rasped into his throat mic. Then he wiped the blood from his knife across the dead man's chest.

"You look like you've been busy," Walsh said, as the men rejoined Freeman by the truck.

Freeman nodded, still shaken by the close call.

Rose filled Walsh in on Freeman's kill.

Walsh placed his hand on Freeman's shoulder. "Nice job killer." He then turned to his men and said, "Let's get away from this hellhole before someone finds these bodies." He saw Morton's face floating in front of him. Not yet, he told himself, not until we're back onboard Buffalo. "Get this guard in the back of the truck. Let's hope we don't run into any more of these guys."

Chapter 48

SEAL Team 6; Bandar-e-Abbas, Naval Base, Iran –

Rose, scouting ahead on the pier, scanned the surface of the harbor. At first, bubbles popping to the surface didn't register. Then he heard a low whining sound. He saw the sub was heading toward the harbor entrance. Damn! What a shitty time for you assholes to show up, he thought. "Walsh, mini-sub heading to the net," he hissed.

'Click, Click'

Walsh waited for the others to join him on the pier. "Rose spotted a mini-sub heading out toward the net." He glanced at his chronometer. "We've got twenty minutes until detonation. The divers, if they come close, eliminate them." He studied the water. "OK. It looks quiet."

The SEALs climbed down to the bottom of the ladder. They replaced their fins, masks, and picked up their scooters.

"Let's move," Walsh ordered. "Detonation 15 minutes."

With the assistance of the outgoing tide and the scooters, the men closed on the harbor net in record time.

Walsh spotted the light from the mini-sub. "Barns, Rose, to the right," he ordered into his mic. "The rest stay left. If we're lucky, they won't spot us."

Rose dropped his scooter and cocked his spear gun. "I'll

take the lead diver," he said to Barns.

Barns pulled out his knife.

The sub closed on Rose's position.

Rose saw the divers in the mini-sub.

The first diver saw Rose's hulking form kneeling in the sand off the left side of the sub. The diver pointed his hand in Rose's direction and then reached for a speargun as the two men mini-sub dropped to the sea bottom.

Rose saw the diver raise his speargun. It was aimed at him. "Oh, no, you don't," Rose said, squeezing the trigger of his speargun.

The four-foot-long spear hit the diver in the chest, knocking him against his seat. The diver sagged over, lifeless, air no longer bubbling from his mouthpiece.

The second diver tried to spring out of his seat, knife in hand.

Freeman, coming up from behind, slammed into the driver and plunged his blade under the Iranian's rib cage, pushing it into his heart. Blood merged with saltwater as he withdrew his blade.

The frogman, still strapped in his seat, was dead.

Walsh scanned the water for more divers. "Clear. Let's get the hell out of here. Rose, take the mini with us."

Rose pulled the diver from his front seat in the mini-sub and draped him over the sub's mid-section. He then got into the driver seat and manned the controls. He turned on the small motor and aimed the sub toward open water.

Walsh checked his watch. "Hurry, ladies! Detonation in less than five minutes. We gotta clear the area. Freeman, get that net up. Rose, go through."

Rose steered the sub under the net.

The SEALs swam after the sub.

Seeing the team was past the chain barrier, Freeman dropped the net and rejoined the team.

As the team moved farther away from the harbor, there was a massive explosion.

Walsh looked back. He counted seven violent blasts. "Time to haul ass ladies," he said.

The black sea and night concealed the team as they increased the speed of their scooters and headed to their rendezvous with the ASDV in deeper water.

Walsh caught the sound of high-speed screws. "Here they come," he shouted in his face mask.

"They're closing fast," Freeman said.

"We need a decoy," Walsh said. "Rose, use the sub."

Rose knew what Walsh wanted. He searched quickly and pulled off the dead diver's facemask. He tied the strap around the steering wheel and jumped out of the mini-sub. "Done," he said in his mic.

"Get out of the way," Walsh shouted.

The mini-sub's propeller chopped the water as it headed away from the team.

Rose and the others dove deeper, high-speed chain saw sounds of jet skis overhead.

Squeezing the maximum speed from their scooters, the team raced for deeper water.

"They took the bait," Walsh said, once they were out of range of the jet skis.

Barns smiled but then heard a much lower thrashing sound. "Walsh, they're coming again."

Freeman hissed, "*They must be emptying their arsenal looking for us.*"

"I see a dim light ahead," Walsh said.

"It's the ASDV," Hamerman said.

"They're taking the bait," Rose called, as the sound of the speed boats became fainter.

Almost there, Walsh thought, nearly exhausted. The mini-sub with the dead divers aboard had done its job. The Iranians were chasing the decoy. "Great job, Rose," he called.

The ASDV was visible. A few more minutes.

Without warning, the water erupted. The concussion from the underwater explosion smashed the men and their scooters to the sea bottom.

Walsh looked at the ASDV. The light was bouncing. He could tell the explosion had rocked the vehicle, but she was still intact. "Rose, get that hatch open," he shouted into his mic, picking himself off the sandy bottom and swimming up toward the submersible.

Rose dropped his scooter and darted under the belly of the ASDV. He spun the locking ring, pushed the hatch inward, and entered.

"Hamerman, help Rose get the men and gear inside," Walsh ordered.

"Where is Barns," Hamerman asked, looking around.

Freeman shrugged.

Walsh standing below the ASDV waited anxiously. He didn't want to lose anyone.

"Barns?" Walsh called into his mic. "C'mon, man, we've got to get out of here."

"Last men standing," Barns said, handing his scooter over to Walsh. "What a hell of a rush. That blast knocked the wind out of me."

"Well, get your sorry ass inside," Walsh ordered following him into the Lockout Chamber. After pressurizing the chamber and removing the water, he rejoined his men.

"Master Chief get us the hell out of here," Walsh ordered, the sound of explosions still ringing in his ears.

The men stripped off their dry suits and stowed their gear.

Rose opened his shaving kit and removed six miniature bottles of Jack Daniels. "Gentleman, a toast." He passed out the bottles.

Walsh passed on the drink. He wasn't ready to let up his guard. "Master Chief move us to deeper water," he ordered, hearing the underwater explosions nearby.

"Yes, Sir," Norris said and pushed the throttle into the stops. The speed indicator reached the maximum of eight knots.

Once the sub was moving, Walsh felt more relaxed. "Great job, men," he said pulling on a black sweatshirt.

"We only had to takeout four guards and two divers," Freeman said.

"It could have been much worse," Rose replied.

A dull tapping sound on the hull made Walsh look up.

"Shit," Norris got out before the mine detonated.

The shock wave slammed against the ASDV. The submersible was pushed hard against the sea bottom knocking Walsh to the deck.

Freeman was thrown from his seat.

Rose and Barns fell from their bunks.

Masks, rebreathers, and a pair of scooters crashed to the floor. An open box of Meals Ready to Eat flew across the deck.

Walsh sat up, rubbing his head. He turned to Rose. "You, okay?"

Rose nodded, examining his bloody hand.

"Stay where you are," Walsh said as a second wave slammed into the submersible. "Damn!" Blood dripping down his face, he helped Rose to his feet.

"Barns, Rose needs attention," Walsh called, bracing in case of another shock wave.

Barns, medically trained, grabbed his kit, and rushed over to Rose.

"You'll be okay," Walsh said, helping Rose to his chair.

Rose nodded. "Thanks, Commander."

Walsh flashed Rose a smile and then turned to the others. "Freeman, clean up this mess. Stow the gear." He surveyed his men. "Everyone remain here while I see what the hell is going on." He pulled himself to the front of the cabin.

Entering the cockpit, Walsh saw Norris flipping switches. He saw Janice staring hard at her panel. "Okay, Norris? Dr. Lace?" he asked.

Janice nodded. "That was too close."

"The sub okay, Master Chief?" Walsh asked.

"I'll know in a minute, Commander," Norris replied. "That second shock wave hit us hard."

"Are we operational?" Walsh asked.

"Testing her now," Norris said, adding air in the ballast tanks.

Walsh felt the ASDV shift slightly then lift up from the sea bottom. He saw a look of relief on Janice's face.

"OK," Norris said. "Let's see if the thruster works." He advanced the lever forward, applying power.

There was a slight jolt, hesitation, and then the whir of the small motor.

"Ok! We're operational. Heading out," Norris said, watching the speed dial climb.

An alarm sounded. The escape hatch light flashed above Janice's head.

"Water coming in from the lower hatch," Janice said.

Norris checked the panel. "Commander Walsh, can you go check out the hatch?" He asked.

"On it," Walsh replied quickly, moving into the Lockout Chamber. He secured the forward watertight door, sealing Janice and Norris in the forward compartment.

Freeman, hearing Norris's request, jumped up from his seat. "I'll give you a hand Commander," he said, following Walsh into the chamber.

"Shit," Walsh said, "I can't move the ring." He struggled to tighten the hatch cover as water gushed from around the rubber seal. "No luck!" Walsh shouted over the noise of the water.

"I'll try," Freeman shouted.

Walsh stood back.

Freeman strained to turn the hatch ring. "Won't budge," he said.

"Get back into our compartment," Walsh demanded, standing in three inches of water. He stepped back into the SEAL compartment, securing the watertight door. "Master Chief, pressurize the chamber," he said. "We better hope it holds," he said to Freeman.

"Pressurizing now," Norris replied, releasing high pressure air into the chamber.

"She's holding," Walsh said.

"We're okay," Norris said. "She's holding."

Janice's voice came over the PA, "Is everyone all right back there?"

"A few bumps and bruises. Thanks for asking," Walsh replied. "Master Chief, now stop fooling around and take us home. You might want to take the long way around to Buffalo.

We don't want anyone following us to her."

Norris glanced at Janice and saw the worried look on her face. "We'll be fine," he said. "Buffalo can handle anything."

If we make it, Janice thought.

The submersible lumbered slowly toward the commercial channels.

Norris reached up and pressed the battery and aft compartment warning lights, cycling them from red to green then back to red. "Commander, battery compartment secure," he said. "Electrical motors operational. No indication of leaks or damage from the explosions." He turned to Janice. "Sonar up and running, Dr. Lace?"

"Yes, Master Chief. The auxiliary power breaker snapped open, but I was able to reset and restore power to the navigational computer and sonar."

"Good job, Dr. Lace. All systems are operational, Commander Walsh. ETA to the Northern shipping channel in 15 minutes," Norris reported, sounding relieved.

"Master Chief, locate a tanker to cover our transit," Walsh said. "Any more bombs like that last one, and we'll be on the bottom."

Janice was thinking the same thing.

Chapter 49

Bandar-e-Abbas; Naval Base, Iran –

Always a heavy sleeper, it took eight phone rings to wake Islamic Naval Commander, Admiral Al Jujair. He picked up the phone, primed to yell at whoever disturbed his much-needed rest. Then he heard his Chief of Staff, Captain Tousi's voice, "Sir, the weapons...our facility at Bandar-e-Abbas Naval Base—"

Jujair jumped from his bed. "Is this a joke? What are you saying?"

"The factory...it was destroyed."

"Destroyed?"

"I'm afraid so."

"How? Who did this?" Jujair was dressing furiously.

"We do not know," Captain Tousi replied. "Sir, we're waiting for base security to examine the ruins. Once it's safe to enter."

Jujair felt faint. Execution was the penalty for failure. "What the hell are you waiting for? Get my driver. Assemble my staff. Get everyone!" He slammed the phone down on its stand and hurried to the door. "Someone will pay for this," he rumbled, racing to the waiting limo.

Entering his underground command center, Admiral Al Jujair was saluted by Captain Tousi, his mind homicidal in rage. "What the hell happened?"

The Naval officers were at attention, anticipating their fate from his scowling face. They knew what was at stake.

The only person who did not avert his eyes from Jujair was Mr. Khadem from the Ministry of Intelligence and National Security. A shadow in a long trenchcoat, he sat waiting for the scimitar to fall on whichever officer Jujair would sacrifice for this incredible blunder. He hoped it would be the Admiral himself whose head might be separated from his arrogant uniform.

Slamming his fist on the table, Admiral Al Jujair shouted, "I want answers! I want them now!" He glared at the men, still at attention. "You, Captain Firouz," he pointed to the head of base security, "What have you discovered?"

The head of security lacked his usual firmness. "Admiral, Sir, we don't know what caused the explosions."

The Admiral's face darkened.

"Sir, our security teams are searching the entire base, from water's edge to the chain-linked fence. Our divers are trying to determine if intruders came from the sea—"

The man in the trenchcoat interrupted, "Two charred bodies were found in the plant's rubble. Until we identify their remains, we assume they were guards posted in the factory building area." He aimed his icy stare at the head of harbor security. "My staff will conduct an autopsy."

Firouz gulped. "So far...our search teams found no indication of intruders."

The man in the trenchcoat spoke again. "Then how do you explain the two badly burnt bodies in the truck?"

Jujair shivered every time Khadem, the Intelligence officer, spoke. He thought of him as knife-like, not quite human. "There were burnt bodies in a truck?" he asked.

The security head nodded. "Yes, Sir. We found one behind the wheel of the cargo truck... and one in the back."

"And you didn't conclude there were enemy invaders from this?" Jujair said menacingly, leaning forward, his fingers splayed on the table.

"Admiral, Sir, the truck was nearly destroyed by the blasts. We want to wait and examine all the bodies before we jump to conclusions—"

"Jump to conclusions?" Jujair shook his head in disbelief. "Well, now we know the explosion was not an accident." He aimed angry eyes at the officers before him. "Whatever it takes, we'll find who did this." He smiled grimly at the harbor security head. "Jump to conclusions?" He glanced at Mokri. "What have you done to secure our fleet in the harbor?"

"I immediately issued orders to send two fast attack craft to search for possible sea breaches, and as precaution against further attacks. As yet, we've no evidence of outside interference from the sea. But we're still looking—"

Jujair interrupted. "While you're looking, someone else may be attacking. Vice Admiral Salehi, have you checked that mines have not been placed under your submarines by these intruders?"

"Our divers are searching. Nothing has been found yet," Salehi said, relieved that he had anticipated Jujair's question.

The trenchcoat stood. "You have not mentioned the obvious."

Jujair had deliberately avoided this. Admitting that the Americans, or worse yet, the Israelis, may have done this under his nose, was not only the ultimate humiliation but a death warrant. He stared at the Intelligence Officer and knew he no longer had a choice. He turned to Mokri and said, "Issue orders for Kajami, and Gahjae, to immediately put to sea. These mini-submarines can search the shallow waters around the Naval Base in case those bastards are still here." He glanced at the trenchcoated man and then aimed hard eyes at his officers. "Unless our investigations determine differently... we must assume the Israelis, or the Americans are responsible for this attack."

None of the officers spoke. They understood that such a determination by their nation's leaders would mean death to someone in the room, even to Jujair.

Mahbod Khadem's soft-spoken voice and sharp-featured face were frighteningly icy. "I recommend you recall all personnel to their duty stations immediately. I will send my security police to interrogate everyone here, individually." He looked at Jujair. "Someone must know something. We'll get it out of them."

Jujair nodded.

Khadem continued, "We'll have our coroner conduct the autopsies of the dead."

"We have facilities here—" Jujair began.

Khadem interrupted. "We'll have our men conduct the autopsies." He again smiled at Jujair. "I'm sure we'll find an American company manufactured the bullets that killed them."

"I agree," Admiral Al Jujair responded quickly. "We

must search for enemy submarines. That's the most likely source—"

"You should have done that already," Khadem hissed, "before this unforgivable outrage."

"Admiral," Vice Admiral Salehi said, breaking the uncomfortable silence, "I issued orders to our submarine squadrons to prepare for sea."

"Yes. Hurry," Jujair said. We must establish a barrier to stop the American fleet from leaving the Persian Gulf. Admiral Mokri," he addressed the Commander of Islamic Surface Forces, "What are our surface fleet doing to stop American ships from escaping into the Straits of Hormuz."

Mokri said proudly, "I deployed a fleet of fast patrol craft to search for any sign of divers or enemy vessels. They have orders to board all surface craft in our area—"

Jujair interrupted. "Not enough. We can't let the perpetrators of this outrage escape our grasp. What if they came in submarines?"

Mokri replied, "I've already ordered our craft to drop explosive charges at the entrance to the harbor and surrounding area. I also ordered our new destroyers, Damavand and Jamaran, to search near the base." He smiled. "Due to my initiative, Jamaran reported earlier she sighted a submarine moving into the Straits."

Jujair felt hopeful. "Were they able to determine if the submarine was an American? Was it Israeli?"

"No, Sir," Admiral Mokri said reluctantly. "We're not sure. It could have been Israeli, American, or a German submarine."

"This is hopeless," Khadem interrupted. "Our supreme leaders will not like us looking like incompetent fools."

Jujair shivered. "Continue, please, Admiral," he said, hoping Mokri could offer something more positive, something that could save them all.

Mokri, feeling the pressure, said, "The USS Blue Ridge, an amphibious assault group, left Hawaii three weeks ago. It's due to arrive in the Straits toward the end of the month—"

Jujair brightened. He glanced at Khadem who showed no sign that this news made any impact on his icy expression. "Admiral, how do we know this?" he asked.

"Sympathetic sources in Italy shared this with us. The Americans have careless lapses in security. Sailors on the USS Carl Vinson Carrier Strike Group do not know how to keep their mouths shut," Mokri said.

Khadem nodded his head. "The Americans are fools."

Jujair smiled. "Well, we've a rare opportunity here." He glanced again at Khadem. "Admiral Mokri, have your fleet continue to mine our waters. Outfit our combat ships with a full complement of missiles. A shipment of Shkval torpedoes from Russia is expected in two days. Distribute them immediately."

"Admiral," Admiral Mokri said, "Our boats need to be sent to Bandar-e-Lengeh, to rearm—"

Jujair saw Khadem shake his head. "Just do it. I'm not interested in problems, just results," he snapped.

Khadem sighed, rose from his chair, and left the room.

Jujair, free of his critical observer, aimed his eyes at the officers. "Do you realize what you've done?" He placed his hands firmly on the table.

"I will not hang for this. But I swear on Allah that one, more, of you, will pay. How could you let this happen under your noses?" He was about to say more when he saw the door open, and Khadem reenter.

Khadem said, "Admiral, I was just informed two divers checking the harbor net did not return last night after their patrol."

"They never returned?" Jujair's head throbbed.

"There is no sign of them or their mini-sub," Khadem replied coldly.

"When was their scheduled check?" Admiral Jujair asked, weighing the implications of this latest bad news.

"The log indicates they left base around midnight. There's no entry that the divers returned." Firouz trembled. "I swear, I didn't know—"

Jujair could barely contain his fury. "Captain Firouz, I want the background of those divers checked. Get out and get it now."

Khadem said. "Wait." He looked hard at Jujair. "I don't like what I hear." He formed a fist. "Those two could be Israeli Mossad implanted to destroy our base."

Jujair screamed, "Captain Firouz, get those dossiers back here as fast as you can."

Khadem held up a photograph of the explosion site. "One thing is clear. This attack on our beloved Islamic Republic was foreign in origin. Most likely, the infidels came from a submarine. What country? We do not know yet." His gaze at the officers, still standing before him, looked almost paternal. "I promise you this. We will know everything once my investigators complete their work. I also promise you someone will pay." He gave them a broad smile, shark-like, and, without looking at Jujair, marched from the room.

As soon as Khadem left, Jujair fell into his seat. He knew that if he didn't catch the Americans or Israelis who managed this attack, his life would be over.

309

EPILOG

Scott was relieved SEAL Team 6 were back safely on board. In his stateroom, he closed his logbook and leaned back in his seat. It had been a challenging mission, for the SEALs, but they succeeded. He had approved Walsh's report: the destruction of the Iranian torpedo factory with no loss of American lives. He was pleased by the reports that there had been only minor damage to the ASDV, and that Janice had returned with its crewmembers. He had listened intently as Walsh described killing those Iranians?

"Could you have avoided killing the guards?" Scott had asked after Walsh reported to him.

"No Sir," Walsh replied. "It was them or us."

Scott regretted they had to kill the Iranian guards and divers, but the safety of the American Fleet and his men had to be his top priority.

"Captain, may I come in?"

Scott rose when he saw Janice at the door. "I'm glad you're safe," he said. "I was concerned each time there was a report of an explosion near your position."

Janice nodded. "Joe, I stopped by to answer your question. The one you asked earlier."

Scott remembered. "And what did you decide?" He braced himself for the negative response he was sure was coming.

Janice gave him a small smile. "I love you too... and when you're ready...I accept your proposal." She turned and left the room.

Scott stared at the closed door.

THE END

Coming Soon: Shallow Water Predator 2

Join Commander Scott and the crew of Buffalo as they sail into new danger in adventures too close to what is happening now.

Characters in Shallow Water Predator

President's Security Council/Advisers
Mr. Jack Kindly, Vice President
Mr. Ian Williams, President's Chief of Staff
Mr. Chuck Aspin, Secretary of Defense
Mrs. Margaret Rice, Secretary of State
Mrs. Sally Wheatfield, Deputy National Security
General Richard Shaw, Chairman to the Joint Chiefs of Staff
General McAllen, Ret. Director of National Intelligence
Mrs. Beverly Yancy, President Secretary

U.S. Navy Senior Command
Admiral Samuel Westfield, Commander Naval Special Warfare Command
Rear Admiral Tom Armstrong, Commander Submarine Group Seven
Vice Admiral Charles W. Clarke, U.S. Fifth Fleet, Manama, Bahrain
Captain Whitfield, Commander Submarine Squadron 15 Apar Harbor Guam

National Geospatial-Intelligence Agency
Colonel Bill Johnson
Lieutenant Colonel Sandy Day
Technical Sergeant Wallace

USS Carl Vinson CVN-70

Rear Admiral Stan Dussault, Commander Carrier Strike Group One

Captain Jim Wills, Rear Admiral Stan Dussault's Chief-of-Staff

Captain Clarence Newhouse, Carl Vinson Commanding Officer

Commander Gary Langdon, Air Wing Commander

Commander Robert Connors, Command and Control and Electronic Warfare

Captain Gene Grubs, Sea Combat Commander

USS Buffalo SSN-715

Lieutenant Commander Dennis Fender, Engineering Officer

Lieutenant Jeff Obermeier, Navigator

Lieutenant Steve Wilkinson, Weapons Officer

Lieutenant Junior Grade, Terry Washington, Supply Officer

Senior Chief Fire Control Technician, Jack Russell

Senior Chief Sonar Technician Submarines (STSCS) Paul Richardson

Sonar Technician Submarines (STS) First Class Lefty Sorenson

Chief Machinists Mate (Weapons), Juststone

Information System Technician First Class Carl Weathers

Sonar Technician Second Class, John Price

Culinary Specialist Second Class, Chad Brady

Dr. Fred Stone, NUWC Mechanical Engineer

Dr. Glen Thomas, NUWC Electrical Engineer

Dr. Aslan Mehman, Iranian Nuclear Physicists

USS Winston S. Churchill DDG-81

Commanding Officer, Captain Rusty Smith
Lieutenant Tom Ralph, Tactical Action Officer
Lieutenant Lester Philips, Launch Safety Officer
Sonar Technician Submarines First Class, Fredstone

USS Mahan DDG 72

Commander Mark Damon
Lieutenant Bob James Navigator/Communication Officer
Hospital Corpsman Master Chief John Danielson
Lieutenant Sam Gross
Lieutenant Baston
FTG 2 Wilson
HM1 Wayne

MK V1-1 Patrol Boat

Master Chief Boatswain Mate Rick Jackson
2nd Class John Cain

Helicopter Anti-Submarine Squadron Light (HLS) 42 Detachment 7

Lieutenant Will Peterson, Pilot
Lieutenant Junior Grade Brendan Tan, CO-Pilot
Airborne Tactical Officer, and a 1st class Aviation Antisubmarine Warfare Operator

USS Oscar Austin DDG-79

Commanding Officer, Captain Lenard Willard
Lieutenant Peter Blair, Tactical Action Officer

U.S. Navy SEALs

Machinist Mate First Class Willy Hamerman

Boatswain Mate First Class Bob Rose
Boatswain Mate Second Class Mark Stanley
Information System Technician Second Class Bruce Freeman
Hospital Corpsman Third Class Chad Barns

Iranian Kilo Diesel Submarine K-901
Commander Atash Karini, Commanding Officer
Lieutenant Commander Mohsen Pejman, Executive Officer
Sonar Technician Specialist, ShahrAm Pahlavi

Converted Landing Craft
Lieutenant Commander Saman Lajani
XO, Lt. Basir Mohsen

Iranian Kilo Diesel Submarine K-903
Captain Giv Alizadeh, Commanding Officer
Lieutenant Commander Dalir Gilani, Executive Officer
Sonar Technician Specialist, Jamshidi

IRIN Damavand, M-77
Captain Javadi, Commander Officer

Bandar 'Abbas Naval Station Iran
Vice Admiral Salehi, Commander of Islamic Submarine Forces
Admiral Mokri, Commander of Islamic Surface Forces
Commodore Garshasp Yazdi, Islamic Submarine Squadron 10
Mahbod Khadem, Ministry of Intelligence and National Security of the Islamic Republic of Iran

Captain Tousi, Admiral Al Jujair Chief of Staff
Captain Husseini Firouz, Base Security
Petty Officer Bamdad- Special Forces
Petty Officer Hijazi- Special Forces

Iranian Qaaem Diesel Submarine Q-100
Commander Ardeshir Naceri, Commanding Officer

Iranian Qaaem Diesel Submarine Q-104
Commander MortezA Kashani, Commanding Officer
Lieutenant Commander Nouri Azizi, Executive Officer
Sonar Technician Submarines 2nd Class, Rashid Namazi

Tannin SSK Dolphin
Colonel Lev Zak
Lieutenant Colonel Pfeffer, Executive Officer
Sonar Staff Sergeant Dan Kahan

W/T Seed
Captain Dalir Sassani, Ship's Master

Glossary

The following terms and definitions may help in your understanding of Shallow Water Predator:

1MC Main ship-wide announcing circuit on U.S. submarines.

ADCAP Advanced Capability. The newest version of the Mark 48 torpedo onboard U.S. submarines.

AN/WLR-12 Acoustic Intercept Receiver found on U.S. Navy submarines.

Angles and dangles A test conducted by a submarine to ensure that everything is stowed before beginning its mission. The procedure calls for making large up and down movements with the submarine as well as using large rudder angles at moderate speeds.

ASDV Advanced SEAL Delivery Vehicle. ASDS was built to address the need for stealthy long-range insertion of special operations forces on covert or clandestine missions. The program was abandoned after the only prototype example of the class was damaged beyond economic repair in an accidental fire.

VLS ASROC Vertical Launch Anti-Submarine rocket carries a Mark 54 homing torpedo.

ASW Antisubmarine Warfare.

AUTEC Atlantic Undersea Test and Evaluation Center, Andros Island. An acoustic test range located off Andros Island in the Bahamas.

Bridge Small observation area on top of the fairwater. The OOD stands his watch there when the submarine is on the surface.

Cavitation The formation and collapse of tiny vapor bubbles on the trailing surface of a propeller when the propeller moves through the water rapidly. The collapse of these bubbles and the attendant noise is called cavitation. Cavitation can make an otherwise quiet Sub audible to sonar

CENTCOM U.S. CENTral COMmand.

CIWS Close-in Weapons System. Fast reaction, a rapid-fire 20-millimeter gun system capable of firing 3,000 or 4,500 rounds per minute.

CO Commanding Officer. The title was given to an officer in command of a ship. Often called 'Captain.' or 'Skipper.'

COB Chief of the Boat. A senior enlisted man in the crews of the submarines usually a senior, our master chief petty officer. Interfaces with the XO on issues that affect the enlisted personnel.

Control room Area on a U.S. Navy submarine where the submarine's ship control, fire control, periscopes are located. All primary submarine functions are controlled from this location. The OOD stands his watch here when the submarine is submerged. In communications, the areas referred to as the conn.

CPA Closest Point of Approach. An estimated point in which the distance between two objects, of which at least one is in motion, will reach its minimum value.

DRT Dead Reckoning Table. In navigation, **dead reckoning** is the process of calculating one's current position by using a previously determined position, or fix, and advancing that position based upon known or estimated speeds over elapsed time and course.

EAB Emergency Air Breathing system. A low-pressure air system that crewmen can plug in to and obtain breathable air. The system provides a source of air in an emergency, such as a fire, when the ship's atmosphere has toxic gases.

Emergency Blow Process by which high-pressure air is rapidly introduced into the submarines' main ballast tanks. An emergency blow makes the submarine positively buoyant, and it will rise to the surface quite quickly. The system was instituted as part of the safe-sub safe program following the loss of the USS Thresher.

EOOW Engineering Officer of the Watch. Officer in charge of the team that is monitoring and manipulating the submarines reactor and propulsion system. Main responsibility is to maintain propulsion safely.

Family Grams Short [forty to fifty words] messages that U.S. Navy submarines can receive from family members about once a month while on patrol.

FLIR Forward-Looking Infrared. Also known as thermal imaging.

ESM Electronic Support Measures. A passive receiver system designed to detect radar emissions from aircraft and surface ships.

Gertrude (AN/WQC-2) Old WW II phrase used to describe any equipment whose function is underwater communications.

GPS Global Positioning System. A constellation of Navstar satellites that can vary accuracy determine the location of the submarine.

Harpoon [UGM – 84] U.S. Navy anti-ship missile, fired from an SSN's torpedo tube.

Kilo SS latest Russian diesel-electric submarine. The Kilo is a medium-range coastal defense submarine that is being offered on the export market. Using state – of – the – art Russian sensors and torpedoes, the Kilo-class compares favorably against older Western designs. Russia has 20 Kilos in their naval order of battle, and approximately 14 have been sold to various countries.

INS Tannin. First Dolphin Batch II class German-made SSK sold to the Israeli navy.

IRGCON Islamic Revolutionary Guards Corps Navy.

LOFAR Low – frequency analyzing and recording. A term used to describe the process by which narrowband 'totals' are displayed on a modern sonar system.

MAD - Magnetic Anomaly Detector is streamed from a wire behind the fuselage. It is used to identify disruptions in the earth's magnetic field caused when a large body of metal passes under the sensor.

Maneuvering The reactor and propulsion control area located in the engine room. The EOOW stands his watch here.

MK V1 PB1 Patrol Boat At 85 feet in length, the MKVI-PB1 was one of two of the Navy's brand-new Mark VI class patrol boats. Commanded by a senior enlisted and a hand-selected crew, these new littoral patrol crafts were supreme in their element. Designed for inshore shallow water patrols and operations with only a 4-foot draft, it could reach speeds of 45 knots from the 5,200 horsepower diesel and pump-jet propulsion. They were also heavily armed, with four operated 50 caliber machine guns, and 25 mm remote-controlled Bushmaster chain guns, their star offensive weapons.

NIXIE Towed Array Decoy. Towed torpedo decoys used on US and allied warships.

NUWC Naval Undersea Warfare Center. The Naval Undersea Warfare Center (NUWC) is the United States Navy's full-spectrum research, development, test and evaluation, engineering and fleet support center.

SCBA Self-containing Breathing Apparatus. A portable system that chemically generates oxygen for between 2 to 4 hours. Used by damage control teams to fight fires.

OOD Officer of the Deck. U.S. Navy officer in charge of directing a ship's movement and ensuring that essential actions are conducted. The primary responsibility is to keep the ship out of dangerous situations and to keep the captain informed.

OPNAV Office of the Chief of NAVal OPerations.

ORSE Operational Reactor Safeguards Examination.

Otto Fuel The monopropellant (oxidizer and fuel combined) used in Mark 48 and Spearfish torpedoes.

Oxygen Generator & Carbon Dioxide Scrubbers https://-cosmosmagazine.com/technology/oxygen-generators-and-carbon-dioxide-scrubbers-explained

Radar RAdio Detection and Ranging.

S6G the designation of the pressurized water reactor installed in 688 – class SSN.

SCRAM an acronym for an unplanned reactor shutdown, derived from "Safety Control Reactor Axe Man," the name given to the man at the University of Chicago, where the first nuclear core was tested, who was responsible for cutting the rope holding the control rods should something go wrong. The method of inserting control rods has changed considerably, but the term has been retained with a rapid insertion of control rods the reactor will be made subcritical and will no longer support a sustained nuclear fission reaction.

SEAL SEa–Air–Land. U.S. Navy special forces/commando units.

Signal ejector A small (usually three-inch) torpedo tube-like system for launching flares, noisemakers, and torpedo decoys.

SINS Ships Internal Navigation System. A set of gyroscopes that monitor and project a submarine's position once determined from a periscope satellite fix.

Snapshot Term used to describe the procedure for launching a torpedo in an emergency situation. In a snapshot, the submarine crew doesn't have time to conduct TMA but simply shoots a torpedo down the bearing of an incoming weapon or close contact. The rapid reaction is the basis for the snapshot mode.

SNR Signal–to–Noise Ratio. A measure used in science and engineering that compares the level of the desired signal to the level of background noise.

SOSUS SOund SUrveillance System. A series of fixed passive sonar raised used by NATO to provide early warning of deployments into the open ocean of former Soviet submarines.

SSXBT Submarine Expendable Bathythermograph. A small torpedo-shaped device that holds a temperature sensor and a transducer to detect changes in water temperature versus depth.

SUBGRU SUBmarine GRoUP

SUBRON U.S. SUBmarine SquadRON

TB – 23 First U.S. Navy "thin line" array found on SSNs and is equipped with AN/BSY – 1 and AN/BQQ – 5E. This array is about four times longer than the TB – 16 series and is stored entirely on a reel located in the aft ballast tank area.

TMA Target Motion Analysis. The process by which computers or man determines a target course, speed, and range so that the torpedo or missile can be fired accurately.

UHF Ultra-High Frequency. Designation for radio frequencies in the range between 300 megahertz (MHz) and 3 gigahertz (GHz).

Waterfall Display phrase used to describe the appearance that a modern passive sonar display makes while showing bearing versus time information. A contact will look like a bright line on a CRT against a speckled background of other noise sources.

XO Executive Officer. U.S. Navy term for the second in command of a ship.

Note: Several Glossary definitions were taken from Tom Clancy's Military Reference Submarine: A guided tour inside a nuclear warship
   https://en.wikipedia.org/wiki/List_of_U.S._Navy_acronyms and https://www.history.navy.mil/research/library/online-reading-room/title-list-alphabetically/d/dod-acronyms.html

Acronyms

The following acronyms are used in Shallow Water Predator:

- **ADCAP** Advanced Capability Torpedo
- **ASDV** Advanced SEAL Delivery Vehicle
- **AIP** Air-independent Propulsion
- **ASW** Anti-Submarine Warfare
- **AUTEC** Atlantic Undersea Test and Evaluation Center
- **ASROC** Anti-Submarine Rocket Vertical Launch
- **BOQ** Bachelor Officers Quarters
- **BUD** Basic Underwater Demolition
- **BM** Boatswain Mate
- **CASREP** Casualty Report
- **CIA** Central Intelligence Agency
- **CIC** Combat Information Center
- **CDC** Combat Direction Center
- **FTC** Chief Fire Control Technician
- **COB** Chief of the Boat
- **COW** Chief-of-the-Watch
- **STSC** Chief Sonar Technician Sonar
- **CNN** Cable News Network
- **CCS** Combat Control System
- **CO** Commanding Officer
- **COMSUBRON** Commander Submarine Squadron
- **NAVCEN** Commander, United States Naval Forces Central

Command
- **COMMS** Communication
- **CON** Control
- **CIWS** Close-in Weapon System
- **CPA** Closest Point of Approach
- **DDG** Destroyer Guided Missile
- **DRT** Dead Reckoning Table
- **DARPA** Defense Advanced Research Project Agency
- **DOD** Department of Defense
- **DOOW** Duty Officer of the Watch
- **ECM** Electronic Countermeasures
- **ELINT** Electronic Intelligence
- **ESM** Electronic Support Measures
- **XO** Executive Officer
- **ENG** Engineer
- **ETA** Estimate Time of Arrival
- **FTCS** Fire Control Technician Senior Chief
- **FITREPS** Fitness Reports
- **FLTA** Flat Line Towed Array
- **FLIR** Forward Looking Infrared
- **GQ** General Quarters (Surface)
- **HMI** Hospital Corpsmen
- **ID** Identification Card
- **IFF** Identification Friend or Foe
- **IDF** Israel Defense Force
- **IT** Information Technician
- **IRGCN** Islamic Revolutionary Guards Corps Navy
- **LIDAR** Light Detection and Ranging
- **LED** Light Emitting Diode
- **LT** Lieutenant
- **LCDR** Lieutenant Commander

- **LAMPS** Light Airborne Multi-Purpose System
- **1MC** General Announcing System (Navy)
- **CMMW** Chief Machinist's Mate Weapons
- **MATE** Manual Adaptive TMA Evaluation
- **MIT** Massachusetts Institute of Technology
- **MS** Master of Science
- **MC** Master Chief
- **MMCM** Master Chief Machinist Mate
- **NATO** North Atlantic Treaty Organization
- **NAV** Navigator
- **NAVSAT** Navigation by Satellite
- **NUWC** Naval Undersea Warfare Center
- **NIXIE** Towed Torpedo Decoy
- **CVN** Nuclear-powered Aircraft Carrier
- **OOD** Officer of the Deck
- **OP** Operations
- **OPORDER** Operations Order
- **OSCM** Operations Specialist Master Chief
- **PD** Periscope Depth
- **PCO** Perspective Commanding Officers
- **Ph.D** Doctor of Philosophy
- **PrtScn** Print Screen
- **SEAL** Sea Air and Land
- **SECNAV** Secretary Navy
- **SCUBA** Self-Contained Underwater Breathing Apparatus
- **SSMG** Ship Service Motor Generators
- **SNR** Signal-to-Noise Ratio
- **SIPERNET** Secret Internet
- **STSCS** Sonar Technician Specialist Senior Chief
- **SOA** Speed of Advance
- **SSBT** Submarine Expendable Bathythermograph

- **SUBLANT** Submarine Atlantic
- **SUBPAC** Submarine Pacific
- **SUBRON** Submarine Squadron
- **SIM** Subscriber Identity Module
- **TMA** Target Motion Analysis
- **TLTA** Thin Line Towed Array
- **TM** Torpedoman
- **TRE** Training Readiness Exam
- **UHF** Ultra-High Frequency
- **UCLL** Ultra Large Crude Tanker
- **UN** United Nations
- **US** United States
- **USCM** United States Marine Corp
- **UUV** Unmanned Underwater Vehicle
- **WDM** Weapons of Mass Destruction

Subscribe to the NCG Narrative

FREE Book for Subscribing to The NCG Narrative

Subscribe to our free newsletter, The NCG Narrative, to immediately receive a **FREE** eBook from Newhouse Creative Group.

Be the first to learn about NCG's newest releases, get behind the scenes of NCG, enter NCG Narrative exclusive contests and giveaways, and much more!

Subscribe today at NewhouseCreativeGroup.com

More from Newhouse Creative Group

Visit NewhouseCreativeGroup.com for more books and other products from NCG Key and the rest of the Newhouse Creative Group family!

About the Author

William Russell holds a Master of Business from Salve Regina University in Newport R.I. and has spent his career working in Naval programs. As a Program Manager, he supported the Surface Ship ASW Effectiveness Measuring Program (SHARM) developing tactical guidelines and publications to assist the surface community in localizing, tracking, and detecting, threat submarines. He developed and participated in at-sea training programs for SURFLANT, and worked at the Naval War College, Naval Lessons Learned library. During the latter part of his career, he supported the DDG 1000 Integration Verification and Validation (IV&V) program as a Software Test Engineer responsible for developing test procedures and verifying software dealing with Surface Ship Combat Operations. Bill and his wife Margaret are enjoying their retirement in sunny Florida with two golden doodles.

Also by William S. Russell

The Guardian of the Tomb Series

Join Steven, a young gifted boy, who suddenly finds himself thrown into a quest which will take him halfway around the world! In the Guardian of the Tomb series, you'll learn about exotic places as you read about the harrowing adventures of a boy facing the problems all teenagers face today.

www.ingramcontent.com/pod-product-compliance
Lightning Source LLC
Chambersburg PA
CBHW070803180626
46818CB00001B/85